SECOND ACT

The Claudia Series by Marilyn Todd

I, CLAUDIA
VIRGIN TERRITORY
MAN EATER
WOLF WHISTLE
JAIL BAIT
BLACK SALAMANDER
DREAM BOAT *
DARK HORSE *
SECOND ACT *

* *available from Severn House*

SECOND ACT

Marilyn Todd

severn
House

This first world edition published in Great Britain 2003 by
SEVERN HOUSE PUBLISHERS LTD of
9–15 High Street, Sutton, Surrey SM1 1DF.
This first world edition published in the USA 2003 by
SEVERN HOUSE PUBLISHERS INC of
595 Madison Avenue, New York, N.Y. 10022.

British Library Cataloguing in Publication Data

Todd, Marilyn
    Second act
    1.   Claudia Seferius (Fictitious character) - Fiction
    2.   Private investigators - Rome - Fiction
    3.   Rape - Investigation - Rome - Fiction
    4.   Rome - History - Empire, 30 B.C. – 284 A.D. - Fiction
    5.   Detective and mystery stories
    I.   Title
    823.9'14 [F]

    ISBN 0-7278-6008-9

Typeset by Palimpsest Book Production Ltd.,
Polmont, Stirlingshire, Scotland.
Printed and bound in Great Britain by
MPG Books Ltd., Bodmin, Cornwall.

To Janet Hutchings, whose support is beyond price.

*A*utumn had transformed the Alban Hills into a patchwork of colour ranging from dull rusts to flame, sulphur yellows to amber.

The air was warm.

Humid, even.

But the air was misleading.

Soon, frosts would arrive to desiccate the woodlands and kill off the food supply. The creatures of the forest had to move fast. Squirrels busily hoarded their caches of acorns and seeds. Dormice, fat as barrels on hazelnuts, ferried grass to their winter nests and badgers, having gorged on elderberries, concentrated on building up their body fat with plump, juicy earthworms. The woods were virtually silent. Birds were using every ounce of energy to feed, not to sing, and the only sound which echoed across the valley was the measured dig-dig-dig of a spade as it turned over the heavy, black soil.

Stripped to the waist, the Digger leaned on the shovel to mop up the sweat with a piece of coarse woollen cloth. A pheasant clucked in the distance and a viper slithered through the leaf litter, tasting with its tongue air rank with the urine of rutting fallow bucks. The Digger unstoppered the goatskin and drank deeply, watching a proliferation of painted lady butterflies on their colourful migration south. There was no wine in the skin. That had been emptied out, to be refilled with water from the little stream that babbled close by. The water was cool. Refreshing the

Digger before the blade once more sliced through the soil.

Gradually, the black, aromatic earth piled up. From time to time, there would come the faint clop of ox hooves, the slow and steady rumble of wagon wheels, the whinny of a mule. Reminders that the highway ran by less than a hundred paces up the bank and that Frascati itself lay only half a dozen miles to the west. Lying at the crossroads of three main routes out of Rome, and with its wealth of patrician villas, post houses and taverns, the little town made for a popular stopover.

Finally, back aching, head pounding, the Digger tossed the spade to one side. Enough, the humid air decreed. Enough, enough, enough.

With the gentlest of nudges, the naked corpse rolled tidily into the hole.

As graves go, it was shallow in the extreme. But the Digger was unused to manual labour, and the leaves would fall soon, then the snow. It was unlikely the body would be found before spring. By then, it wouldn't matter.

The Digger's gaze ranged over the cadaver's belongings. Heaven knows, there wasn't much. A couple of tunics which had seen better days, a few personal items such as comb, faded cloak, the wineskin which the Digger had emptied. But there, at the bottom of the pack and carefully wrapped between layers of brown felt, nestled a trio of theatrical masks.

All three had been delicately carved of wood and had a wig attached. One mask had its gaping mouth curved upwards in an exaggerated smile, for comic parts. The mouth of the second was turned down for tragedy. The third, painted white and with its fair hair curled into ringlets and pinned, was for when the actor played female roles. Admiring the workmanship, the elaborate brush strokes, the sturdy ribbons by which the masks fastened behind the actor's ears, the Digger prepared to toss them in after the corpse.

No, wait.

Back in Frascati, a company of strolling players had been hiring. Convinced they could do better alone, certain members of the troupe had broken away to form a rival splinter group, leaving the original company in the lurch. With Saturnalia but two months away, a lucrative time for strolling players, the diehards of the original group were desperate to take on new artists and train any amateurs willing to roll up their sleeves and pitch in.

Why not, the Digger wondered.

It wasn't as though it was such a transition.

Aren't all killers actors at heart—?

One

Six weeks later and the vicious desiccating wind that sweeps down from the mountains in the north, known as the tramontana, arrived in Rome with a vengeance. Leaves which had managed to withstand autumn storms and winter frosts now scattered like chaff in the wind and the soil, as with a defenceless crowd of peasants facing mounted Persian hordes, shrivelled and receded beneath its icy blast.

'Makes you think about those Briton barbarians,' Claudia said to her bodyguard, as they pushed their way through the crowds. 'I mean, what kind of people find blue skin attractive?'

There had been no question of travelling by litter today. Snug as she would have been beneath a pile of bear skins with heated bricks at her feet, the chair would never have got through. Half the universe descended on Rome for Saturnalia and the crush of handcarts and donkeys, despatch riders and pedestrians, soldiers and slaves clogged every road. Traders and students jostled shoulder to thickly cloaked shoulder with athletes and letter carriers in a kaleidoscope of colour and customs. Dark-skinned Abyssinians, pantalooned Dacians, Cretans with their thickly oiled curls swarmed in on everything from camels to stilts, bringing with them the scents of the Orient, new breeds of sheep, panther claws, pepper, silver-coated drinking horns, turbans, marmots and liquor.

They came armed with stories, as well. Of ants that mine

gold in the Indus. Of virgins auctioned off in Illyria. Of headhunting Gauls and Teutonic warriors sending their sons tobogganing down snow-covered slopes on their fathers' bronze shields.

All these things congested the streets, filling the air with laughter and awe, while prisoners of war rattled their chains and sang songs of defiance in incomprehensible tongues and children rode piggyback on their fathers' shoulders, squealing, tugging, dripping pastry crumbs as they passed. Wrestling her way through beneath the Capitol, Claudia noticed that not even weather as cold and drab as this could dull the gold on Jupiter's chariot on the apex of his temple. But the sun, what little of it percolated the grey, leaden clouds, was sinking faster than she would have liked.

She was already late.

Crossing the vegetable market, finished for the day, empty-eyed beggars pressed together for warmth against the walls of the warehouse. Cripples in rags moaned with the pain. For a fleeting moment, she faltered and the past rushed up to meet her. Suddenly, she, too, was smelling the vile stench of poverty, feeling the icy cold hand of despair grip her shoulder . . . Then pfft! The moment was gone. She was back in the open plaza, the twenty-five-year-old widow of a wealthy wine merchant on her way to an urgent appointment.

The flower market afforded little variety in midwinter and for the most part stallholders displayed identical wares. Early white Cretan crocus feathered with amethyst, black-eyed anemones forced under glass (and which were already wilting in the freezing air) or pots of late Damascan crocuses, although one booth offered iris, narcissus and the white bells of snowflake for a vastly inflated price, gambling on wealthy womenfolk paying through the nose for exotic, unseasonable blooms. Nevertheless, the bulk of today's trade was in greenery, and trade was brisk. With Saturnalia just one week away, Roman matrons were out in force, sniffing out the best of the bargains in fir, yew, holly and myrtle to deck out their apartments or hang in their halls.

Claudia glanced around. Pretended to peruse the foliage displays. Curled one booted foot round the leg of a collapsible stand. With a crash, the table pitched forward on to the cobbles, spraying evergreens in every direction.

'Junius!' She extracted a prickly holly leaf from the hem of her gown and snapped her fingers. 'Help this poor woman with her table, will you?'

'Must be the cold,' the stallholder muttered, gathering up armfuls of fragrant fir before they were trampled. 'Got into the hinges, I'll wager.'

She was extremely grateful to the young noblewoman for lending her a strong arm to help.

While Junius rushed to lift the collapsed stand, Claudia slipped away. In theory, of course, she should have been able to order her slave to stand guard while she kept her appointment, but theory had no place with the young Gaul. Closer than her own shadow, orders meant nothing when it came to protecting his mistress. Guile was the only solution.

Daylight was fading fast and the smell of the Tiber was sour in Claudia's nostrils as she negotiated her way through the maze of twisty lanes. The din of commerce receded with her every footstep. With the seas closed from October until March, the only traffic on the river in December came from local barges and the occasional coaster. The docks were deserted and Claudia's boots echoed over the quayside.

Funny how circular temples remained so popular in the provinces, yet had long fallen out of favour here in Rome. There were only three of them left – the one she was making for, the Temple of Portunus, Hercules's shrine across the way and, of course, Vesta's temple in the Forum. But whether they were situated in the heart of the Empire or the back of beyond, every circular temple toed the same architectural line. Fluted columns round a circular cell. Domed roof. Elaborate bronze grating between the columns.

In the temple precinct, she paused. 'Captain Moschus?' She could have sworn she'd seen a figure. 'Moschus, is that you?'

A skinny black cat shot out from behind the sacred laurel. Unless the gods had been turning men into animals again, safe to assume it's not the trusty captain. She shrugged off her unease, mounted the steps and pushed open the door.

'I'm a tad late,' she said, and her breath was white in the air.

The man with his back to the altar stone struggled to his feet, dirty hands scrubbing the sleep out of his eyes and pushing greasy, greying locks back from his face. 'No problem, missus. It's your show.'

The tidal wave of body odour sent her reeling. Hygiene, Claudia remembered belatedly, taking in the greasy stains down his waterproof goatskin cloak and the ingrained grime round the neck of his tunic, did not top the captain's list of priorities. But hungry dogs eat dirty puddings, or so the proverb goes. Putting a hand across her nostrils, she got straight to business.

'The *Artemis* is officially recorded as sunk?'

'S'right.' He smiled a black-toothed smile. 'Old Moschus put the word round good and proper.' He sniffed noisily to emphasize his point. 'To all intents and purposes, 'er ribs is scattered over Neptune's sandy soil from Naples to the Messina Straits.'

A simple yes would have done, but never mind. 'You had no trouble convincing the merchant, Butico, that his consignment of Seferius wine went down with her?'

'Word for word like we agreed. "Risky business, shippin' this time of year," I tells him. "Storms whips up outta nowhere and wallop. Lucky to be alive meself," I says. "Me crew escaped by the skin of their teeth."'

'And Butico believed you?'

7

'Looked 'im straight in the eye and said I got fifty witnesses what saw the old girl go down.' A grimy finger tapped the side of his nose knowingly. 'You can trust old Moschus, missus.'

Anything less likely Claudia could not imagine, but under the circumstances, a girl can't afford to be choosy. Especially when the idea had been his in the first place!

When Butico had approached her with a view to purchasing a large consignment of wine for his estate in Sicily, the seas were already closing.

'I'm afraid shipping it would be logistically impossible,' she told him.

'There is a boat, the *Artemis*, which is leaving shortly to lie up in Syracuse for the winter,' Butico pointed out. 'Perhaps she might be willing to oblige?'

Perhaps she might, Claudia thought, but if you don't have the goods to sell, you don't have the goods to sell, although she saw no merit in mentioning that minor detail to Butico. Consequently, she thought no more about it, until Moschus knocked on her door two days later.

'I hear you might have a cargo for me?'

She'd had to come clean then. Admit that she didn't have the quantity in stock that Butico wanted. But instead of shrugging and turning away, the old sea dog had laughed.

'Don't see that as no problem, missus. I mean, Butico ain't to know, is he?'

Suppose they pretended the shipment went down in a storm? With his estate on Sicily, Butico, more than most, would know the unpredictability of the Ionian Sea, the storms that ravage her coasts. And old Moschus could sure use the money, he'd added, almost drooling.

'Uh-uh. This is out and out robbery,' Claudia had replied. 'Bargepoles aren't long enough for me to touch this.'

Besides. Not only would they be defrauding some poor slob of an awful lot of sesterces, but if she was caught, she would be stripped of her assets and exiled. No fear!

'Butico's richer than Croesus,' the captain spat. 'Small change to 'im, that.'

'Maybe so, but—'

'Trust me, he won't even miss it, and if it's your pretty skin you're worried about, forget it.' The old sea dog had wiped his nose noisily with the back of his hand. 'Once I gets the *Artemis* refitted and sailing under a new name and canvas, you and me's got no worries.'

Claudia glanced at the statue of Portunus the harbour god and hoped to heaven he was right. 'As agreed, then.' From her purse she withdrew five bronze receipts, each stamped with the hallmark of the Temple of Castor and Pollux. Each token would redeem a thousand sesterces from the depository.

Moschus's price was high. Very high. But there was his crew to be bribed, as well as the *Artemis*'s refit, but even then Claudia had made a comfortable three thousand on the deal. Outside, daylight was almost gone, but she was taking no chances being seen with the captain. She would allow Moschus a slow count of thirty before following.

Nine, ten, eleven—

A figure appeared in the doorway. Taller. Broader. Better dressed than Moschus, and a decade younger.

Call it the twilight, but to Claudia, inside that tiny circular shrine of Portunus the harbour god, the figure looked extremely reminiscent of Butico. *The merchant whose consignment of wine was supposed to have washed into Neptune's sandy soil from Naples to the Messina Straits.*

Two

Bastard! Double-crossing, dirty, filthy bastard. But whatever Claudia's feelings towards Captain Moschus, they would have to wait. Butico was advancing across the floor towards her, menace oozing from every well-shod pore.

'Eight thousand, I believe, was the sum I paid you for that wine.'

The very coldness of his tone forced Claudia's mouth into a smile. Teeth, teeth, show him more teeth. Let him see you're not afraid. 'It's not what you think, Butico.'

Suddenly there were no more teeth left to show.

'Well, now, I'm sure we can come to terms,' Butico said smoothly.

With exaggerated slowness, he flipped one length of cloak over one shoulder, then did the same for the other. Dusk might be falling, but there was no mistaking the gleam of steel on each hip.

Claudia had been a dancer before she changed her identity and dancers, by their very definition, must be light on their feet, fast and, above all, they have to be flexible. She was past him before he could blink, and suddenly she was cursing the wide open space of the quayside. Where were the sailors, the stevedores, the labourers when you wanted one? Where was the crowd she could lose herself in? Cursing her own stupidity for giving her own bodyguard the slip, she flew down the steps, cloak billowing behind like a sail. Halfway across the precinct, she heard Butico

10

bark a command. Two heavies stepped out from behind the sacred laurel, blocking her path.

'All right, Butico, you win,' she said, skidding to a halt.

The heavies turned to each other, grinning smugly. That was all the time she needed. In the split second they locked eyes to congratulate themselves on their intimidation tactics, Claudia dived between their legs. A huge paw lashed out, but the eel was too fast and before they could turn, she was racing across the quayside for all she was worth. Footsteps pounded behind her. Which way, which way? The obvious course was to backtrack, follow the route she'd come by, but goddammit they were running like Olympic athletes and at this pace they would be upon her long before she reached the flower market and the crush of safety. Her only chance was to lose them by ducking and diving.

She realized her mistake almost at once. Not only were the thugs keeping pace as she ducked and dived round the alleys, Claudia was being sucked deeper and deeper into the slums. Between the tall tenements, the last of the twilight was obliterated. Moans and wails unfurled from every window. A gagging stench permeated the air, a combination of rotting meat, dog piss, sewage and despair. Many of the cobbles were missing, making every step a hazard which threatened to trip her or turn an ankle, leaving her helpless and stranded. On she ran, feeling her way with her hands. She heard screams from open windows. Fists connecting with flesh. Babies bawling, dogs baying, but loudest of all were the footsteps behind her.

Desperate now, she flung her purse on the ground, scattering the coins noisily over the stones to bring out the slum dwellers and impede her pursuers. Too late. A hand spun her round. Sent her crashing against the tenement wall, knocking the breath from her lungs. In the blackness, she saw the oaf grinning, and this time the grin didn't fade.

'Well, well, well! Thought you could lose us, didya?'

The second set of footsteps drew up alongside. Both men

laughed. The laugh made Claudia's blood turn to ice. 'Touch me again and I'll cry rape, you fat bastards.'

One smelled of garlic, the other of straw. They both stank of sweat.

'She did say rape, didn't she?'

Oh god, they meant it. She could see the gleam in their eyes, felt their arousal through her thick furs. Even if she screamed, who would come? One lonely scream among hundreds. One more lost soul among thousands. Unseen hands could be heard, scrabbling in the blackness for her coins, but they would not come to her aid. Within seconds, they would disappear back inside the crumbling death traps, unconcerned where the coins came from, only where they were going. Six storeys of hopelessness pressed down upon her as hands clawed at her flesh, fingers probed without subtlety.

'Enough!'

Butico's implacable tones cut through the howls of the slums like a scythe. The mauling stopped.

'One thing you need to be aware of, my dear,' he said quietly. His hand cupped her jaw. 'No one gets away from Butico.'

He glanced up at the crumbling plaster, wrinkled his nose at the stench.

'Now, before you so rudely walked out of our meeting, I believe we were discussing the eight thousand sesterces you owe me.'

'I don't have eight—'

His hand turned into a vice, crushing her cheeks. 'Plus interest.' He leaned over, his cold eyes level with hers. 'You see, me, I like the good things in life. Greek sculpture. Gourmet foods. Vintage wines. You get my drift?'

She nodded as far as his grip would permit.

'But my boys, here.' When he smiled, Claudia felt a chill to her marrow. 'Well, the fine arts, I'm afraid, pass right over their heads, though they still appreciate pretty things. Don't you, lads?'

'Sure do, boss.' A paw clamped over Claudia's breast and squeezed to prove the point.

'My rate of interest,' Butico said, releasing his grip on her jaw, 'is thirty-two per cent.'

'*Thirty-two?*' Terrified as she was, that was still an outrageous amount.

'Effective the day I handed over the cash,' he continued smoothly. 'Which, as I recall, was exactly one month ago, bringing the outstanding balance to—'

'Yes, yes, I can do the maths, thank you very much.'

She couldn't. Was in no position to think, much less calculate. She just needed to claw back her dignity, regain some kind of control. Pointedly she swatted the paw off her breast, thankful her trembling hand could not be seen in the dark. She felt sick.

'Then we understand one another,' he said.

'We do indeed. I pay you back, with interest, or you throw me to your dogs as a bone.'

'No, no, no.' Butico tutted gently, and the sound made the hairs on the back of her neck stand up on end. 'Either way, I get my money back, Claudia. Whether my boys get to play with you is dependent entirely upon yourself.'

He brushed bits of crumbling plaster from his cloak. 'Fair's fair, after all.'

He smiled.

'Fuck with me and they fuck you.'

Three

Crossing the Forum, her beaver fur drawn tight around her chin, Claudia hoped to Juno that her pinched, white face and chattering teeth would be attributed to the cold. What a mess. What an absolutely bloody awful mess. Oblivious to the fire-eaters that had drawn a crowd over by the Vulcanal, or the crush of hot-pie vendors pressing in around her, the captain's words echoed in her ears.

You can trust old Moschus, missus.

Couldn't you! You could trust the bastard to go straight to the Temple of Castor and Pollux after leaving her, so that by the time she arrived, it was to find the depository locked up for the night and the records showing all too clearly the sea dog's mark where he'd redeemed five tokens for a thousand sesterces each. Claudia's fists clenched. When I catch up with you, Moschus, those will be *your* ribs scattered over Neptune's sandy soil from Naples to Messina. So help me, I shall personally break them off and drop them in the ocean one by one – and you can bloody watch me!

Meanwhile, there was Butico. Eight thousand plus thirty-two per cent interest? Her stomach churned, her limbs felt like jelly and her hands couldn't stop shaking, so she exchanged a silver bracelet for a flagon of warm wine spiced with cinnamon, and pretty soon her teeth ceased to chatter. The Rostra, the splendid new orators' platform at the end of the Forum, was eighty feet long, forty feet deep and forested with an assortment of marble,

14

bronze and gilded heroes. Sheltered from the biting wind by the Record Office behind, Claudia leaned her back against the bronze grille of the balustrade and dangled her feet over the edge. Far below, a cosmopolitan sea swirled around the temples and basilicas, the fountains and the arches – revellers, hawkers, bankers and astrologers, dogs, mules, fortune-tellers and jugglers, even a string of roped ostriches.

No point in trying to negotiate with Butico, asking him if he'd accept wine in lieu of cash. She'd already made her bed by double-crossing him, she had to lie in it and the main thing now was to ensure she didn't end up sharing it with two hulking great thugs! For the life of her, she couldn't understand why she didn't just sell this wretched business and be done with. It was why she'd married Gaius in the first place, wasn't it? For the money?

Slowly, the scroll that was her past unravelled.

It revealed a young girl taking elocution lessons – and the identity of a noblewoman who'd died in the plague. Of that same girl exchanging marriage vows with a man nearly three times her own age. Signed, sealed and delivered, what more could a girl from the slums ask for? Son of a humble road builder and a self-made man himself, Gaius hadn't noticed any shortfall in the social niceties. All that concerned him was that he had a beautiful, witty young wife to parade and, had Claudia died before him, no doubt he would have had her stuffed and mounted on his office wall. But of course she hadn't. Instead, and with unaccustomed expedience, it was Gaius who'd whistled up the Ferryman to take that long ride across the River Styx. That had been fifteen months ago, shortly before the sixth anniversary of his wedding, and, to the horror of his blood relatives, he bequeathed his trophy widow the lot. Large house in Rome. Vineyards in Tuscany. Investments in housing, in shops, in numerous commercial enterprises.

Happy ending? Dream on.

Before his ashes were cool, the Guild of Wine Merchants were muscling in to take over his patch. They tried everything. Buying her out, bullying her out, cajoling, seducing, flattering, beseeching, and all to no avail. At first Claudia hung on out of stubbornness. Gaius might have been bald and fat and in the grip of terminal halitosis, but dammit, he'd worked his whole life to build up his network of trade. Those vultures should not be allowed to simply move in and pick the bones clean. *She* would be the one who decided what and when to sell. Gradually, though, she saw how profitable the wine business was. By hanging on to it, not only could she continue to live in the style to which she'd grown accustomed without dipping into her capital, it would be one in the eye for the Guild of Ghouls.

Only it wasn't that simple. Normally fiercely competitive in the marketplace, the bastards put their differences aside and united. Anything to force Claudia Seferius out of business.

Over her dead body!

On the platform behind her, a living statue painted head to foot in white lime was posing motionless in imitation of the genuine articles lined up on their plinths. Small children tried lobbing pellets and stones to distract him, but the statue remained a study in muscular rigidity.

It wasn't that Claudia was felonious by nature. She drained the last of the warm, spicy wine. Hand on her heart, she would not have ripped Butico off had her hand not been forced. To survive the cut-throat world that she'd inherited, she was having to meet dirty trick with dirty trick and her current strategy was to undercut the Guild with prices so low that buyers simply couldn't say no. Seferius wine was synonymous with quality, so why not get the punters hooked, then gradually increase the price to market levels? So far, so good, and Claudia had a stack of purchasers lined up for the next vintage. Unfortunately, she was selling at such a thumping great loss that resources were currently stretched to breaking point. And now, of course, it was Saturnalia.

Below her dangling squirrel-lined boots, a cart delivering bricks locked wheels with another delivering cotton in the tight space in front of the sacred lotus tree. Within no time, fists and bales, insults and cobs were flying over the Forum as both drivers claimed right of way. Mules bucked in the harness. The donkey with the cotton cart brayed and kicked anyone who tried to intercede. Claudia lifted her gaze to the Palatine.

Saturnalia, when it was customary (compulsory) for merchants to cross the palms of their clients with silver. Five to six pounds in weight, to be exact. *Apiece!* Dear god, how was she supposed to find that kind of money with Butico's shadow looming over her? Silver was the yard-stick against which clients measured success, and if she didn't deliver, they would smell a rat and default. The business would sink without trace.

The stench of conspiracy was all over this scam, but by heaven, she would not let the Guild win this battle—

'It's funny,' a melodious baritone murmured in her ear, 'how nothing travels through the universe faster than a rumour.'

Claudia turned in time to see a pair of red patrician boots easing themselves over the grille, followed by a long patrician tunic encased in spotless white patrician toga. Terrific. That's all I need. The Security Police.

'I tend to think of rumours as fires,' she said. 'Ignore them and they fizzle out.'

'Then I must have been a blacksmith in a previous life,' he replied. 'Or maybe a bathhouse stoker.'

He smelled of sandalwood, with just the faintest hint of the rosemary in which his clothes had been rinsed. The unmistakable scent of the hunter—

'What do you want, Orbilio?'

'Who said I wanted anything?'

17

'Then why are you attaching yourself to me like a rash?'

'You could always try rubbing ointment all over me and see whether I vanish.'

The eyes might be twinkling, but make no mistake. Petting lions in the arena carried less risk.

'Isn't there a law against the harassment of grieving young widows?' she asked, as he made himself comfortable on the stonework beside her.

'Edict five-eight-three, sub-section twenty-two, paragraph six and a half,' he said happily. *'Provided the widows are grieving.'*

'Very funny.'

'I thought so.'

Ah, yes. The more urbane, the more dangerous . . .

From the corner of her eye, she watched him comb his mop of dark, wavy hair with casual hands. Noted the crisp, dark hairs on the back of his forearm. And contrasted them with fifteen years of penniless exile.

'So then.' He folded his arms over his chest and leaned his back against the metal grille. His legs were long enough for his feet to rest on one of the gleaming bronze prows set in the wall of the Rostra, trophies from ships captured in Rome's naval victory at Antium. 'How's business?'

Claudia's gaze swung to the tall, gabled building to the east of the Rostra, with the letters SPQR over the door. Ambitious as he was cultured, determined as he was handsome, Marcus Cornelius Orbilio had his sights set on a seat in that building some day. The question was, how soon was that day? The more results he chalked up, the closer his maiden speech in the Senate – and let's face it, a nice juicy fraud would close the distance considerably.

'Senators Please Queue Respectfully,' she said.

'Excuse me?'

'The letters,' she said. 'I was wondering what they stood for. "Small Profits, Quick Returns"? "Sleeping Politicians' Quiet Recess"?'

'I always thought it was "Sharks, Pimps, Quacks and Rogues".'

'Yes, but you're biased. Half your family sits there.'

'That's slander,' he protested. 'My kinsmen are far too busy rogering their popsies to waste time on trivia like laws and foreign policy. Anyway.' He brushed an imaginary speck from his toga. 'You never did tell me how you're coping, a lone woman in a pit of hungry tigers.'

'If you mean the Guild, you've read them wrong. Underneath the stripes, they're just a load of pussy cats. Did you know, they've invited me to join them?'

'Can you smell something?' he asked, twisting his head to look over his shoulder. 'Only I thought I smelled a bull on the Rostra. One that hasn't been house trained.'

'Good heavens.' Claudia pointed towards the sacred lotus tree lit by torches. 'I do believe I see my best friend Antonia down there. Must dash, Marcus, so lovely to see you again.'

Skipping nimbly over the balustrade, Claudia ran across the platform and skipped down the steps without a backward glance. Strangely though, despite the shouts of the hawkers, the cries of the alms-seekers, the cracks of the bull-whips and the creaking of carts, the only sound she could hear was the echo of Orbilio's words inside her head.

'One day, Claudia Seferius.' He hadn't even bothered to unfold his arms or uncross his ankles from where they were resting on the bronze prow. 'One day, you'll realize that I'm the best friend you have.'

Come into my parlour, said the spider to the fly.

Pausing to let a chariot pass, Claudia laughed. Honestly, Marcus Cornelius. Do I look like I have wings?

Four

For a woman on her own, the Forum after nightfall was safe enough. Reeds burning in sconces on every plinth and wall illuminated the place like a midsummer noon, and the greatest risk to Claudia's person came not from pickpockets or muggers, but from a hobnailed boot crushing her toes or a poke in the ribs from an elbow. Which was not to say the same philosophy applied to the streets leading off! The further from the Forum, the greater the danger, and not just from pickpockets, either. There had been talk of Augustus setting up a corps of *vigiles*. Servants of the State who could police the dark alleyways and backstreets and protect travellers from the gangs of roaming thieves and footpads who valued silver more than human life. But so far only a few vague political promises had materialized, and Claudia decided to invest another bangle in a litter to take her home. There was a stand near the prison, on the corner of Silversmith's Rise, and it was here she set out for.

It wasn't coincidence, the Security Police turning up this afternoon. Somehow, Orbilio knew the *Artemis* hadn't sunk in any storm. She edged her way round a knot of kilted Syrian archers and past a Gaulish merchant selling silky deer-skin tunics. He'd know exactly whose mythical cargo she'd been carrying and was most likely on his way to Butico's right this minute, with a view to getting him to testify against her. Wasted journey, chum. Butico wasn't the type who'd write off his investment in the name of justice. Butico would want his money back, plus interest. *Then* he'd testify against her.

On the steps of the Senate, a bearded Arab with bangles round his wrist was selling bottled lizards' tongues mixed with seal rennet and yellow spiders as a cure for obesity and pots of sticky purple cream, guaranteed to restore hair, while a boy of no more than nine made dogs with ribbons round their collars dance through hoops.

For the first time this afternoon, Claudia felt a faint stirring of hope. Strange as it might seem, Butico's procrastination might actually work in her favour. Defrauding merchants was undoubtedly a crime, but quite how far the Security Police were prepared to push the matter was moot. Give him a good old-fashioned conspiracy and you wouldn't see Marcus Cornelius for dust, and this was Rome, after all. Plots hatched faster than lice, all she had to do was hold on to her nerve.

She was approaching the corner by the prison on Silversmith's Rise when a rainbow exploded from a tavern.

'Get out and stay out!' the landlord was bellowing. 'All of you!'

'Good sir, I must protest,' the smallest and most portly element of the rainbow complained, as it picked itself up from the flagstones. 'These dear ladies—'

'Them ain't ladies, and them ain't expensive, neither. Set one foot within ten yards of this establishment, you *or* yer cheap tarts, and I'll set the dogs on yer.'

'Go to hell!' one of the ladies in question retorted, and the shortest and most portly component of the rainbow groaned.

'Such sentiments, dear Jemima, aid our cause not.'

To prove his point, a volley of trunks, packs and cases came hurtling through the hostelry door, much to the delight of the crowd which was starting to gather. Far from being embarrassed by the concourse, his little fat face brightened.

'An audience,' he breathed, and when he bowed, the feather in his bright blue turban swept the ground. 'Ladies and gentlemen, allow me to acquaint you with "Caspar's

Spectaculars". Pantomime, opera, tragedy—'

'Ham!' someone shouted.

'—comedy, drama, political satire—'

'Your actors are so wooden,' another wag called, 'I've seen better performances from oak trees.'

The crowd quickly warmed to the theme. 'Oak-smoked hams!'

'With lots of stuffing,' someone added, indicating Caspar's rotund belly.

Then a wagon delivering jars of olive oil to an address up the hill came rumbling round the corner to spoil the fun and, with one last rattle of good-natured insults, the audience dispersed into the night. Claudia would have gone, too, only she was stuck between the cart and the tavern wall.

There were about twenty members in Caspar's patchwork troupe, she counted. Mostly male, but the group also included half a dozen well-upholstered girls.

'Madam. I am utterly charmed to make your acquaintance.'

This time Caspar swept off his turban when he bowed, revealing a gleaming bald head encircled by tight black shiny curls. A better arena for staging a performance Claudia hadn't seen, even in the Theatre of Marcellus. He replaced the turban and brushed the dust off his rose-red embroidered tunic.

'I trust this ugly contretemps will not deter you from coming along to enjoy one of Caspar's Spectaculars whilst the company is in Rome?' He flicked a piece of stale pie crust off his elbow. 'Mention my name at the door, dear lady, and you are assured of the best seat in the house.'

Don't mind if I do. 'Which house might that be, exactly?'

'Ah.' Plump hands spread in an open-palmed gesture as his fellow thespians collected up the baggage. 'The appropriate venue, alas, is proving troublesome.' He flashed a caustic glance at the landlord. 'I shall have to advise you in due course, dear lady, of our next theatrical address.'

'Which particular Spectacular do you recommend?' Not that it mattered. Any one of them must be a hoot.

'My word, you pose some tricky questions,' Caspar said, wringing his hands and inspiring Claudia to wonder whether his appendages were ever still, even when he slept. 'A major problem for touring companies such as ours lies in the transient nature of the workforce,' he explained. 'Most of these lovely people have been with me for only a matter of weeks, and one can hardly train them in the nuances of the classics when they're still wet behind the ears.'

'Which reduces the options to what?'

'To writing the scripts myself,' he sighed. 'And therein lies another problem. An impresario runs the most terrible risks if his scripts owe more to plagiarism than originality.'

Claudia was getting the drift. 'In other words, you're without a play and you don't have a venue to put it on, even if you had one?'

'Staging a production is nothing if not a challenge, madam.'

Notoriously slow movers at the best of times, the oxen had ground to a halt, refusing point-blank to turn the corner into Silversmith's Rise. Caspar, his shivering troupe and Claudia seemed doomed to spend the evening squashed together in the tavern door, and the drop in trade wasn't improving the landlord's temper any.

'This is yours 'an all, mate,' he growled, tossing down a marble bust from the balcony overhead.

Caspar just managed to catch the statuette before it lost its nose on the rear wheel of the ox cart. 'That, sir,' he called up, 'is no way to treat the dear departed.'

'Your wife?' Claudia asked, watching him tenderly brush the painted face and blow the dust off the smiling cheeks of the figurine. Like the other female members in his troupe, the dear departed had been far from the final throes of starvation.

The feather in the turban nodded sadly.

'How did she die?' Claudia asked. He certainly liked his women big, did Caspar.

'Die?' His little eyebrows rose. 'Good heavens, madam, the good lady didn't die, she just departed.' He tucked the bust underneath his arm and patted it. 'Somewhere around Athens, if my memory serves me correctly.'

Claudia sucked her cheeks in. 'You obviously miss her.'

'You have no idea,' he intoned sombrely. 'Damn good playwright, that woman. Oh, I beg you not to laugh, madam. The company faces a serious predicament this year. Once upon a time, we could put on a show and people would just be pleased to see us. Today every pleb's a critic and when certain criteria are required of one's production, it can prove difficult.'

Caspar was referring to the stringent rules which governed every script, be they enacted on the streets or in stone amphitheatres, where every play had to conform to a stereotyped cast list.

'Between ourselves, madam, not all the dramatics in the range I proclaimed are performed by our company.'

'No opera?'

Gloomy shake of the turban.

'No tense dramas?'

Again, the turban shook sadly from side to side. 'Even tragedy is out of the question,' he said. 'When things go wrong, as they are prone to do in a small touring company whose thespian turnover is faster than the blink of an eye, a laugh on a child's deathbed scene makes the difference between being showered with silver and being showered with distressed vegetable waste.'

'Which only leaves comedy.'

'I do not pretend to understand modern audiences when I tell you that the best laughs come from storylines involving pimps and prostitutes,' Caspar said. 'But sadly they've been done to death this season. What I'm left with are plots revolving round swaggering soldiers who think they're the gods' gift to women, grasping misers who get their comeuppance and beautiful girls without brains in love with penniless poets. Of course, I need the obligatory mix-up surrounding identical twins, and if the poor playwright can throw in a couple of cuckolds, so much the better.'

Caspar rubbed the statuette with affection.

'A sad miss, my dear wife, a sad miss.'

'So why don't you write a play round a grasping miser with an airhead of a wife who conspires to relieve him of his gold so she can elope with her handsome, but penniless, poet lover?' Claudia asked.

'Ho!' Caspar was jumping up and down, and not from the cold. 'Magnificent, madam, absolutely magnificent. Dear me, you possess more creative talent than the dear departed! Now if I could only devise a happy ending, whereby the lovers run off with the money and make the husband look small . . .'

'How about the poet has a secret identical twin who agrees to recite his poetry before a group of drunken, swaggering soldiers to provide his brother with an alibi for the time of the robbery . . . ?'

'Sublime!' For a moment she thought he'd wet himself. 'Utterly, brilliantitiously sublime!'

'Not utterly, brilliantitiously implausible, you don't think? To the point of, say, ludicrous and far-fetched?'

Caspar calmed down enough to roll his eyes at the very suggestion. 'We are looking at comedy here, madam. At pantomime. Farce. Escapist entertainment. Nudity.'

'*Nudity?*'

The entrepreneur gave an exaggerated wink. 'Nudity pays the rent, dear lady. Especially volumptuous beauties like mine.' He laced his little fat fingers. 'And since musical farce is the one area in which women are allowed on the stage, it would be a shame to waste their plumptious talents.'

Nudity. Claudia smiled as the oxen were finally coerced

into moving. Never let it be said that this had not been one eventful afternoon!

Caspar took advantage of the space to envelop her in his arms and shower her face with kisses that smelled of rose-water. 'You have bestowed upon me a veritable triumph, madam. This play will be the talk of all Rome.' More kisses rained down on her cheek. 'How can I *ever* thank you?'

The oxen had plodded off and were out of sight round the corner. Claudia drew her beaver fur around her. The litter stand was just across the street.

'Well, Caspar. It's funny you should ask.'

Forget the five to six pounds of silver. This latest Spectacular, with its 'volumptuous' beauties and musical farce, couldn't fail to impress potential clients. And with four days of public holiday, that was a lot of clients Claudia could squeeze in to be impressed!

As Caspar said, bawdiness was the order of the day as far as Roman comedy was concerned, and Claudia could see her clients' eyes popping out on stalks when the girls were on stage and a mischievous wind, manufactured in the wings, accidentally blew aside the thin scarves that draped round their bodies or forced their clothes to cling tight to their spectacular curves.

Best of all, though, by staging the revue at her house, no financial outlay was required. She looked around the rainbow group, shivering in the cold as they staggered under their burdens of chests, trunks and baggage, their stomachs rumbling from hunger, and marvelled at this amazing new direction that her life was taking.

Not taking on a string of gadfly actors.

Going straight.

Excitedly, the company gathered up the array of trunks and clutter.

Packed in the tight, concise way that only travelling

people manage to achieve were all the things essential to a theatrical performance. Costumes. Buskins. Musical instruments. Masks. Painted scenery boards were far too bulky for a troupe of strolling players to cope with, and for that reason painted canvases served as backdrops. These could then be rolled up tight and hung quickly and easily by means of a simple pulley system.

Gripping the leather strap of one of the prop chests and oblivious to the running chatter of the young lad on the other, the Digger smiled.

A lot of things had happened since autumn.

And they kept getting better and better—

Five

Claudia's lanky Macedonian steward did not so much as blink when his mistress charged into the atrium, threw her fur cloak into his arms, chafed her hands over the charcoals in the brazier, then calmly announced that there would be twenty strolling players arriving shortly who would be staying over Saturnalia, oh and could he prepare a hot bath, please, her feet were blocks of ice.

Leonides didn't blink, for the simple reason that he couldn't.

He just stood there, beaver fur halfway up his nostrils, paralysed.

God knows, when Master Gaius was alive, there was a constant traipse of clients, scribes, secretaries and messengers buzzing in and out. It wasn't that he couldn't cope. Or that there had been any less traffic in the house since the master's death. Admittedly, it was a different kind of busy and heaven help him, it was nothing to have the master's carping relatives in one room, members of certain law-enforcement agencies in another and irate moneylenders in a third, whilst he ran back and forth between them like some demented monkey, serving wine and honey cakes while the mistress was out implicating herself in an even deeper jam.

But all the same. Strolling *players*!

Leonides dragged himself to his senses. No point in lamenting. The deed was done and the person who could talk the young mistress into changing her mind hadn't been born yet.

28

'Lock up the silver,' he urged the household slaves. 'Take everything away that might be flogged before we've had a chance to notice that it's missing, plan on four to a room and don't forget to count the blankets on the bed.'

Outside, voices, common ones at that, were growing louder. The dog next door began to howl. Leonides knew exactly how it felt. Within seconds, a laughing, shivering, grumbling prism of colours, shapes and textures surged through the vestibule door, filling the atrium with odours of wet wool and leather, cheap scent and cosmetics. What had he done to offend the gods, he wondered? He, who led the household prayers piously every morning and poured generous libations with conscientious regularity.

'Dear lady.'

A small tornado in scarlet embroidered kaftan and what looked for all the world like a blue parrot bobbing on his head pushed his way to the front of the crush, his shining eyes on Claudia.

'Allow me to compliment you on your charming house. Utterly enchanting, madam. Just like your wondrous self.'

'Enough with the flattery, Caspar, I've already allocated you a guest bedroom,' Claudia laughed. The others would have to take their chances in the slave quarters.

'Dear lady, my motives are entirely selfless,' Caspar said, affecting a mock wound. 'Your domicile positively oozes taste. Sophistication and elegance weep from every marble column.'

Claudia was glad he approved. Many of the features were additions (costly ones at that) she'd had installed upon her husband's death. Features designed to impress potential business contacts, proof that Gaius's business ventures were not merely ticking over in his widow's hands, but prospering. A lie, of course, but image is everything when it's a man's world, dog eat dog. Her eyes ranged with pride over the soaring atrium with its exquisite mosaics, marble busts and Nile frescoes, the fountain which babbled gently night and day, the aviary of tiny birds which sang their little hearts out. Not all new, of course. But combined, the house was the embodiment of commercial success.

'Allow me, madam, to introduce the cast, starting with the star of our Spectaculars—' Caspar presented a tall, blond chap whose hair owed more to art than nature '—the sinuous Felix.'

On cue, Felix bent himself backwards so his palms touched the floor behind his heels and then effortlessly performed the splits.

'Felix is our mime solo,' Caspar added proudly. 'And this is Jupiter.'

As with all strolling players, every male member of the company was typecast in certain roles, but towering over everyone, with his curled beard and long black hair falling to his shoulders, his olive skin and saturnine good looks, the actor could easily be mistaken for the King of the Immortals.

'Should I swoon or curtsy?' Claudia asked.

'With Jupiter, you should probably be taking your clothes off,' the young man laughed, 'but sometimes Caspar forgets that I'm only the Sorter of Problems on stage. My name,' he added with a broad grin, 'is Ion.'

But before Claudia could reply, a swarthy individual with thick, bushy eyebrows was kissing both of her cheeks.

'I'm Urgularius Philippus,' he said. 'But you may as well call me what everyone else does. Ugly Phil.'

The nickname was unfair. He had a pleasant face and green eyes that twinkled, but you could see how he'd got the name.

'And because I'm the shortest, I'm cast as the Satyr.'

'He doesn't need much by way of costume, either,' quipped a craggy-faced actor, whose shaven head marked him out as the Buffoon. 'The furry leggings are natural,' he chortled.

The introductions went on. She met Periander, a fat

youth, who'd been castrated at the age of twelve to keep his soprano voice clear and pure, but her attention had wandered. It was attracted by a young man with finely chiselled cheekbones whose eyes bore a thin but nevertheless distinctive trace of kohl and who was watching her closely.

'Finally, madam—' with a sweep of his little fat hand, Caspar ushered forward the female members of the troupe, '—please welcome my splendiferous harem of beauties.'

Good grief. Claudia had no idea that fat could be broken down into so many different categories. There was solid fat, wobbly fat, provocative fat – this latter category being Jemima of the bright red hair and unfettered tongue, who seemed perfectly oblivious to the amount of bosom she was showing, goose pimples and all. Then there was fat that tried to hide it, fat that tried to enhance its beauty with cosmetics and, finally, there was fat that simply didn't give a damn.

Behind them, the men were admiring the acoustics more than the décor and had already launched into their stereotyped roles. Jupiter was courting an effeminate Venus, while the leering Satyr prowled behind him, playing his imaginary pan pipes. The Poet, on bended knee, was wooing his Lover into adultery with verse. But it was the Buffoon who stole the scene, launching alternately into monkey walks, then pretending to trip over invisible obstacles before being chased by his own shaven-headed shadow.

'Renata,' Caspar said, having to raise his voice over the babble as he kissed the hand of the woman whose face was a stiff mask of white chalk and rouge. 'Our musician and our rock. She plays flute for Felix's mime, but clever girl that she is, Renata also plays the pan pipes and tuba.'

'Don't forget the twin pipes, the horn and the cornet,' Renata chided.

'The way she carries on,' Wobbly Fat snapped, 'you'd think she played all six at once.'

'Ah, the lovely Adah,' Caspar said, patting Wobbly Fat on her ample bottom. 'Then we have the plumptious Fenja.'

Tall as a legionary, solid as a dam, fair of hair and blue of eye, the girl had to be of Nordic origin.

'You ferry kind, inviting us to stay wid you.'

Claudia thought of those quaint Nordic customs that so endeared them to the Roman populace. Punishing homosexuality by pressing the offender under a stone until dead. Public flogging for adulterous wives. Criminals executed by being pegged down in a peat bog.

'You hef luffly villa,' Fenja said, cracking her knuckles. 'Much good taste.'

Claudia had an idea that when Fenja talked of moving house, she meant picking it up and physically carting it off on her back.

'Jemima, of course, you already know.' Caspar's eyeballs nearly disappeared down the redhead's magnificent cleavage.

'Everyone knows Jem,' Adah put in cattily. 'Leastways, half the men in Rome do.'

'Bollocks,' Jemima said, winking at Claudia. 'It's less than a third, yer jealous cow.'

To prevent a catfight, Caspar thrust forward a girl whose frizzy hair was escaping from her hairpins to give her the appearance of a startled hedgehog. 'Hermione.'

'It'th tho kind of you to thponthor uth,' Hermione lisped. 'We won't be no trouble.'

Claudia sincerely hoped not. She had enough to contend with, thanks to Butico, Moschus and the Security Police.

'And last, but never least,' Caspar gushed, 'the lovely Erinna.'

If Hermione was the one who tried to hide her shape, Erinna was the girl who didn't give a damn. Unlike the others, who were slaves to fashion with their cheap, but trendy pleated gowns and bright, embroidered hems, Erinna's long, chestnut hair wasn't contorted into fashionable styles with hot tongs. She'd merely twisted it into a dark, glossy bun.

Were there really only six of them, Claudia wondered, counting the splendiferous harem for the umpteenth time? And would they *ever* fit into just two rooms?

'Fine house this, damn fine,' Caspar murmured, accepting a goblet of wine from his hostess. 'I had hoped, you know, that as a producer and director of some years' standing, I would have owned a residence such as this myself by now, but alas, alas. Certain ill-advised investments . . .'

'I had some like that,' Claudia replied. Indeed, a couple of them were still running, she believed.

Across the atrium, the Buffoon was mimicking Leonides behind his back, mirroring the steward's every action and exaggerating it. The more the servants laughed, the more he piled on the comedy, adding a mincing walk as he switched to mimicking Chiselled Cheekbones, then snatching a kiss from an outraged, macho Ion.

'I don't suppose,' Caspar said, fingering an ivory statuette, 'there's a vacancy for a husband in this magnificent establishment?'

'Only a rich one,' Claudia said. 'And besides. You're already married.'

'A technicality, madam, which I assure you would be no impediment, none at all, to any nuptials, should you consent.' He took a long hard glug at the wine. 'Truth to tell, dear lady, there have been three, possibly four, such technicalities during the course of Caspar's travels.'

'You don't remember how many women you've married?'

'Madam!' he protested. 'I recall with the greatest sentiment and clarity the four charming creatures to whom I plighted my troth. There's merely a little question mark over the legality of a certain ceremony in Carthage, an issue which was never entirely resolved. Still.' He brightened visibly. 'One less divorce to worry about, what.'

Claudia sighed contentedly as she retreated to her office. Oh, yes, Caspar's latest Spectacular was going to put a lot of business her way. An *awful* lot. She took a sheet of parchment off the pile, dipped her stylus in the inkwell and began to draft a list of invitees. How could the glitterati fail to be impressed by such a comedy, when half of it did not need any scripting?

Six

Seven hills of Rome. Each very different from its neighbour. The Aventine, for instance, rising from the wharves, had covered its slopes with warehouses and was pretty much the plebeian quarter of the city. The Esquiline, on the other hand, with its cleaner, clearer air, abounded with parks and public gardens and was where rich patricians chose to site their homes. The Capitol, of course, precipitous and once completely forested, stood testament to the Empire's wealth and superiority, which was now symbolized by soaring temples which dominated the skyline.

But it was the Palatine Hill where the seat of power lay.

It was here, on the Palatine, that the most influential of all Rome's temples had been built, the Temple of Apollo. Commissioned by Augustus to commemorate his victory over Mark Antony and Cleopatra, and constructed of solid marble from the quarries of Numidia, the temple housed the great Greek and Latin libraries, as well as the ancient Sybilline prophecies, and was the wonder of its day.

It was on the Palatine that the Imperial Palace stood guard above the Forum, solid and secure as the Empire itself, where hundreds of civil servants busied themselves like bees in a hive to service the massive administration that was Rome.

And it was on the Palatine, in the very shadow of the Emperor's private residence, that the Arch-Hawk of the Senate, Sextus Valerius Cotta, was putting the finishing touches to his speech.

Forty-two years old, lean as a tiger and with a thatch of hair the colour of ripe corn, Cotta cut a figure of envy among an Assembly who, for the most part, were strangers to a full head of hair and their back teeth. His military record was admirable, too, particularly that outstanding victory in Cisalpine Gaul when he was General, and materially he was up there with the best of them, as well. Prestigious address on the Palatine. Large estate in Frascati. Handsome wife who'd borne him four sons. (Not to mention Phyllis, the beautiful and undemanding mistress who had spurned a Consul in favour of Cotta's protection.)

Tonight, though, he was in no mood for socializing and the door to his private office was locked. Crammed with antique furniture, its walls painted in rich, dark, military reds and smelling far too strongly of leather, the room appeared much smaller than it actually was. An effect exacerbated by an array of wall-mounted trophies in the form of antlers, tusks and animal heads, and a floor littered with the skins of various hunted beasts from panther to lion, which, with a bizarre sense of irony, now trapped the heat pumped out by the bronze brazier standing on a tripod in the centre of the office.

'*Stagnation, gentlemen, will be the ruin of Rome,*' he read aloud. '*We should be thinking not of how best to employ Parian marble in our temples, but how best to employ the plunder of the Dacian goldmines.*'

Test the King of Dacia enough and he'll eventually fall to Rome's sword.

'*How best to maximize the potential of the shipping round the Black Sea.*'

The Scythians can't hold out for ever. They'd have to release their grip some time, why not sooner rather than later?

'*And finally, gentlemen, we must consider what treasures might await us, once we finish the job started by the Divine*

*Julius and storm the white cliffs of Britannia in a properly
organized military campaign.'*

Cotta leaned back in his chair and steepled his fingers.
None of these prizes were beyond Rome's capabilities.
Especially now that Augustus had reformed the army to
comprise professionals on twenty-year contracts, rather than
a bunch of raggle-taggle farmers who'd only sign up for a
campaign provided it suited them. Cotta picked up his
stylus.

*'With twenty-eight legions, seven hundred warships,
superior cavalry and the best auxiliaries money can buy,'*
he wrote, *'the eagle's shadow already soars over half the
civilized world. All we need are another five, possibly six
legions and Dacia is in our pocket, Scythia next, then the
whole of the maritime trade round the Black Sea becomes
ours.'*

Fine for Augustus to stand up there and spout about how
peace feeds the people, but son-of-a-bitch! Subduing Dacia,
Britannia and Scythia would bring in a huge influx of slaves,
working even more land, which would lead to even greater
prosperity.

'Arabia,' he scribbled, *'would follow, our stepping stone
to the treasures of the Orient—'*

He scrumpled the parchment and tossed it on to the floor.
He was wasting his breath and he knew it. Hawks were as
popular as the plague in the Senate these days. The
Assembly shot them for sport.

Which was rich, coming from doves.

The trouble was, the governing classes had grown fat on
Rome's victories. Lazy as walruses, they had no desire to
risk their own skins when they could be doing nothing. Tch!
Cotta kicked the leg of his desk. There was no such thing
as 'doing' 'nothing'. Either one did something or one did
not and if Rome was becoming complacent, you could bet
your boots the enemy at the gate was not. Before you know
it, that enemy will have patched up its differences with its

neighbours to become a hundred-headed monster attacking from every direction, and then it'll be too late for the eagle to start fighting back.

Expansion was the only way forward. Conquer the world, and you can be assured of exactly where your enemies are and what they are plotting.

Cotta pushed his chair back and rested his feet on the desk, crossing them at the ankles.

Their counter-argument was that long-term stability lay in consolidating the peace, as opposed to expanding the boundaries. Three generations of civil war had taken their toll, they argued. Neither Rome nor its citizens had the stomach for war, and more importantly nor did their neighbours, they said. A generation was growing up with sons burying their fathers, not the other way round, trade links had been forged and these had raised the living standards of the conquered nations to levels far above their expectations. Moreover, they insisted that many of the smaller tribes actually felt empowered by Rome's military protection, rather than oppressed.

Fine. If Sextus Valerius Cotta couldn't change the views of the Senate, then there was always the other option.

He would have to change those who sat in it.

'Don't say I didn't warn you,' he murmured. 'Don't ever say you weren't fucking warned.'

Seven

As another grey December dawn poked its way through the clouds, Marcus Cornelius Orbilio yawned, put out a hand and found a nipple. It was a very pretty nipple. Pink and perky. And it wasn't one of his. Under his hand, the nipple began to stir. He opened his eyes and got another shock. This wasn't his house. Hell, it wasn't even a house. Just one cramped room, and instead of gazing upon porphyry inlaid with tortoiseshell and silver, at gilded stuccoed ceilings, water clocks and ivory statuettes, the furniture was functional and worn, the bed little more than a wooden shelf jointed to the wall, and if a chap wasn't careful, he'd bang his head on the cooking stove when he rolled off.

From the flat next door, a baby howled and dogs barked in the yard. Footsteps stomped overhead, rattling the ladles which hung over the oven. Most depressing of all, though, in place of sturdy, draughtproof shutters, light from the single window was shut out by a sagging curtain which hung limply on a hook. But at least the curtain was clean, the floorboards scrubbed, the plaster on the walls spotless and the blanket covering him smelled of violets. At home his bedroom would be perfumed with aromatic herbs and resins. Here, the smell of stale cheap wine predominated. Overlaid with sex.

Under his hand, the nipple let out a girlish giggle. 'Who's woken up a naughty boy, then?'

Jupiter in heaven, please, who is she? Where was he? How had he ended up in this impoverished little bedsit? Orbilio tried to think, but was prevented by the relentless clack of castanets behind his eyes. Last night, last night. Where had he been? What was he doing? Dammit, never mind last night. This morning was troublesome enough. Croesus, not only did he have to contend with a perfect little breast swelling in his hand, there was a corresponding swelling in his groin. He groaned, which she mistook for pleasure and began feathering her fingertips lightly down his chest. Lower, lower, lower, until he had to push her hand away.

'Taking it slowly, huh?'

In the early morning light, her face was beautiful. A small, round, pixie face flushed pink with sleep, surrounded by a halo of frothy honey curls. Any man would feel it a privilege to wake up next to such an enchanting creature. Any man except Orbilio. How the blazes had he got here? Why couldn't he remember?

'Slow is fine by me,' she whispered, running her tongue inside his ear.

'I have to be on duty early.' Despite himself, a shiver of desire rippled through his loins. 'Today's the day the new tribunes assume elected office.'

Being the sole member of the aristocracy attached to the Security Police, this meant Orbilio was the only person his boss could call on for assistance with the protocols of the governing classes. Another resentment Callisunus could then add to his list, since, being equestrian class himself, he bitterly begrudged having to rely on a patrician for advice on social matters. A subordinate, at that. By way of retaliation, and as though it was Orbilio's fault that he was born to the nobility, Callisunus would proceed to toss him every rotten assignment that he could. But today the Head of the Security Police needed his patrician subordinate at his shoulder when the tribunes were sworn in. Just in case of gaffes.

'You don't have to go,' the pixie wheedled. 'You could send a message saying something's come up.' She giggled again. 'After all, it's the truth.'

'I'd love to stay, darling,' he lied, 'but this is a big day.'

'It certainly is,' she giggled.

He groaned. 'No, really. I have to go.'

Croesus, she was lovely. Sexy, too, with her slim white hips and soft white skin. Her legs went on for ever. But he didn't know the woman. Couldn't even remember her name, for heaven's sake – and whatever rapport the drink had established between them last night, it did not constitute a relationship in the true sense of the word. Therefore, it followed that, if he consummated the urges his body was telling him to, he was reducing the pixie to the level of a whore and himself to— To what? What worm was lower than the man too drunk to know – or care – who gave him satisfaction?

Images of another woman burned his brain. A woman with flashing eyes and dark, tumbling curls, and although he had as much chance of taming Claudia Seferius as he had of throwing a harness round the wind, when he made love, he wanted to experience all the passion, all the red-hot anguish, pain and pleasure that the act entailed. His gut wrenched as he imagined himself burying his face in those dark curls. Inhaling the scent of her intense Judaean perfume. Running his tongue round that little dip in her collarbone. To submit to copulation for its own sake in the cold, clear light of sobriety was not the same and whilst he supposed a man could argue that succumbing to his sexual urges when he'd hit rock bottom didn't make a scrap of difference at this stage – just be stronger next time, Marcus, and *try* not to end up naked in a bed with any more attractive nympho-maniacs – he wasn't fooling anyone, much less himself.

'I'm already late,' he told the pixie, swinging out of her exquisite nibbling clutches and narrowly missing the edge of the stove.

'You'll call round tonight, won't you?' Moist pink lips formed a half-open pout through which he could see her tongue. 'After work?'

'Of course I will,' he promised, taking extra care as he buckled his belt to avoid meeting her gaze.

'Miss you.' She planted a kiss on her fingers and blew it across to where his hand was already closing round the door handle.

'You, too, darling.'

As an afterthought, Marcus winked. He had a feeling women liked that sort of thing.

The play was going well.

Considering it hadn't actually been written.

Caspar, however, felt he knew enough about musical farce to rush ahead, confident of shoring up any shortfalls at the end. Improvisation was his middle name, he declared grandly. And since he was the Narrator from whom the actors took their cue, Claudia suspected that more than one previous production had owed more to frantic ad-libbing than a script.

She was also beginning to understand what had prompted several members of the previous cast to break away and form their own company last October!

But credit where it's due, the whole troupe was pulling together on this. Leonides reported – sourly, it must be said, since it involved much burning of coals through the night and no consideration whatsoever as to the number of oil lamps that were lit – that few of the company had been to bed last night, scratching away on rolls of parchment in a bid to get the dialogue down and start rehearsals as soon as possible.

'Teamwork wins the day, dear boy,' Caspar had told him with a firm clap on the back. Before requesting bread and cheese for eight, even though the hour was after three.

Far from showing the strain, however, the portly impresario's face glowed and his little dark eyes shone. Unmistakably, a man in the grip of ecstasy!

'These,' he had announced, sweeping out of Claudia's

office with a sheaf of rustling parchments, 'shall be billed as the *Halcyon Spectaculars* and our play – your play – I have called *The Cuckold.*' He planted a loud kiss on the back of her hand and failed to notice that his hostess was shielding her eyes against his narcissus-yellow robe, lime-green bejewelled turban and turquoise belt. 'Alas, I can't stop to brief you on it now, dear lady, I must get started on the scenery, but rest assured you will be given progress within the hour.'

With that, the little tornado scurried off in a flurry of rosewater scent and Claudia felt quite breathless as she settled down for breakfast. Hardly an original title, *Halcyon Spectaculars*, but appropriate enough – and catchy. She tucked her feet underneath her on the couch and sipped the spiced apple juice Leonides had warmed up in advance. Halcyon reflected perfectly the fourteen days that bridged the winter solstice, the time when the sea is calm enough for the fabled halcyon bird to lay her eggs upon the waves. Idly, Claudia wondered what else might be about to hatch—

She was slicing off a wedge of pecorino cheese, her favourite, when Chiselled Cheekbones, he who had been watching her so intently yesterday, minced comically into the room, tossed back his fringe and perched cross-legged on top of the chest containing the silver.

'I'm Doris,' he announced. His voice was soft and slightly husky. 'The name means bountiful, you know.'

'Wasn't Doris the nymph who married a sea god who could change his shape at will?'

'And your point?' The young man tilted his head to one side as he grinned. 'Be a love, would you, and toss me a roll. Caspar said to brief you on the Spectacular, but he never said to do it on an empty stomach.'

'I thought actors perform best when they're hungry.' Claudia threw across a hot roll peppered with poppy seeds, which he caught with one hand.

'Not this thesp, kiddo,' he said, catching the chunk of

spicy sausage that came winging after it. 'Right then,' he said through a mouthful of dough. 'The programme's as follows.'

Claudia wasn't interested in the programme, only the schedule. 'Just tell me, yes or no, will the show be ready for the eighteenth?'

That was the day after Saturnalia, traditionally a day of anticlimax following the exchanging of gifts, the Great Sacrifice outside the temple in the Forum, the games and feasting throughout the day before. It would not impress jaded merchants much if the play wasn't ready!

'If you can trust the great lord's propaganda, I'll be in Miser's costume by this afternoon,' Doris said. 'I play First Lead, which means I'm the cuckold of the title, wouldn't you believe. Listen, are you sure you aren't even a tinksy bit curious about what twenty strangers will be doing in your house? It's more than putting on just the one play, you know.'

Eyelashes like a giraffe, Claudia thought. Thin, feminine hands. And, of course, those fine chiselled cheekbones.

Doris took her silence as a cue. 'The Spectaculars open with Felix doing his dance solo. This time he's enacting the Judgement of Paris accompanied, as usual, by Periander our castrato and the delectable Renata on the flute.'

The likelihood of one bleached blond miming Paris, two goddesses plus Helen of Troy without Claudia's atrium walls ending up splattered with fruit was a slim one. She could only pray that Periander had a voice like an angel or that Renata fluted so loudly it distracted the audience from everything else.

'Then Skyles and I perform this wicked little domestic scene between the Emperor and his lady wife – in which yours truly naturally plays Livia.'

'Skyles?' Claudia queried, selecting a date.

'Big butch bitch who shaves his head, but put a wig on him and, dear me, that boy's a ringer for Augustus.'

Claudia remembered Skyles now. The Buffoon with his

monkey walk, who tripped over invisible obstacles and who, this morning, had chased the kitchen maids with a feather duster. But acting, acting, all the time acting. She wondered whether Leonides wasn't wise to send for padlocks for the silver.

'If I wasn't the very *soul* of discretion,' Doris said, 'I could name you twenty aristocratic wives who have not so much surrendered their virtue to that boy as lobbed it at him.'

'I hope Skyles is gentleman enough to refuse?'

'Charity begins at home,' Chiselled Cheekbones trilled, rattling the bangles round his wrist. 'Just look at the little knick-knacks my admirers have given *me*. As I said. The name means bountiful.'

'Don't confuse admirers with groupies, Doris. Tell me what you know about Skyles.'

He assumed a pose of mock indignation. 'Honestly, do I *look* like someone who dishes dirt like an ostler dishes oats? Don't answer that. Anyway, after Skyles and I have finished, the girls launch into their song-and-dance routines and then – ta-da! One "splendiferous" musical farce as the great lord would call it.'

'With nudity.'

Doris hopped down from the chest. 'When it comes to the exposure of female flesh, kiddo, the audience likes their arena filled.'

Well, they'd certainly get that with Caspar's girls. If not overflowing.

'Me,' Doris said, pulling a gold pendant out from his tunic. 'I go for subtlety. Get the jewels in first, I say. *Then* show 'em what you've got.'

The swearing in of tribunes was a solemn business. These, remember, were the justices elected by the people to defend their rights. A heavy weight of responsibility hung on them. These men now held the power of veto over elections, laws, edicts by the Senate, hell, they could even overrule the decisions of the all-powerful magistrates if they felt so inclined. Charged with the protection of the lives and property of the working classes, and with their own legislative body, the newly elected tribunes were today accorded privileges akin to senators and cuirasses special to legates in honour of their role.

Orbilio stifled his yawn.

Too much toga posturing for him. Subtly, he shifted his weight and tried to ignore the throbbing behind his cyes. No one doubted that the ten men currently swearing to uphold their tribuneship were genuine in their intentions. It was everybody else, he thought. How broad a purple stripe you had on your toga. Whether your shorter, military tunic was more impressive than your magisterial neighbour's long one. Who cared?

In front of him, and a whole head and shoulders shorter, the Head of the Security Police oiled his way through the ceremony in a way that only a man with a narrow purple stripe hoping to get a wider one can do. But then Callisunus would sell his mother into harlotry and throw in his sisters for good luck if it secured him a promotion.

Orbilio made a mental calculation. Another two mind-numbing hours, if he was lucky. The way things were going, though, it might be three.

On his face, his patrician breeding showed nothing but encouragement and interest, the expression of a man stimulated by long-winded procedures, as he reviewed his current case notes in his head.

December being a particularly active month for criminals, there was quite a pot on the boil. Too many festivals combined with too many layers of thick clothing equals too many purses snatched and secreted, but that wasn't the concern of the Security Police. Nor was the fact that, because people went to bed earlier to save lamp oil and thus unwittingly improved working conditions for burglars, incidents of rape and murder went up in proportion, often as a result of those burglaries going horribly wrong. What did concern the Security Police was that, with the courts closed from the beginning of November, jails were over-crowded through lack of trials, while the crime rate continued to soar.

Perfect conditions for anarchy to breed and Rome was positively rife with plots to bring down the Emperor. Small wonder Augustus had installed the Praetorian Guard!

But apart from conspiracies requiring sharp nips in their buds, he had a killing down in the Subura to deal with. A domestic, which the husband tried to pass off as the work of an intruder, but Orbilio was gathering witnesses and evidence. No challenge there, he'd have the man in irons by tomorrow. And then there was that forgery ring oper-ating out of an old warehouse on the edge of town. Small-scale stuff, just the duplication of dole tablets, and that wouldn't take long to wrap up. Orbilio had the place under twenty-four-hour surveillance and the next time the master-mind dropped in – a swarthy, low-ranking civil servant from the Water Department – that was that.

Callisunus, even though he'd taken no interest in either case, would nevertheless scoop the credit for both. Orbilio glanced down to where his boss was smarming away to Olympic standards, and knew his only course of action was to congratulate him on the outcome with a smile. Nothing got up the little toady's nose more than the knowledge that his younger, taller, good-looking patrician subordinate didn't give a damn. Petty tactics, Orbilio admitted. But a soldier is trained to employ any weapon in his armoury, even if it's only a pin, and he hadn't spent two years in uniform for nothing. (Which was another thing that raised Callisunus's low-born hackles. That he hadn't been given a commission.)

From the corner of his eye, Marcus noticed a legionary slip into the hall and murmur something to the soldiers on guard. His mind turned to another item on his case load, one involving a certain Claudia Seferius. He shook his head in amazement. Mother of Tarquin, what was it with that woman? Couldn't she ever stay out of trouble? A smile twisted up one corner of his mouth. He bloody hoped not. But what amazed him about this particular business was that someone as sharp as Claudia had been taken in by someone as obviously slippery as Moschus. Was she growing careless, or just desperate, he wondered? Either way, if she'd only thought to check how many ships the captain had lost in various storms, she'd have realized that the authorities would have caught on sooner or later and that, when they did, Moschus was the type who'd squeal like a litter of piglets.

As the fourth tribune approached the rostrum to a deafening applause, Orbilio realized that the legionary who'd just entered the hall was edging through the crowd in his direction. The legionary's nose was pinched with cold, but then legionaries, unfortunately, don't have nine yards of woollen toga in which to swaddle themselves in winter.

'For you, sir,' he mouthed. 'Urgent.'

It wasn't difficult for Marcus to unroll the parchment quietly, not the way the soldier had been gripping it until it had turned soft, but he resisted the urge to use Callisunus's head as a rest upon which to read it. Suddenly the ceremony, his case review, even his normally restful musings on Claudia were sent spinning into oblivion. Every muscle in his body seemed to have been paralysed. He couldn't breathe. He read it twice. And then again. Unable to believe what he was seeing.

The note was from a colleague. Dymas. The note was brief.

'*The halcyon rapes*,' it read. '*They've started again.*'

Impossible.

Orbilio's hand shook as he folded up the note and tucked it into the folds of his toga.

48

Impossible.

Starting a year ago to the day, fourteen women were raped, one every day for the two weeks bridging the winter solstice. The attacks were the most brutal Marcus had ever known, had shocked everyone involved in the hunt for the rapist, traumatizing the victims beyond belief. In broad daylight, girls were dragged off the streets, stripped, forced to commit oral sex on their masked attacker, then buggered and dumped on the middens. Once the halcyon days were over, the rapes stopped, but the search did not. It was the end of March before Orbilio tracked the bastard down. Luckily, three of the victims had been able to identify him as their assailant. The incriminating mask was found under his bed. His clothes stank of the aniseed his victims had mentioned. More importantly, the rapist eventually signed a confession.

The bastard could not be on the rampage again, it was impossible.

Orbilio had personally supervised the execution.

Eight

One of the best things about Saturnalia was the atmosphere in the run-up to the holiday. Wall-to-wall with festivals beforehand, this was a time of jollity and fun. Of decorating houses with greenery and garlands. Of celebrations. Banquets. Aid to the poor and needy. A time of exchanging gifts, of mooching round the craft market in the Colonnade of the Argonauts, which specialized in presents to exchange at Saturnalia. The ultimate time of revelry; of peace and goodwill to men; an end to grudges.

There was always an exception . . .

'Sister-in-law.' If Julia had spent the morning chewing alecost and washed it down with vinegar, her expression could not have been more sour. *My house*, stomped her footsteps down the peristyle. *My marble pillars. My fountains. My sundial. My black hellebores in bloom.*

My arse, they were. Julia had just never come to terms with the fact that her brother hadn't just cut her out of his will in favour of the young chit whom he'd married, but he hadn't made any provision whatsoever for the daughter that he'd foisted on her and her husband years before. To Julia, it flew in the face of decency and reason, not to mention Roman law – and *how* Gaius got past that she would never know, but you didn't need to look too closely to see that A Certain Party Not A Million Miles Away had had a hand in that!

Forget the extenuating circumstances that existed at the time he made his will.

Second Act

Forget that the widow had been supporting the family ever since, even though Marcellus was an architect and should have been more than capable of supporting himself.

And forget that, legally, Claudia didn't owe them one black bean.

Curdled milk ran in Julia's veins. Grudges every bit a part of her as her long, thin nose and propensity for summer colds. The closer she approached along the garden path, the easier it became to compare Claudia's fur cape with her own. Finding the other's lusher, more lustrous, just like her clothes, her slippers, her jewels – even the money-grubbing bitch's skin and hair. No silver strands requiring walnut juice in those curls, dammit, and her bosoms didn't need padding, either. Julia's own linen wodges had started to slip halfway along the Via Sacra. Must remember not to take her cloak off. Better a flat chest than to be seen with breasts around her waist.

'I need to speak to you about your daughter,' she said without preamble. To her immense irritation, a dunnock started to sing in the cherry tree.

'Gaius's daughter,' Claudia corrected. There were times, and this was one of them, when she had to remind herself that Julia was only a decade older than herself. Ten years, but she might as well be another species. 'What's the sulky little cow been up to now?'

'These last few days have been a nightmare. An absolute nightmare, I tell you.' Julia sniffed and the dunnock wisely flew off. 'Teenage daughters are always a problem, I know, but Flavia is giving us so many sleepless nights, now she's acquired an interest in boys.'

'She's fifteen. It would be unnatural if she didn't.'

'I've been trying to drum into her the importance of securing a good marriage, but she simply repels potential suitors.'

Repel was the right word. Spotty, fat and moody, Flavia was hardly catch of the day.

51

'The child insists she will only marry for love, and this selfish attitude is scuppering any headway Marcellus and I make to fix her up with a husband—'

'To get her off your hands, you mean.'

'—and all the time the wretched creature keeps mooning about over the most inappropriate youth you could imagine. The son of an artisan. Imagine!'

Teenage crushes come and go. It wasn't the first one Flavia had had, it would not be the last, and this hardly constituted a crisis.

'What's really troubling you, Julia?'

'*Me?* Good heavens, there's nothing wrong in *my* life, nothing whatsoever – Well. Actually, I suppose there is a little matter I might take the opportunity to discuss in confidence, seeing as I'm here.' She glanced round the garden to make sure no one else was within earshot. 'After all, dear, you are *family*.'

Claudia preferred her sister-in-law as a bitch.

'I am not exaggerating when I say Flavia's been a pain, but—' Julia stared at a rearing stone horse. 'Marcellus has been behaving strangely, too.'

'How can you tell?'

Indignation flared the older woman's nostrils. 'Don't get impertinent with me!' But the need to confide had engulfed her, she couldn't turn back the tide now. She looked at the holly bush, awash with bright red shiny berries, and the rows of clipped laurels and the aromatic myrtle, and came to a decision. 'I think Marcellus might be having an affair.'

Honestly, who could blame him?

'Do you know who?'

'I would have preferred you to have asked, do I know *why*. After all, it's not as though there are cracks in our relationship.'

'What do you call not letting Marcellus in your bed for two years?'

'Lots of couples sleep in separate rooms,' Julia reminded her, pointedly swivelling her eyes towards the house behind her, with its wide double staircase leading off the atrium. With Claudia's bedroom on one side of the gallery, Gaius's on the other . . .

'Anyway, I made it clear a long time ago that I don't like That Sort Of Thing.' Julia's thin lips pursed white. 'But that doesn't mean he has to go elsewhere.'

'Actually, I rather think it does, although I agree about you not having any cracks in your relationship. They're bloody great canyons, Julia.'

'How dare you!'

'Well, what would you call a marriage in which one party is frustrated and unhappy while the other claims that it's faultless?'

The luck of the draw?

'For gods' sakes, Julia, life's not a straight road paved by other people for you.'

Believe me, it's crazy paving – and worse, you have to lay it yourself.

'But—'

'But nothing. Try talking to Marcellus instead of at him, see what happens. Oh, and you might consider offering him an incentive to stay home.'

'Bribing my own husband with sexual favours?' Julia snorted derisively. 'I should have known better than to come and seek advice from you! Anyway.' She pulled her fur tighter to her body. 'What's all that nonsense in the atrium?'

Moving down the path, to where tubs of fragrant pale purple irises provided a backdrop to the stunning white Stars of Judea, Claudia informed her sister-in-law of her plans to sponsor the Halcyon Spectaculars.

'But you can't *possibly* allow that troupe to live here!' Julia protested. 'Think of the gossip! The scandal! If he knew what you were doing, my dear late brother would be rolling in his grave!'

Wouldn't he just! Rolling about with laughter at Caspar's gaudy dress sense, his 'volumptuous beauties', the little castrato, the dancer who could fold himself backwards in two. Funny the things you remember, she thought suddenly, plucking a Damascan iris and holding it to her nose. For instance, when Gaius laughed, he'd tip his head right back and bellow like a bull in a meadow full of heifers. Whereas his baby sister's face would crack if she so much as smiled.

A thin claw laid itself on her arm. 'My dear, if you'd only heard the piece they were rehearsing when I came in. Quite frankly, there's no other word to describe it, it was lewd. Absolutely vulgar. In fact, disgusting would *not* be too strong a term.'

Claudia inhaled the scent of the yellow iris. 'So you'll be staying for Saturnalia, then?'

'Very well,' Julia sighed. 'If you insist.'

It was all hands to the pump for Caspar's Halcyon Spectaculars. Just like the big productions staged in giant, stone-built theatres which were watched by thousands of spectators, the backdrops still had to resemble three adjoining house fronts, complete with marble columns, statues and mosaics, and even though they were made of canvas and operated on a pulley system and the audience was small, the scenery must look fresh as well as realistic. For that reason, half the troupe were sprawled on their knees with paintbrushes in one hand and script notes in another.

The Digger among them.

Deft strokes from the Digger's paintbrush filled in the blue bits on the canvas spread across the floor as Periander, the castrato, warbled his soprano solo. Light banter was the order of the day as red paint pots jostled with yellow brush-strokes, interspersed with practical jokes and good-natured backchat. There was no option for a small unit locked together for months on end but to rub along. Friction was a commodity everyone could do without, so you closed your eyes to faults and niggles and concentrated on the positive and, since the company came almost exclusively from low-born or slave backgrounds, this way of life came naturally. For the same reason, no one asked probing questions. And if they did, those questions didn't get answered.

A plump female hand reached out and tickled Leonides's leg as he passed, the whole group shrieking at the steward's equal mix of outrage (that the unseemly incident had happened) and relief (that the hand had not belonged to Doris).

There was a unity about this company, the Digger reflected, filling in the clear blue summer sky, even though the very nature of their business meant that it was transitory. The female members fluctuated more than most, hooking up with men they met along the way, returning when the love affairs had soured, but the ambience went deeper than that. The group as a whole symbolized acceptance. Come or go, it doesn't matter a flying fig to us was their attitude. We take you for who – or what – you are.

Quite who had stayed and who was new to the company after last October's breakaway was not entirely clear. Renata, bless her plastered face, was one of the old gang, the fat boy who'd been gelded at the tender age of twelve another. Felix the dancer quite possibly another. But just as the Digger had been incorporated seamlessly into their society, so had everyone else.

At last, the blue parts of the canvas, at least this canvas anyway, had been refreshed and now the whole backdrop radiated brightness and sparkle. Just like the new play. The Digger leaned back, admiring the handiwork, not only on the canvas, but the production as a whole. For instance, too small to sustain a separate orchestra, Renata's talents were augmented by the cast, who had been given training in at least one percussion instrument, whether cymbals, tambourine, castanets or sistrum. That was how it was with Caspar's Spectaculars. Teamwork all the way. They were like raisins in a bun, the Digger thought. Separate, yet bound together in a warm and pleasant setting.

It took a moment before it filtered through that, for the word 'they', one should substitute the word 'we'.

The Digger was also one of the raisins in the bun.

And the body in the grave pointed an accusing finger.

'I am not the last,' it said. *'Am I?'*

Nine

There is no point being a sponsor of a Halcyon Spectacular if no one gets to hear about the wretched thing. Advertising is everything these days, and Claudia had no intention of her support being anything less than the talk of the town. Impossible, of course, if the players never set foot out of doors. They were, after all, her advertising hoardings. Let them bloody advertise.

'I am not sure we have the time, dear lady, to indulge in the luxury of relaxation,' Caspar protested, his turban askew and little round face daubed with paint. 'Think of the scenery, the costumes, the script, the choreography!'

'Think of the money.' Once word got round, he'd be booked solid right through the summer.

'Doris, Jemima, Erinna, Skyles, drop what you're doing and get your glad rags on,' Caspar ordered. 'Adah, Ion, you go with them.'

'But—' they chorused in unison.

'Butts are for billy goats.' Caspar clapped his little fat hands. 'Come along, come along, we haven't got all day, we have an important engagement lined up.' To Claudia he asked under his breath, 'Which might be what, exactly?'

Actors! Don't know the time of day it is. Don't even know what day they've lost track of time on.

'It's the Festival of the Lambs,' she reminded him, tapping the calendar nailed to the wall right in front of him and wondering, was wolf fur thick enough to wow them at the sacrifice or should she stick with beaver? Decisions,

decisions. Quality or colour. Dear Diana, whatever was she thinking of! There would be more than enough colour with Caspar's rainbow troupe. Especially if Jemima opened her mouth.

Slowly, so that everyone could get an eyeful, the multi-coloured snake made its way down to the Forum. Being market day, the city was thronging with farmers, shoppers, beggars, hucksters, but all heads turned at the procession which stopped outside the tiny Temple of Janus. Claudia had deliberately taken her litter, looping up the drapes and sod the tramontana, to catch as many gawpers as she could. Gossip was still one of the best publicity devices on the market, and the sight of Gaius Seferius's young widow bumping along in a litter draped in turquoise and silver and shouldered by eight hunks in matching tunics with a peacock of a companion was enough to set tongues wagging, never mind the human billboards bringing up the rear.

'They know what to do?' she murmured, alighting from the litter.

'Trust me, madam, they are *professionals*.' Caspar righted his turban and hitched up his belt. 'Well, some of them, anyway.'

Claudia glanced at the preparations being made for the sacrifice. No knives laid out, no incense burning, the fire barely lit. Excellent. Another half an hour to the start, unless she missed her guess. Just right. By the time that poor ram was led up to the altar, no one except the priest would be interested in its fate. Even Janus would have both his faces trained upon the show.

There had been a bit of a problem at the beginning. Since it was sacrilege for women to attend a sacrifice without their heads veiled, how was Claudia to make the volumptuous beauties stand out from the crowd? The men were easy. Unlike the big theatres, strolling male actors relied on the age-old technique of gurning to bring about laughs, and Claudia was convinced that Doris and Skyles would have the crowd regretting they'd not practised their pelvic-floor exercises more meticulously But that didn't solve the problem of the plumptious beauties, when women were only allowed on stage providing their heads were covered. (Exactly. Even though convention encouraged them to end up wearing nothing else, they still had to wear a veil!) Today, the solution was simple. Keep the girls veiled, but have the boys wear proper theatrical masks, then no one could have any doubt about what the group could be. *Or who was sponsoring them!*

'. . . this is but a detail,' Doris was saying, supposedly reading from a script on the portico of the basilica adjacent to the temple. 'We must address the fundamental issue here—'

At which point, Jemima bent down and touched her toes. The veil, naturally, slipped off.

'Some fundament *there!*' Ion shouted from the steps.

'I wouldn't mind getting to the bottom of it, that's for sure,' Skyles jeered from the other side of the group.

The crowd shuffled closer. Jemima promptly lifted her hem and peered at them through her chunky ankles.

'What are you lot laughing at?' She straightened up and looked from left to right, adopting a puzzled air. 'No, come on. *What?*'

Skyles and Ion both held up innocent hands. Doris pretended to get cross that rehearsals weren't going according to plan. The crowd began tossing coppers.

'O Janus,' the priest intoned solemnly, 'god of beginnings, porter of heaven, guardian of the gates, may your powers be great from this offering.'

No one heard him. No one heard the poor ram bleat as it tugged on its lead. No one noticed that the temple doors, kept permanently shut during peacetime, had been opened by a pair of sombre, white-robed acolytes so that Janus might watch the sacrifice in his honour.

'Don't you accuse *me* of buggering up rehearsals,'

Jemima told Doris, hands planted on her ample hips. 'It's them two fat ugly cows.' She jerked her head at Adah and Erinna. 'Distracting people from the ceremony, you want to keep 'em indoors, out the way.'

'*Me* fat?' Erinna shrieked. 'You're the one whose favourite food is seconds!'

'At least I haven't reached the point where food's a substitute for sex,' Adah sneered.

'No?' Jemima shot back. 'Then why's there a mirror above yer bleeding dinner table?'

Copper coins became bronze.

The priest raised his voice. He had long ago given up any hope of silence during the sacrifice, his best hope now lay in incense. Choking grey clouds tried to draw the attention of the masses, but fat remained triumphant. Only a pious young widow and a rotund individual dressed like a kingfisher strained to listen to the prayers as the young ram was purified with holy water. Adah lunged at Jemima, Erinna tried to pull Jemima off, handsome Ion leapt off the steps to rush to Erinna's aid and whoops! Erinna's tunic came off in his hands.

Uproarious cheers.

Silver showers.

The ram went to its doom unmourned.

'You dirty devil!' Erinna gasped, torn between slapping Ion round the ear and covering her embarrassment. 'You know damn well I don't wear underclothes!'

Ion, in his Jupiter-chasing-the-nymphs mode, managed to convey to the crowd that, no, he hadn't actually forgotten that aspect of Erinna's attire . . . In the background, Doris searched the script for something he'd missed. Jemima and Adah clung like virgins in a brothel, in case their own clothes came under assault. The audience were agog. Then, just when they thought it couldn't get any better, Skyles whipped off his yellow woollen tunic to protect Erinna's modesty, but in doing so, exposed his own form for inspection. Bulging muscles, rippling pecs, with just a tiny loin-cloth to cover the essentials. Claudia could see what attracted the ladies. (And one or two of the men, she couldn't help noticing.) The crowd went wild.

The priest had finished. With the longest face this side of the Tiber, he had flayed the sacrifice, passed its liver to the haruspex for inspection, and was now sprinkling the flesh with holy salt before roasting it in strips over the fire. Oh, Caspar, what magnificent timing your people have! No wonder you call them Spectaculars! And now it was her turn. Wrenching herself away from the solemn ceremony, the young widow was mortified to discover that her house guests had been causing chaos alongside the basilica.

'I am *so* sorry,' she told the crowd. 'This is all my fault. They were rehearsing for the show I'm putting on at my house—'

She didn't get a chance to finish. 'When?' 'Where?' 'How much?' 'Can we get seats?' bellowed from every direction. Oh, yes. And this was only the start. Tomorrow, to cele-brate the Festival of the Seven Hills, there was chariot racing in the Circus Maximus. Word would have spread, there'd be even more spectators at tomorrow afternoon's perform-ance.

A total of fifty thousand potential sales.

'That went well,' Ion said to Doris, wiping the sweat from his face beneath his mask.

'Fat jokes always do,' Doris retorted, comically mopping the outside of his tragedy mask. 'They unite both sexes and bridge every generation. Well. Them, and Gaulish virgin jokes. Did you hear about the one who sat in the chair right through her wedding night?'

'Go on, tell me,' Ion groaned.

'Her mother told her it would be the best night of her life, so she stayed up so as not to miss it.'

*   *   *

'That went well,' Skyles told Erinna, belting up his spare tunic.

It was the first time he had seen Erinna at such close quarters, and he'd rather liked the view. Unblemished olive skin, full firm breasts, hips that he could grip when he . . . If he . . .

He cleared his throat. 'Don't you think?' he finished hoarsely.

'That went well.' Leaning against a pillar in the portico, Adah adjusted the strap of her sandal, which had come loose.

'Bleeding did an' all.' Jemima combed her red hair with her fingers, replaced her veil and shook out the hem of her tunic. 'Got meself another admirer out of it.'

'Don't tell me. You're meeting him down the side of an alley?'

'Behind the temple, if you must know. But that's one more gold piece to put away for me old age, Adah, which is one more than you'll have.'

'That went well,' said Claudia, relieving Caspar of the takings.

'And with extreme rapidity,' Caspar commented dryly, watching them disappear into the depths of her cloak. 'But you were quite right, dear lady. A better advertisement for the Halcyons I could not have envisaged, and should you wish to reconsider my proposal of marriage, you will find my betrothal ring on your pillow within the hour.'

'Sorry to disappoint you, Caspar, but if my future husband can't respond faster than that, then he's of no interest.'

The bejewelled turban was still bobbing with merriment as it led its little masked snake home to continue work on the genuine Spectaculars.

'That went well,' a baritone murmured in Claudia's ear.

She caught the faint hint of sandalwood before she turned.

There it was again, the unmistakable scent of the hunter.

'Any chance of a box?' he asked mildly.

'I presume you're not raising my hopes by asking for a coffin?'

'My health is perfectly sound,' Orbilio replied. 'But your concern is most touching. I was referring to a ringside seat at the show.'

'What a shame we're fully booked.'

Bowing reverently backwards from the open temple doors, white-robed acolytes passed round platters piled high with strips of chargrilled sacrificial lamb. Inside the tiny sanctuary, the bronze statue of two-faced Janus gleamed from the reflection of the firelight. Both profiles were positioned so that they could watch across the city's gates and doorways, and around the statue stood twelve minute altars, one for each month of the year. December's was hung with shiny, aromatic, dark green myrtle, symbolizing the love and peace appropriate for Saturnalia, and sprigs of the shrub lay wreathed at Janus's feet. The god of new beginnings, Claudia reflected, selecting a sliver of crispy lamb. The god who, because he could see the past, watched for the future. She wondered what he was looking at when he saw her with the Security Police.

'I thought you might be interested to know we're holding a man prisoner,' Orbilio said. 'A sea captain called Moschus. Ring any bells?'

Funny how, even inside a fur cloak and squirrel-lined boots, she still felt the tramontana's icy bite. 'Moxer, you say?'

'Moschus.'

'Sorry, Orbilio, don't know any Mushers.'

In front of her, the bronze-clad doors ground shut. They would stay closed until the next Festival of the Lambs came round in January. By which time, of course, Claudia's own future would be assured. *One way or another.*

'The good captain's keeping his counsel at the moment,

but the fascinating thing about this case is that Moschus isn't a Roman name.'

'My, my, you Security Police are a mine of information,' she trilled. 'But if you want my advice, Orbilio?'

'Yes?'

'Eat your lamb before it gets cold.'

'The thing about non-Romans,' he continued, 'is that the same rules of interrogation don't apply. Unlike citizens, they can be put to the torture to extract information.'

'You have my undivided indifference.'

'My grapevine informs me that Moschus has a very low threshold of pain.'

Claudia swallowed. *One day you'll wake up to the fact that I'm the best friend you have.* Was he warning her, she wondered? Or was the spider more likely spinning a web for the fly . . . ? About to toss out another flippant retort, she suddenly noticed something different about him this morning. Wrapped in a heavy woollen toga over a long patrician tunic and with the wind baffled by the high buildings all round the Forum, his face should not be white and pinched, his expression should not be frozen. His eyes should not be dead. Jupiter, Juno and Mars, I'm going to regret asking this, I know, but—

'Marcus, is everything all right?'

He hadn't so much as looked at the sacrificial roast. Just held it between his fingers, spots of grease congealing on his nails.

'I suppose that largely depends on your definition of all right,' he said, tossing the lamb to a shaggy wolfhound, whose beseeching eyes had been on him for several minutes. 'The halcyon rapes have started again.'

Claudia shivered. 'But the man confessed. H–he was executed in the arena.'

'*A* man confessed,' Orbilio corrected. '*A* man was executed, but—'

'But nothing,' Claudia said.

Second Act

Marcus Cornelius Orbilio was renowned for his near-perfect record. Not because he was cleverer than the rest of the Security Police, although he was certainly better educated. But because his patrician training made him thorough to the point of pedantry. Even in those instances where he could not bring the perpetrator to book – itinerants, for instance, and those protected by High Society and the government – he nevertheless satisfied himself that he had done everything within his power and had at least some gratification in knowing that the case was closed. Dogged wasn't the word, and that was why Claudia walked on eggshells around him. She hadn't dragged herself out of the gutter to watch everything she'd worked for washed out to sea. Upright, conscientious and thorough, if Orbilio had nailed the Halcyon Rapist, then the Halcyon Rapist was nailed.

'This has to be a copycat crime,' she said.

'That's what my colleague, Dymas, thinks. That some arrogant bastard wants to prove himself smart enough to outwit the authorities.' Orbilio tried for a smile and failed. 'Well, my colleague is right on *that* score. I spoke to the girl who was attacked yesterday morning and I've just come from questioning the second victim now and it's exactly the same as last year. Not similar,' he said wearily. 'Identical, Claudia, right down to the aniseed and the mask, and you know what that means.'

The lamb she'd eaten as part of the sacrifice threatened to regurgitate itself over the cobbles. No wonder he hadn't been able to face it.

'Yes,' she said softly, and something tightened inside. 'I know what it means.'

It meant Mr Conscientious-Upright-and-Thorough had made a mistake.

As a result of that error, an innocent man had been sent to his death.

Ten

Out in the Alban Hills, a few miles from the bustling town of Frascati, a woodsman paused for lunch. The meal was humble – a hunk of cheese and a sweet chestnut scone – but he was glad to rest his weary bones, he'd been on the hoof since dawn. There was quite a nip in the air, but the woodsman was warm enough in his soft hide jerkin and leggings to brave untying the stout thongs of his leather cloak while he ate.

'Xerxes!' He whistled his dog. 'Here, boy!'

Daft mutt. Gone lolloping off on a scent. The woodsman shrugged. All the more for him. He broke off a chunk of the cheese, hand-churned by the best cheese maker in the Alban Hills, his own wife. Aye, she knew how to make cheese, did his missus. One denarius of lamb's rennet to every pail of milk, then she'd toss in a few wild thistle flowers and leave nature to take its course. Once it had thickened, she'd transfer the curds into a wicker basket to be moulded and pressed, salted then pressed again, before she added yet more salt and left it to mature under weights. This particular specimen had been hardened in brine and left smoking over the hearth through the summer until the rind had turned a rich, oaky brown, but his wife turned out everything from soft pungent goat's cheese to fresh curds to ewe's cheese which she made only in March when milk was at its most plentiful.

She sold many of her cheeses in the market in town and was a treasure house of gossip when she got back. Sited at the junction of no fewer than three main routes in and out of Rome, Frascati saw everyone from bone workers to horse breakers, soothsayers to purveyors of fine linen towels for the nobility. Musicians passed through, auctioneers, freaks, tax collectors, viper tamers, midwives, wagoners, you name it, and each with a tale to tell. The evenings were never dull when his wife had been into market.

There was that slave who had run away from Senator Cotta's estate, what had been recaptured half a mile out of town. What a fight she put up, according to his missus. Kicking, biting, screaming as they carried her back to the house!

Then there was that kerfuffle with the strolling players last autumn, when half of them (no, more than half) stormed off, leaving the original troupe well and truly in the doodah and taking on anyone stupid enough to sign up and not being too fussed about who they hired, either, because Saturnalia was coming up fast.

The woodsman smiled as he chomped on his scone. All good fun, those stories, but none of them was a patch on the one where Senator Cotta's old man blew himself up.

What a hoot that was! For more years than anyone could remember, the old boy had been babbling on about the Elixir of Immortality, bragging to anyone who'd listen that he'd toured the world to track down the ingredients, listing everything from iron pyrites to cinnabar to realgar. Lord alive, half the town was expecting him to die writhing in agony from his experiment, because realgar was a form of arsenic, but no. Give the old man his due, he mightn't have gained everlasting life, but he certainly went out with a bang.

The whole of Senator Cotta's west wing went up like a thunderbolt!

Laugh? The town of Frascati nearly wet itself. They were sorry about the old man, of course. Harmless old duffer, but at least he didn't suffer. (Not like the wife's mother, poor cow.) No, what was so funny was the Senator's reaction. Talk about odd.

'Xerxes!' The woodsman called louder this time. 'Come on, boy. Dinner.'

Still no response, so he polished off the piece of cheese that he had saved for the dog and sank his teeth into the last of the scone. Aye, and she baked a bloody fine loaf as well, his old lady. Chestnut bread was her speciality, and these scones fair melted in the mouth.

Maybe it was the suddenness of the old man's death or just the stupid bloody manner of his dying, blowing the house up like that, that made the Senator react so oddly. But whatever the reason, he'd driven straight from the old man's funeral to Cumae, outside of Naples. He had to consult with the Oracle, he had said. Urgent. And when he came back, someone up at the big house overheard him telling someone else that he'd visited Hades, ridden with the Ferryman across the River Styx, heard the bark of Cerberus, the three-headed hound of hell, the whole lot. Apparently while he was down there, he'd also met with the ghost of his father, if you can believe that.

Which the woodsman could not.

'Xerxes?'

Stupid mutt. He could hear him snaffling in the under-growth over the way, too, his paws rootling through the cold, crisp leaves which lay scattered across the woodland floor.

'Ah, there you are, boy. Wondered what you was up to, you daft bugger.'

The dog was thumping his tail so energetically that his whole body waggled. Amber eyes shone black with excitement.

'Wrrrf.'

As the woodsman leaned down to pat his ears, a human hand plopped at his feet.

'Wrf–wrf.'

Amiable as ever, Xerxes was more than willing to share his find. With a sour taste in the back of his throat, the woodsman followed. Some creature, a fox in all probability, had already unearthed the remains. He could see gnaw marks on some of the bones. But one thing was clear.

'This ain't no barbarian burial, boy.'

The grave was too shallow for one thing. Too far off the road for another. Also, he knew of no pagan ritual where loved ones were despatched to the afterlife naked. And another thing he couldn't help noticing.

'Death weren't from natural causes, neither.'

The skull had been caved in at the temple, most likely by the spade whose wooden handle protruded from under a thin layer of litter.

'Poor little bitch,' he said over the grave, as he made the sign of the horns to avert the evil eye. 'Didn't deserve to end up like this, did she?'

He wondered what had lured her into the woods. Sex? Was she some prostitute who'd ended up taking her last walk with a pervert disguised as a punter? Or was he looking at the outcome of an execution, the body stripped to prevent identification? Had she suffered? Was she scared? Whatever the circumstances of her murder, she must have been a bonny lass, the woodsman thought. Her long black hair still streamed round her shoulders.

Eleven

Hearing that Moschus was in custody was a development Claudia hadn't envisaged, and Orbilio's announcement had caught her right off her guard. If the old sea dog talked . . . So far, his mouth seemed to have stayed shut tighter than a clam, but if Moschus was put to the torture . . .

Claudia shivered. There was only one option open to her now. Prevent the bastard from talking.

Two hours after the Festival of the Lambs had wound up, she returned home to find a problem in the boiler house filling the atrium with clouds of steam. Swirling in and out of the vapour, like ships in a fogbank, Caspar's Spectaculars rehearsed with scripts that resembled limp lettuce and did not turn a hair. As Claudia tossed her cloak in the general direction of the porter, Drusilla, her blue-eyed, cross-eyed, dark Egyptian cat, jumped down from the roof of the aviary.

'Mrrrow.'

'Yes, I know, poppet. Not much fun for you, is it, all these strangers over the house?'

Not much fun for the birds in the aviary, either. Furious that her territory had been usurped, Drusilla had vented her spleen by taking up sentry duty on top of the bird house. There were several advantages here. First, she was out of range of cat-strokers, although in truth these were few and far between. (Those individuals who'd naively imagined that Drusilla would benefit from their endeavours reeked of the opobalsam with which their wounds had been dressed.) Secondly, from her lookout on the top of the aviary, Drusilla maintained the territorial advantage in that she could still follow everything that went on in her domain. And thirdly, and by far the most rewarding, was the effect her presence had on the aviary's twittering inmates.

'Prrrrrr.'

As Claudia's nails raked Drusilla's backbone, she glanced across to where Caspar was putting the cast through their paces. The squawking in the aviary had subsided as the birds regrouped and preened their ruffled feathers, so that the words of the castrato came as sweet and clear as a mountain stream. Accompanying him on the flute was Renata.

'Prrrr,' Drusilla repeated, rubbing her head under her mistress's chin.

'I know,' Claudia replied. 'Isn't his the voice of an angel? And just look at Felix!'

The bleached blond had reached the point in his balletic mime where Paris was weighing in his hand the golden apple engraved 'To the Fairest'. That one human body could express so many emotions without the aid of speech was utterly amazing. Fear: of snubbing at least one, possibly two goddesses at the risk of divine retribution. Pride: the privilege of being asked to judge the contest. Anxiety: that he might make the wrong decision. Nor was Claudia the only person mesmerized by Felix's performance. No mosaic had been swept more meticulously, no bronze statuette ever polished harder, no niche and crevice dusted quite so often. Small wonder the boiler house had set off so much steam, with no one in there to attend the fire!

Claudia took a piece of bacon that Doris had left on his trencher and fed it to Drusilla, while she drank the libation from the household shrine (and now the slaves would have another excuse to pass through the atrium slower than a sleeping snail) and nibbled on Ion's chive bread.

'Mrrr.'

Stuffed with ham, plus a few prawns that her mistress

had found underneath the chive bread, Drusilla rearranged herself round Claudia's neck to wash her whiskers. Up on the gallery, Ugly Phil appeared to be chiselling lumps out of the support rails to secure the pulleys for the backdrops. Claudia tried not to think about the cost of repairs, and turned her attentions to her Saturnalia banquet.

The festival covered four full days from the seventeenth to the twentieth of December, with the morning of the seventeenth devoted to the Great Sacrifice outside the Temple of Saturn in the Forum. Schools, law courts, even shops closed on this day, and the whole of Rome gathered to propitiate the God of Agriculture in the hope that the seeds already in the ground plus those about to be sown would flourish into a bountiful harvest. Afterwards, many citizens would join in the famous public banquet, where they'd dress up in funny hats, gorge themselves stupid, drink until they were ill, play party games and generally have a bloody good time. The merchant and noble classes celebrated in pretty much the same style, only they had the good sense to do it in the warmth and comfort of a private home. Preferably not their own. Otherwise, how could they expect to collect five to six pounds of silver plate from every supplier?

Claudia had given a lot of thought to the theme of her own Saturnalia banquet. 'What do you think about setting it round the zodiac?' she asked Drusilla.

'Prrrr.'

'Yes, I thought so.'

Beef to represent Taurus, the bull. Crabs for Cancer, mutton for Aries, mullets for Pisces and so on.

'But it probably won't do to serve spit-roasted virgins or stuffed water bearers,' she told the cat, draining the last of the sacrificial wine. 'This is where I'm relying on the expertise of our illustrious Cook.'

Aromas of smoked garlic, honeyed hams, poached pears and yeasty bread met her in the kitchen doorway. In the flurry of activity, bronze ladles clanged against baking pans, earthenware pots clunked together, baskets scraped the tiled floor. Someone winced, cursing in a guttural Teutonic tongue as they burned themselves on the water heater as they passed by, and voices became raised as two of the slaves fought over who should clean the cauldron, it was their turn yesterday, and who should get the job of pickling onions, you know it makes their eyes water. Twenty extra mouths were taking their toll, then. Not, perhaps, the most judicious moment to raise the subject of zodiac banquets with the Cook. Especially when that happened to be his guttural Teutonic tongue cursing the water heater back there! But this was the eleventh and there wasn't time to spare.

Suddenly, she felt Drusilla stiffen against her collarbone. The purring stopped.

'Hrrow.'

Her expression was that of a leopard on a fresh kill who had just spotted a lion approaching. Claudia followed Drusilla's gaze and saw one of the actors sidling in through the back entrance, pinching the bottom of one of the kitchen maids before snatching a leftover rissole and skipping out the door to the slave quarters.

Skyles, of course.

Skyles, who had taken off his tunic in the Forum, ostensibly to spare Erinna's modesty.

Skyles, who'd left the Forum two hours ago with the maestro and the others.

Skyles. Who had only just returned . . .

Tail wide and thrashing, Drusilla jumped down and ran off. Across the atrium, Claudia watched as the young castrato muttered something to Renata and scampered down the corridor as fast as his chubby legs would carry him in the direction Skyles had taken. Claudia followed. No doors sealed off the rooms in the slave quarters. Only Leonides and the Cook were afforded the luxury of privacy, the rest had to make do with heavy tapestries hung across the opening of their rooms.

'Well?' Periander's girlish voice was rendered even higher with breathless excitement. 'How did you get on, then?'

Skyles chuckled. It was a deep chuckle, made all the more resonant in a small room. 'The minute I didn't come home with the others, Peri my mate, you knew exactly how I got on.'

'So tell me what happened.'

The actor laughed again. 'For a boy with no balls, you have one helluva sex drive.'

'For the last time, Sky, I'm not a boy, I'm sixteen, and will you bloody hurry before Renata comes looking for me. Who was she this time, eh? Was she patrician? What did she say when she picked you up? Where did she take you? Come on, Sky, what did you do?'

'You're a little pervert, you know that, Peri?' There was a creak as Skyles made himself comfortable on the bed. 'No, she wasn't patrician,' he said. 'But she had a nice house on the Quirinal—'

Behind the curtain, pale blue and embroidered with dolphins and seashells around a rather portly Venus rising from the waves, Claudia eavesdropped on a concise but graphic description of his latest conquest's charms and sexual foibles. That was the last time she'd look at *this* tapestry in the same light, she thought. Talk about a new dimension to the term sky blue.

'Blimey!' Peri's breath came out in a whistle. 'The dirty slut! *And* she made you shag her in the atrium, where anybody might walk in?'

'I think that was the point of the exercise, Peri. The danger.'

'Ju–p–es,' Periander said, incredulity stretching out the single syllable, and Claudia could almost picture his rosebud mouth dropping open in astonishment. 'You don't half pick 'em, Sky.'

'I don't pick *them* at all. They pick me.'

There was a scraping sound, which Claudia identified as the boy scuffing his sandal on the flagstone, the sort of action people take before embarking on contentious issues.

'Don't take this the wrong way,' Peri said carefully. 'I mean, you're a great guy and everything, but what I don't understand is: why don't these women throw themselves at Ion? No offence, Sky, but he's tall, bearded, handsome as sin and with shoulders like a bleedin' ox. You'd think the tarts would be tossing their knickers his way, but they don't. Why always you?'

'Haven't a clue, mate,' Skyles laughed. 'What's your opinion, milady?'

Bugger. Claudia pushed the drape aside. No point in asking how he knew she was there. Hell, perhaps every woman he encountered listened at his keyholes? Tapping her fingertip against the wooden door frame, she glanced at the eager-faced castrato sitting on the opposite bunk, plumpness bulging out his maroon and yellow tunic just as amazement bulged out his dark-brown velvet eyes. A greater contrast to the man sprawled out on his pallet, hands behind his head, his legs crossed leisurely at the ankle, could not be imagined.

'Well?' Skyles prompted quietly.

Peri was right. There was nothing out of the ordinary about Skyles. Sure, his body was lean and hard, but he was of average height, average build, and shaven skulls flatter very few men. Hardly a head-turner, then.

At least, not on paper.

But how does one define sex appeal? The white scars that criss-crossed his back? The craggy, lived-in face – a face far too old for a man of thirty-five? Maybe it had something to do with that taunting-the-world look in his eye? The air of indifference about what people thought of him? Or was it a combination of all these things?

'Frankly, I have no idea,' she said.

'Liar,' Skyles countered softly, patting the solid lump that

75

passed for a mattress and indicating to Periander to make himself scarce.

'Candied cherries?' he asked.

Claudia curled her legs underneath her and wondered what Julia would make of this. Rich merchant's widow and commoner alone together in a windowless broom cupboard lit by a solitary candle. With the actor offering luxury goods to a woman who could afford the whole tree.

'My mother told me never to take sweets from strange men.'

'I strike you as strange, do I?' He laughed softly under his breath. 'Wine, then.'

It wasn't a question. He leaned over, poured two mugs of red wine and handed one to her. The mug was chipped, and read 'Drink me dry' on the outside.

'To success,' he said, chinking the rim of his earthenware cup against hers.

'In what?' she asked. The wine was fruity and coarse, dry enough to strip paint, and Skyles wasn't a man to water his wine. Or indeed any other aspect of his life, come to that.

'You tell me.'

He shifted the weight on to one elbow, and now his thighs were but a sylph's breath from her shins. She could feel the heat pulsing out from his tanned, naked flesh. His pallet smelled of cool, mountain forests. She sipped from the mug and tried to remember whether his gaze had ever left hers from the moment she'd stepped into his room.

'Do they pay you, these women?'

He drew a deep breath, held it for a count of three, then exhaled slowly. 'They offer, but I never accept.'

He waited for her to ask the inevitable, but Claudia remained silent, and the question hung in the air between them, heavy as a thundercloud, every bit as loaded.

In silence, coarse wine was sipped from chipped mugs.

* * *

The day commemorating the Festival of the Lambs was drawing to a close. Four times a year, in December, January, March and May, a ram would lay down its life as the priest invoked the sun's rays to shine favourably on the soil, that there might be neither drought nor deluge and that Rome, therefore, would not starve. Fat chance of that happening, Orbilio thought, his weary legs tramping up Piper Street towards the Esquiline. A quarter century of peace had brought a stability to the Empire that its citizens had never known before, and with peace came prosperity. Slaves outnumbered Romans ten to one on farms, tending the land better than a wet nurse. Armies of labourers were constantly manuring, irrigating, pruning and weeding to ensure maximum harvests, optimum qualities, all at a price people could afford. Droughts and deluges might be a problem, but thank Jupiter, they were no longer a crisis, and this was down to the work of one man. Augustus.

His boast was that he had inherited a city of brick and had turned it to marble, eighty-two temples alone. Now Rome gleamed from every angle that the sun's invoked rays hit, blinding in its brilliance with the gold on the columns and the bronze on the statues, but the glints reflected far more than one man's building programme. These marbles and metals, the intricate frieze work, the skill of the men who laid the mosaics and painted the frescoes reflected serenity. A nation that was no longer burying young men in the prime of their life was a nation which thrived. It had grown strong on food that was as cheap as it was plentiful. On the fresh water that came in on the aqueducts and kept the city clean. On the sharp fall in street crime (December excepted!)

Orbilio turned into Fig Street. The ancient tree from which the road got its name had long since withered away, but several of its cubs scrambled over the walls of the shops and apartment blocks, scenting the street with the smell of ripe fruit in the summer. From behind a shutter, he heard the late-night clack of a loom, a cough from an upstairs window. A pack of feral dogs loped down an alleyway, off to scavenge the middens.

But peace did not suit everyone, he reflected. Sextus Valerius Cotta was due to address the Senate, calling for more war, more expansion, more territories, more riches. Despite little support in the Assembly, Orbilio knew that greed was a strong puller of crowds. The Arch-Hawk had many a supporter among ordinary citizens, especially those whose lives could do with a bit of enriching.

'Why should the Empire rest on her laurels,' they cried, carrying his echo into the streets, 'when we can get our hands on the gold mines of Dacia?'

Living in death-trap tenements, where burglary was rife and fire claimed victims every night of the year, Cotta's followers saw a future in which they paid fewer taxes and less tribute once the shipping revenues from the Black Sea fell into Roman hands. They saw valuable minerals from the Orient rebuilding their slums the way the spoils of war had raised temples of marble from brick. They saw Indian spices paying for water coming straight to their courtyards, Britannia paying for their sons to be educated, African campaigns providing them with beds stuffed with feathers not straw, and where the only thing that moved on the mattress was the occupant, not the fleas.

'Rome *can* win,' they rallied. 'Our army is the best in the world, we have wealth on our side, strength in discipline, let's not waste the opportunity.'

Impoverished men with impoverished vision, they couldn't grasp the Emperor's argument that strength lay in holding on. In reinforcing ties with one's neighbours, rather than testing them. Strength lay in trade. In security. *In peace.* Only with stability could the Empire stand firm. One had to consolidate before one moved on.

'Bullshit,' the crowed bayed. 'We've done it before, we can do it again, the eagle and the hawk are invincible.'

All Orbilio could hope for was that, this close to Saturnalia, Cotta's incitements would fall on deaf ears. Young or old, rich or poor, sick or healthy, this was a season when people were happy and heaven knows, no month matched December for festivals. Eighteen, to be precise, with chariot races, dancing, donkey derbies and banquets, processions, dedications and music. This would herald a New Year. A fresh start for everyone. Halcyon days, indeed.

And on the loose, the Halcyon Rapist.

At the top of Fig Street, Marcus paused to tickle the ears of a bright-eyed ginger kitten and found himself trapped as the kitten rolled over and demanded a belly rub, squirming and purring with pleasure.

'It's all right for you, you rascal. The most you ever have to do to keep vermin off the streets is chase rats.'

At which point, the kitten discovered that toga hems were the gateway to a wonderful playground, and it was with considerable difficulty that he disengaged the sharp little claws and repositioned the squirming bundle back on the pavement. Being a kitten, of course, and not a puppy, it instantly dismissed its new acquaintance in favour of phantom moths, squirting up the fig tree like liquid.

The streets were eerily quiet. The fourth Lamb Festival of the year was also a holiday for beasts of burden, so no delivery carts rattled over the cobbles tonight, and no plod of oxen or whinny of mules broke through the silence. Only the odd creak of a barrow, the off-key song of a late-night carouser in the distance, the shuffle of a funeral bier as it was carried away for cremation unmourned. Walking these silent streets without even his own shadow for company, Orbilio could see how a young woman could be hauled into an alleyway and raped. But nights like this were rare in Rome. Day and night the city bristled with frantic activity, and it was a well-worn joke that more people died from insomnia than the plague. Moreover, the rapist snatched his victims in daylight.

Nor were these, strictly speaking, the Halcyon Days. Officially, they didn't start until the fifteenth of December, bridging the seven days either side of the winter solstice, and today was only the eleventh. The name Halcyon Rapist came from the animal himself.

'Remember well your halcyon lover,' he told his victims, before launching into a string of obscenities so vile that the girls couldn't bring themselves to repeat it.

Last year, this self-styled halcyon lover had committed fourteen vicious assaults over the holiday period, with the exception of the four days of Saturnalia itself, his last rape falling on the final the halcyon day. A pattern which, goddammit, was repeating again . . .

Head down, his toga drawn close against his body for warmth, Orbilio turned into his own street just as the herald called the midnight hour. It had been a long day. Trying to find witnesses and not succeeding. Trying to convince himself it was a copycat crime – and not succeeding there, either.

What would he say, what *could* he say, to the mother of the man he'd sent to face the lions?

Round and round, like donkeys on a treadmill, his thoughts had been tramping the same ground. Stale thoughts, because he'd gone through this process last year and was finding nothing new this time round. His only clue was that the four days 'off' suggested the killer couldn't get away during Saturnalia, but dammit that applied to half the men in Rome. Which, at a rough count, left him with a quarter of a million potential suspects. Mother of Tarquin, he needed to sleep. Perhaps in the morning he might be able to get a handle on this. Find a new angle to explore. A crack to probe.

Glancing up as he approached his own house, he blinked. And blinked again. There, in the middle of the street, a woman was . . . *dancing*. Not a drunken sway, or some spontaneous burst of emotion expressing itself in a quick tap of the feet followed by a spring in the air and maybe a click of the heels. This was professional choreography at work. He paused. There was something vaguely familiar about the sinuous Egyptian ballet. About the plaited Cleopatra wig, the silver breast band and tight fringed skirt that barely covered her modesty, the shapely legs that seemed to go on for ever. Then he remembered. Two nights ago, at his cousin's house, this girl had been hired to dance for the all-male party.

'It's Angelina, isn't it?' He vaguely remembered his cousin introducing them.

The dance stopped abruptly. In the light of the torches that burned in sconces either side of his front door, the beads in her black wig shone like jewels.

'Marcus!' She was breathless after her routine, making her pretty breasts heave in a most interesting rhythm, and he couldn't help noticing the effect the cold air had had on her nipples.

'What are you doing here?' He glanced around, noticed her cloak rolled up against his doorstep and flung it round her shoulders.

'Well, I was rather hoping you were going to invite me inside.' Her eyes were bright, either from cold or excitement, and he had a sinking feeling as to which of the two was the culprit.

'I, er—'

Debating whether the offer of money would offend her, Orbilio was saved the bother. She pulled off her wig, shook her head and a cascade of honey-coloured curls frothed around her ears like a halo. Mother of Tarquin, the pixie!

'You stood me up last night, you naughty boy.' She combed her fingers through her hair with professional ease. 'I had dinner waiting and everything, but you didn't even send me a note.'

Shit. 'It was the same thing tonight,' he said truthfully. 'I didn't finish until midnight.'

'Yes, I know, you poor pumpkin.' Angelina linked her arm with his and tousled his fringe. 'You're working on those halcyon rapes. I heard. That's why I came to you, instead of you having to trail over to my place. Makes more sense, doesn't it?'

'Angelina—'

He remembered chatting to her at his cousin's house, where one thing had obviously led to another and, fuelled by wine, he'd ended up in her bed. But what, for him, had been a one-night stand clearly meant more to her.

'Angelina, we need to talk.' Not inside his own house, either. 'There's a tavern three streets away with a crackling log fire, we can warm you up there and, er . . .'

He let the sentence trail. Milo's tavern would be quiet tonight, without the delivery trade. Orbilio would be able to let her down gently over a meal as well as anywhere, he supposed.

'That sounds absolutely wonderful, darling.'

Angelina stood up on tiptoes and planted an affectionate kiss on his cheek. This, he realized dully, wasn't going to be easy. And he had to be up early, as well. Personally, he blamed the wink. Women obviously did like that sort of thing.

The sound of dogs barking across the street woke Claudia from sleep. Any other time and she would not have heard them. The clatter of delivery wagons, the crack of bull-whips, the shouts of the drivers, the braying of mules would have muffled any complaints by angry dogs, and noise was a lullaby to Claudia. Without it, the night was eerily quiet. Unnatural in this city of chaos and turmoil. But even beasts of burden deserve a holiday, she supposed. And slept fitfully as a result.

The barking grew louder. More urgent. Then other dogs joined in, as dogs always will, including the mastiff next door. Claudia slipped out of bed, pulling the warm blankets up round her shoulders. Something was up. And now a different sound had joined in the chorus. A metallic clamp-clamp-clamp, the jangle of armour, the sharp bark of military orders. A blast of bitter cold air made her gasp as she opened the shutter. There was damp in the atmosphere. Below her balcony, the street was a blaze of light from the torches of householders and slaves who had streamed outside to see what was going on.

What was going on was that the linen merchant over the way had called out the army. There had been two men loitering in the street all day, he reported, and after dark they remained in his doorway. Any other time and he would have moved them on, he insisted, but his steward had noticed two more round the corner, all four armed with daggers and cudgels.

Not now they weren't. One large bruiser was being held in an armlock by a tough-looking legionary with a scar down his cheek, while the second suspect was being chained hand and foot.

'It's a damn lie, this rumour that I keep my life savings in a wine jar down in the cellar,' the merchant told the sergeant. 'I use the temple depository like everyone else, but thieves don't always believe what they're told, do they, officer, and I have my wife and five children to think of, not to mention my mother-in-law living with us, as well as the wife's sister and her three young nippers and a cousin up from the country.'

As he paused to draw breath, another group of soldiers came tramping round the corner, dragging two more heavies between them. Blood poured from one of the men's heads, its bubbling stream blinding him as it poured over one eye and dripped off his chin. The other one was missing a boot.

'Got 'em, sarge!' one of the legionaries puffed, prodding one of the prisoners in the small of the back with his fist. 'They tried to make a run for it, but we got 'em.' He was proud that years of hard physical training had given his footsloggers the edge.

'Are these the men you saw earlier?' the sergeant asked the linen merchant's steward.

'Definitely. I remember that one, because of the birthmark.'

'Then you four are under arrest for intent to burgle and rob. Take 'em away, corporal.'

'But we wasn't—' That was as far as Bleeding Head's protest got. One of his companions landed a sound kick on his shin, which silenced him immediately, just as Missing Boot growled a warning which Claudia couldn't hear.

'Is it safe, do you think, officer?' the linen merchant whined. 'Only there are four women and eight children inside and—'

'Perfectly safe,' the sergeant assured him. 'But just in case there's more in the gang, I'm leaving two men here to stand guard for the next couple of nights.'

'It's not true about my savings down in the cellar,' the linen merchant called after him. 'I don't know where these rumours come from.'

Probably because it wasn't a rumour, Claudia thought, staring down at the now empty street. The old miser begrudged paying the temple a fee for holding his valuables safe, no wonder people were always trying to rob him. There had been at least five previous attempts that she knew of.

Except this was no bungled robbery.

She'd recognized Bleeding Head and Missing Boot immediately. The scum from the slum. The thugs whose paws had mauled at her flesh. Whose stale breath had been forced into her nostrils.

Butico, goddammit, had posted a warning.

Only a fool would ignore the message.

Pay up or I'll take my eight grand in kind, he was saying. The bastard wasn't bluffing. Like a shark, he sensed blood in the water and was moving in for the kill. Claudia saw him sending in his thugs to strip her house of its rare woods and marble, trashing whatever they liked in the process, raiding the storerooms, pillaging artworks, and with a bailiff to legitimize the process by undervaluing the goods as they went along.

That he was able to do this was because he had the backing of the Guild of Wine Merchants. With the Widow Seferius bankrupt and humiliated, her business would go down the sewer with her.

Bastards, bastards, absolute bloody bastards.

Still. First thing in the morning, she would send Butico the three thousand sesterces 'profit' she'd made from Moschus. That would keep the dogs at bay and she'd just have to take it from there.

Claudia closed the shutters and climbed back to bed, but the herald had called another hour before she finally drifted back to sleep.

It's unlikely her eyes would have closed at all, had she known she was separated by just a few bits of bricks and mortar from a killer.

The Digger had also been woken by the rumpus. Everyone had.

The Digger also lay awake long after the disturbance had died down, but, unlike Claudia, the Digger did not get back to sleep.

Killers do not know the luxury of peace of mind.

And the body in the grave nodded knowingly.

'You'll never get away with my murder,' she sneered. 'They'll find you in the end. One way or another, they'll find you and then you'll have to pay.'

Twelve

As festivals go, the Seven Hills of Rome wasn't Deva's favourite. She much preferred those which fell around the summer solstice, such as the Festival of Fortune, where she could wear her pretty summer bodices and weave flowers in her hair without crushing them under a woollen mantle to keep out the cold. But still. It was a festival. There would be processions, sacrifices, chariot races at the Circus Maximus later on, and tomorrow, with luck, pottery mugs might be on sale inscribed with the winners' names, and she just might buy one of those for her man, to go with the tunic she was embroidering for him for Saturnalia.

He didn't care too much for embroidery, Deva knew, but she was Damascan and Damascan women didn't let their men go about in plain cloth and that was *that*. He couldn't have it both ways. If he liked the way she wore short bodices that revealed a tight midriff and fringed skirts that came halfway down her calf to show off her finely boned ankles, then he'd have to accept that every once in a while he'd have to look good for *her*. And since looking good in Damascan eyes meant wearing a tunic embroidered in traditional designs, then he could bloody well lump it.

'You'll rue the day you set up with a Roman,' her mother had said. 'It doesn't do, two cultures crossing. No good can ever come of it.'

Deva spat on to the pavement. What did her mother know? The old crone had been a widow these past fifteen years, she'd grown sour and miserable, and you'd think she'd have been pleased her only daughter had found a good man to settle down with. A herbalist, too! In fact, if Deva only had a child to present to him, her joy would be complete. She giggled. Of course, they'd only been together six months, her and her man. He'd hardly leap for joy if she handed him a bawling bundle and said, 'There you are, love, that's your son.'

The joke sustained her as she crossed the Sublician Bridge, its timbers reverberating under the solid clomp of her clogs. Ahead, the sheds and warehouses lined up along the river looked grey and forbidding on this dull, damp day, the shadow of the Aventine Hill looming over them, but Deva wasn't worried that there was no one else around so early in the morning. A pleasant change, not having to step over piles of steaming dung, or sidestep refuse left behind by the delivery carts, or be on the constant lookout for pickpockets and gropers.

Turning up between the spice warehouse and a marble store and shifting her basket to her other arm, she squeezed the small brooch which lay in the palm of her hand. Bronze and engraved with an intricate leaf pattern, she knew her mother would find the gift 'too Roman' for her taste, but then the old crab found fault with everything these days, and you'd think she'd just get on with it and accept that she was a Damascan living in Rome and bloody well get on and enjoy the life and the customs.

'That's because you don't know no better,' her mother would snap. 'You was born into it, Deva.'

'Yes, I do know better,' she'd reply. 'You keep telling me,' and then she and her mother would argue, and then she'd regret going to visit, much less taking the gift she always brought, which was inevitably far more than she could afford, but she did it anyway, because they always parted on a quarrel and even though it was as much her mother's fault as hers, Deva still felt guilty. And it always bloody hurt that the gift was never *good* enough . . .

Between the tall buildings, she found herself sheltered from the wind blowing straight down from the north. There'd be rain later, she thought. Cold, icy rain, but it wouldn't dampen the spirits of the people crushed into the Circus cheering on the chariots, waving their team colours in the air. Out of the wind, Deva paused to pull the shawl from her head, and thought she saw movement behind her. Obviously not. Nothing stirred. Rats, in all likelihood.

The shawl was Damascan, too. Rich red and deeply fringed, it was her best shawl, because today was a triple celebration. Not only the Festival of the Seven Hills, but her seventeenth birthday and the six-month anniversary of her and her man getting together as a live-in couple. He was twice her age and more. A widower with receding hair. But he was funny, clever, good in bed, too, and he knew a lot about a lot of things, her herbalist. Deva was happy. Why shouldn't she be? She had a good life with a good man, and good honey to sell at market this morning which should bring her a good profit to tide her over the holidays. Who wouldn't be dancing for joy? And, of course, if she became pregnant . . .

That was her reason for visiting her mother. The dance. She stopped again, glanced round, but there was no shadow, no echo of footsteps. Just Deva and her lovely red, fringed shawl. She shook the soft, woollen cloth, draped it across her right shoulder then tied the ends round her waist. Tonight, of course, she would not be wearing her winter bodice and thick skirt. She would put on her best beaded top, the white skirt and then, barefoot, she would act out the Fertility Dance that her mother had showed her when she was a child.

'You have to tie the shawl right, Deva. It's all in the knots.'

Bunkum. It was all in the *dance*. But believing's conceiving, and Deva did so want to give her man a son. A little redheaded herbalist, just like his daddy, to fill the crib that her man had carved himself. And if she got the dance just so (and the bloody knots right), then they were looking at a plump little autumn equinox baby!

Singing to herself, the bronze brooch clenched in her hand, Deva hurried up the alleyway towards the apartment above the weaver's that her mother shared with her oldest brother and his family. With luck, she'd have timed it so that her sister-in-law would be coming back from the public ovens with a basket of hot rolls.

The hand that lashed out round her neck and pulled her into the open doorway came so fast, that for a moment Deva didn't realize what was happening. All she knew was a strong smell of aniseed and that the brooch had gone spinning out of her hand, but she had to get the brooch back. It was for her mother, and had cost a small fortune.

'Whore!'

Again, she didn't connect. Whoever this person was talking to, it couldn't be her. She was a virgin when she'd met her man. Had known no other. Wanted none, either.

'Dirty, filthy, common little bitch!' The voice seemed to echo behind her. 'Scream and I'll cut your throat like the worthless trash that you are.'

'P–please. I have no money. Only the brooch.'

What brooch? She'd dropped it, he'd never believe her. Her mind was whirling. He was taking her shawl, her precious shawl, because she had no money to give him. The shawl was worth more than the brooch. Not in financial terms, but it was her *fertility* shawl. The shawl that would give her a baby. Deva began to claw at the cloth until she felt the prick of the knife at the side of her throat. Felt a hot dribble of liquid run down her neck. Instinctively, she stopped fighting.

'There's a good little whore.'

Laughing, he flung her to the ground, the stone flagstones sending a shooting pain through one of her knees as the bone cracked.

'Do as I say and I won't kill you.'

Deva nodded dumbly. He had dragged her into an empty storehouse. Grain from the smell of it, the dry dusty air. A store that would not be used until the harvest was in. Months – light years – away. If she resisted, tried to run, he would kill her and then, when her body was eventually found, it would be unrecognizable. In the meantime, her man would think she had run off and left him.

So Deva obeyed every twisted and deviant command the Halcyon Rapist gave her.

Thirteen

With her elbows resting on the rail that ran round the upstairs gallery, Claudia watched the frenzied activity in the atrium below. Any fears she might have harboured about the production not being professional had vanished. The pulleys had been rigged up for the canvas scenery and Ion and Doris were hauling on one side, Skyles and Felix on the other, and with every run-through, the backdrop was changed that little bit faster.

'That bloody rumpus in the street last night,' Ion grumbled, his handsome face made ugly with a scowl. 'I couldn't sleep a bloody wink after that.'

All four men shared the same room, Claudia remembered. The same room where she and a Buffoon with a craggy, lived-in face had sipped wine . . .

'Oh, really?' Doris laughed. 'Then who was snoring like a carthorse in the bunk above me? It's the rest of us who couldn't sleep, kiddo.'

'Is that why *you* slipped out?' Felix asked.

Perhaps it would have happened anyway, but the rope slithered through Doris's hand, tilting the canvas at a drunken angle.

'The bleach from your hair has washed into your ears and softened your brain,' he said, and Claudia noticed a tightness around his mouth as he replied. 'I didn't go anywhere.'

'If you two girls wouldn't mind,' Skyles called across, his biceps bulging from the strain of holding the heavy sailcloths. 'Only, Ion and me are getting a mite tired over here.'

Doris pulled a face. 'Sorry.'

Stage management was another factor which had to be worked into the production. Among such a small troupe, there was no room for the squad of labourers and skivvies that were employed in the bigger theatres. Like it or not, everyone had to pitch in with scenery and costume changes, even the castrato, and no one saw any conflict between big, bearded Ion wielding a dainty needle or a young man with chiselled cheekbones and traces of kohl round his eyes boasting muscles a stevedore would be proud of. Now, as the four actors hauled on the ropes, aiming for a count of twenty-five to get one backdrop up, then drop the other one, Claudia wondered why had Doris faltered when Felix asked, is that why *you* slipped out? Especially when the question had been addressed to Skyles.

She was still speculating when the door to the porter's vestibule banged open and Julia, Flavia and ten trunks of luggage deposited themselves around the fountain. The old bat wasn't hanging about, then. Come for Saturnalia clearly meant come five days beforehand in Julia's book and Claudia already saw her penny-pinching brain computing how much money she'd be saving.

'I've put you in Gaius's room,' she called down. 'With dear little Flavia next door.'

Julia opened her mouth and then shut it. To complain that she'd prefer one of the other rooms would be to snub the brother she professed to have loved so dearly, whereas to request (in front of strangers, too!) that her whingeing foster daughter sleep further away would sound worse. She shot Claudia a pinched smile.

'Thoughtful as usual, sister-in-law.'

Beside her, Flavia was standing with her mouth gaping at the pageant of tanned flesh and rippling musculature hauling away at the canvas, her eyes popping at the care-less way the men balanced on a mere quarter rung of a ladder. Claudia smiled to herself. Whichever 'highly unsuitable boy' had been the object of Flavia's latest crush, that boy was history. Four objects of passion had taken his place and her gaze jumped from one to the other as she followed Julia up the stairs to the opposite gallery. Frumpy, lumpy and not helped by a breakout of spots on her forehead, Flavia didn't understand what kohl round a man's eyes signalled. She interpreted it as daring and raffish, just as she mistook Felix's bleached hair as an actor's affectation. Dear me, Claudia thought, if Flavia transfers her affections to either of those two, she's in for a shock.

'I hope you don't mind,' Julia said, 'but I've invited a friend to stay, too.'

'Of course I don't mind.' Any more people who could keep her from this harping old fossil would be welcomed with open arms.

'Well, you *did* say they were going to be the talk of all Rome, these productions of yours, and there's this gentleman who could put a lot of business my husband's way—'

'Not exactly a friend, then?' She should have known Julia wouldn't have any.

'It would be an excellent contact for Marcellus to culti-vate,' Julia sniffed. 'He's patrician, an oleiculturist, his family's in the law—'

'Remind me how useful an olive grower might be for an architect.'

Across the gap, Julia smiled condescendingly. 'You don't understand how these things work, dear. This gentleman is nobility, and he assures me that he is in a position to help Marcellus, so it's only right we return the favour.'

'In other words, you're short of the readies to slip him his five to six pounds in silver?'

The smile froze into something approaching a sneer. 'That is not the case at all. This gentleman simply mentioned that he would very much like to attend this particular function, and under the circumstances one could hardly refuse.' The freeze thawed. 'As I say, he's an aristocrat, divorced, stinking rich – and very much taken with our little Flavia, I don't mind admitting.'

'I think I know him,' Claudia murmured. 'His mother dropped him as a baby and he was never the same after that.'

For a moment, she almost felt sorry for the lank-haired, round-shouldered lump goggling down at her four heroes, who'd decided they'd had enough physical exercise for one morning and were now reading through the script. Claudia saw visions of her being palmed off, like some character in one of Caspar's plays, to some doddery old olive grower who had taken a shine to her childbearing hips. Then the sympathy vanished. Over the last year, Flavia had been bombarded with eligible bachelors. Almost from the day of her birth, Gaius had started paving the way with potential husbands and while Claudia had continued his labours after his death, Julia and Marcellus had also worked tirelessly to secure the girl a good future. With what reward? Flavia had insulted every single suitor and the time to be wilful was running out fast. Soon she would have no choice in the matter. Roman law was tough when it needed to be, and if she wasn't betrothed soon, the State would step in and fix her up with a candidate of its own choosing.

Claudia resolved to have a word in her stubborn little ear tonight. Tell Flavia that it was high time the silly cow wised up. Marry someone she can at least get on with. Then have affairs like everyone else.

'In fact, unless I miss my guess,' Julia was saying, 'you may well find there is something in this for you, sister-in-law. My gentleman is extremely well connected and I daresay he will be able to recommend our wine—'

'Whose wine?'

'—to his family and friends. As I say, his people are in law, which means the network's probably spread right across the Empire.'

'You don't think you're getting carried away here, Julia?'

The old bat chose to ignore her. 'You might even know him. Yes, I think you do. He came here, once. I recall the occasion now. Gaius was entertaining – or was it just a family affair? No matter. The point is, you were there at the time, dear. Marcellus, as well, and yes, I do believe little Flavia actually sat next to him.'

'What's his name?' Claudia asked.

If a girl is to be entertaining an influential contact under her roof, best to find out as much about him as she can. Especially if there's a chance he might be part of the family one day. Also, nothing eases trade quite like a buried secret and the sooner she got rooting the better for everyone concerned. But the olive grower's name would have to wait. Caspar chose that moment to emerge from his bedroom.

'Why, good heavens, madam! You failed to mention that you had two such luscious creatures staying with you.'

Julia blushed unbecomingly. Flavia was still gawping at the actors, who had now been joined by half a dozen other men, although you could probably rule out Ugly Phil as a contender for her affections. Pleasant though this face might be, that set of horns and furry leggings were designed for laughs, not winning female hearts. But whatever rejoinder Julia intended to make to Caspar's ostentatious bow did not get past her larynx. From his bedroom, which just happened to be situated next to Julia's, a strapping blonde marched out, her gown ungirdled, her hair awry.

'Is this your wife?' Julia asked, smiling.

'Not exactly, madam.' Caspar's hands made a deprecating gesture before one of them settled happily around Fenja's waist. 'But you know how chilly it gets in the wee small hours before dawn.'

'Ja, ferry cold.' Fenja nodded vehemently. 'Vee heff much keep-fitting to do, not to be goose pimpling.'

A froth of bright red curls then put their head round the doorpost. 'Mornin' all,' it yawned.

'*Two?*' Julia gasped.

'You can come and make it three, if you want, love,' Jemima quipped, one strap slipping from her shoulder as she squeezed beside her pint-sized lover. Caspar's little pudgy hand immediately slipped around her waist, ensuring that both arms were now firmly, protectively, possessively round both girls.

'I presume, sister-in-law, that you do not propose to expose my Flavia to these excesses of licentiousness?'

'Too late, her jaw's already dropped to the floor,' Claudia replied, although Flavia seemed more fascinated than shocked. 'Anyway, Marcellus has been banging on for years about how women should receive the best education possible.'

'Educations, madam, do not come higher than Caspar's Spectaculars,' the little man confirmed solemnly, but Julia did not hear.

The merest mention of her husband's name had sent her retreating to her bedroom as she realized this was yet another problem to contend with. It was bound to give him 'ideas', this bevy of femaleness clad in fabric you could almost read through. What on earth was she going to do? Gaius's couch, goddammit, was a double one. How could she possibly fend him off in that?

Caspar's eyes twinkled wickedly. 'Run along now, my volumptuous beauties, run along. We have a cabaret to execute at the Circus, remember?'

He gave them both a slap on their ample backsides, and, shrieking with laughter, the girls tumbled boisterously along the gallery and down the stairs. The boards were still reverberating thirty seconds after they'd left.

'Madam.' He gave Claudia a sweeping bow. 'I do believe

this is the happiliest household in which I have had the pleasure to perform.'

It wasn't entirely clear whether he was referring to his theatrical productions or his performance in the bedroom, but it didn't matter. Because Flavia had come to a decision in the meantime.

Like a child poring over a litter of puppies and not knowing which to choose, she had finally settled on the one she would adopt for her next crush. Claudia rather hoped it would have been Ion, with his broad back and shoulder-length hair and voice that boomed like a god. It wasn't, of course.

Like everyone else, she picked Skyles.

Fourteen

The second Orbilio opened his eyes he realized he was in trouble. He knew instantly that he'd slept in, something he hadn't done since his school days, but there was more.

For a moment, he wondered whether he might be dreaming. Same cramped bedsit with its scrubbed floors, polished chairs and window open regardless of the weather. Even, he was sure, the same baby bawling. He had to be dreaming. Reliving the nightmare, as trauma victims invariably do.

But Orbilio was no victim of suffering. True, he was under stress – enormous stress – over the halcyon rapes. But surely he would be reliving those moments, not this? Also. He scratched his head. Would he be able to dream of fresh blankets on the bed, green ones, even though they still smelled of violets? Would his imagination pile a plate of honey cakes on the stove? Would his imagination make it drizzle outside? Maybe, he thought sourly. But no way would imagination catch his skin with a fingernail when it made the pixie clamber on top of him!

'You were fabulous last night,' she whispered, rubbing herself against his naked skin. 'After the fourth time, Marcus Cornelius, I thought you'd be too exhausted ever to rise to the occasion again. But—' she giggled '—I see I'm mistaken.'

To his horror, Angelina was right. Mother of Tarquin, how *could* he? How could he have taken her to Milo's tavern, fortified himself with a jug of wine before dumping her, then allowed himself to get so out of his skull that he ends up here. *Again.*

'That feels so–o–o good, darling.'

What the hell happened after him taking her to Milo's and breaking off the relationship?

'Oh, Marcus. Yes.'

Apart from the obvious, that is, and for a moment he experienced a brief surge of something that might have been pride. (Four times? Well, well, well!) But his performance wasn't the issue here. It was the fact that he couldn't *remember* it. In fact, he didn't even remember leaving the tavern. Was he really so stressed about the Halcyon Rapist that it was unbalancing his mind? Or did the answer lie closer to home? In the jugs of wine he had taken to consuming, in an effort to blot out the man he had sent to the lions?

Orbilio licked his lips. They were dry, his tongue felt furred, and there was a sour taste in his mouth. *So that's what a conscience tastes like . . .*

He made a vow. No more wine. Ever.

And all the while, those damn castanets behind his eyes—

'Do you like that?' Angelina moaned, wriggling on top of him.

Like it? It was driving him wild. 'I have an appointment,' he rasped.

'Break it, darling.'

'I can't,' he said, pushing her away, and he wasn't referring to his fictitious appointment. 'I'm sorry, Angelina, I just can't.'

Kneeling on the bed, the pixie pouted. 'You won't stand me up again tonight, will you?'

Orbilio draped his toga roughly over his tunic and hauled on his boots. 'No,' he said solemnly. 'You have my word, Angelina. I'll call on you tonight, after work.'

This time, he would cut the thing dead once and for all.

* * *

Dymas was waiting for him in his own atrium, where Orbilio's steward had provided hospitality in the form of warm tansy wine and dried figs. Rain dripped through the aperture in the roof into the atrium pool via a series of shiny copper waterspouts. Dymas counted the drips. He was not a young man – late thirties and his hair was thinning – and he wasn't particularly big, but he was strong. Greek-born and a blacksmith by trade, he had retained both native cunning and strength. The instant Orbilio returned, he was off the couch and grabbing his cloak.

'Bloody fuck, mate, where the hell have you been? All Hades has broken loose and we couldn't find you any place.'

Marcus had only worked with Dymas twice before, the last occasion, of course, being on the rapes last year. He hadn't enjoyed either mission, frankly, finding the Greek truculent and temperamental, prone to sulks interspersed with bouts of sullen, protracted silences. Small wonder Dymas tended to work alone. No one had ever seen him with a woman. But credit where it's due, the man was thorough. Certainly, on the two cases in which he'd been seconded to Orbilio. And loners, in the Security Police, invariably achieved more than team players.

'I had another case to attend to,' he lied, swiping his wet hair out of his face.

'Well, if you were hoping to freshen up, tough luck, mate. The boss wants to see us. Like an hour and a half ago!'

Marcus felt a punch to his stomach. 'Another rape?'

'Number three,' Dymas confirmed. 'And Callisunus is going ballistic.'

Stomach churning, Marcus stared at the bust of his father glowering censoriously down from his podium. *That's another gel you've failed, m'boy. Another life you've ruined, because you cocked up.* The atrium swam. He was glad to close the door on it behind him.

'Where did it happen?' he asked thickly.

'Near the river.' Dymas kept his eyes to the ground to

avoid stepping in the puddles. Not that he ever looked up when he walked. 'Same modus operandi as before. Masked attacker drags his victim off the street, strips her clothes off with a knife, forces her to have oral sex with him, then beats her to a pulp, buggers her senseless and dumps her in the filth on the middens.'

He might just as well have been talking about the weather or describing a handcart.

In his office, the Head of the Security Police was hopping up and down. Enough that the rapes had started again. Enough that he was looking at full-scale panic in the city right over the holiday period, a time of peace and goodwill and festivals which would bring every young woman in Rome on to the streets to be exposed to the beast who's still stalking them. But that he, Callisunus, should be kept waiting for nearly two hours by some *patrician* underling . . .

'Wait outside,' he told Dymas.

Dymas scowled. 'This is my case, too, boss.'

'Are you fucking deaf, man? *Outside*. And you.' Callisunus's gaze ranged over the tunic Orbilio had been wearing yesterday, the stubble on his chin. 'What the fuck's going on here?'

Marcus tugged at his earlobe. 'I don't honestly know, sir.'

'Well, there's a young kid called Deva who does fucking know, and if you'd been there like you should, at the scene of the fucking crime, you'd have seen for yourself. Seventeen years old today on her way to her mother's, and now the poor cow can't even speak. She just clutches some bit of red cloth to her breast, shouting, "My baby, my baby," and that is not fucking good enough.'

'No, sir, it isn't— Did you say Deva? The Damascan girl from over the river?'

'You know her?'

'Not exactly, but—' He began to pace the office. 'I met her when I interviewed her husband last summer. He's a

101

herbalist, and I was picking his brains over that crackpot who tried to poison the Emperor by putting what turned out to be monkshood in the sweetmeats.'

Two civil servants and a slave died that day. A high price to pay for filching Imperial sweeties.

Callisunus pursed his thick lips and sat down behind his desk. The silence alone should have been enough to set alarm bells ringing, but Orbilio couldn't rid himself of the haunting image of a young woman clutching her favoured red fringed shawl and mourning a baby that she might now never have.

'You realize I have the Emperor's people on my back, don't you?' Callisunus snarled. 'You don't need me to draw diagrams, Orbilio. Thanks to your fuck-up, they blame *me* for the Security Police turning into a laughing stock that can't tell a copycat crime from its elbow. Well, sonny boy, let me tell you, I don't propose to lose my job over your stupidity. I've worked too bloody hard to get my arse on this chair and if it's going anywhere, my arse, it's going bloody upwards, you hear?'

Orbilio stopped pacing. 'Are you firing me?'

'The hell I am!' A fat fist pounded the desk. 'If I were to sack you now, there'd still be another rape tomorrow and with the head of the original investigating team out of the loop, how does that make me look? Use your bloody noodle.'

'You've lost me, sir. What are you saying?'

Callisunus sighed. 'What I'm saying, Orbilio, is that I'm putting Dymas in charge of this investigation.'

'You're not serious?'

'What's the matter? Don't you fancy the idea of reporting to a low-born dago blacksmith's son?'

Sometimes his boss was truly beneath contempt. 'You want results, the Emperor wants results and believe it or not, sir, I want results as well.' Generations of breeding kept his voice level. 'Give me another forty-eight hours.'

'No.'

'Twenty-four, then.'

'What the fuck will that prove? You sent an innocent man to his death, for Croesussakes.'

'Twenty-four hours should prove whether this is a copycat or otherwise.'

'You're pissing in the dark, Orbilio.'

Bloody right. 'Let's not lose sight of the fact that we got a confession,' he said carefully. 'We found the mask under the rapist's bed—'

'*Alleged* rapist's bed.'

'—his clothes stank of aniseed, plus some of the victims were also able to identify the man as their attacker.'

'Exactly why I'm taking you off the case,' Callisunus said, tapping the piles of scrolls on his desk with an irritated finger. 'This bears all the hallmarks of the original rapes, and I ought to know, because while I was waiting for your high-and-mightyship to condescend to pay me a call this morning, I had plenty of time to read through the bloody files.'

Orbilio leafed through the scrolls. 'Where did these come from?'

This was the Security Police, for heaven's sake. Only current cases were ever retained, everything else was destroyed, Imperial policy. Too sensitive by far to keep on file. In the wrong hands, went the theory, stuff like this could destabilize the Empire.

Callisunus smiled the sort of smile that curdled fresh milk. 'Your superior officer kept them.'

'*Dymas?*'

'Obviously he had reservations at the time.' He folded his hands on the table and stared at his patrician subordinate for at least two full minutes. 'You said you knew the girl who was raped this morning.'

'Deva? Sort of. Why?'

Callisunus reached across to a scroll tied in blue ribbon

on the table behind him. 'On the morning before the tribunes were sworn in, the first attack took place just behind
the Temple of Lucina on the Esquiline Hill.' He looked up.
'That's not far from where you live, is it?'

Marcus shrugged. 'A hundred yards, I suppose.' He
wished he knew where this was leading.

'And yesterday morning, a girl called Blandina was
dragged off Armoury Row.'

Orbilio waited for some kind of explanation, but his boss
merely re-rolled the parchment and replaced it on the table
behind him. 'So?' he prompted.

Callisunus leaned back in his chair and considered the
young man standing in front of him. Twenty-six years old,
handsome as hell, muscles like armour, wanted for nothing
his entire life. Hell, the family had even bought him a
commission in the fucking army.

'So, nothing,' he said cheerfully. 'But it's interesting that
she happened to be the daughter of the man who supplies
you with your harnesses. Don't you think?'

Fifteen

'There are many things I might have envisaged happening during the Festival of the Seven Hills,' Claudia murmured to Drusilla. 'But for Flavia to come home laughing wasn't one of them.'

'Hrrrrow,' Drusilla agreed.

We're not talking smiling. We're not talking grinning. We're not even talking about a fit of adolescent giggles. No, for perhaps the first time in her life, Flavia was in the grip of genuine happiness. Well, well, well, will wonders never cease! Eyes which were normally twin balls of resentment set in a perpetual scowl shone like hilltop beacons, transforming her face into something approaching radiance. And not just her face, either. Happiness had loosened the slump of her shoulders, lifted her head, freed her spine from its withdrawn posture. In fact, Flavia looked exactly like a girl of fifteen *ought* to look. Young, carefree, with the world at her feet and a flower in her hair. Oh, and a ring missing from the middle finger of her right hand . . .

'Brrrp.'

'I know, poppet. It was the one set with amethysts.'

But Drusilla wasn't interested in what fate might have befallen Flavia's jewellery. Tickles round the ear were nice, but they didn't begin to compare with tormenting little jewel-coloured birds until they squawked themselves hoarse. With a lithe jump, she returned to her sentry post on the roof of the aviary and began to tweak at the wire with vicious hooked claws. Claudia slipped into a pair of fur-lined slippers warming underneath the brazier. Day Two of the advertising campaign had exceeded her expectations and not purely because of the increased crowd attendance at the Circus Maximus. The players were now established in their roles, firing off the banter that much faster, and Skyles's chivalrous offer of giving Erinna his tunic happened so quickly that it never occurred to the spectators to question whether he couldn't have asked someone for the loan of a long cloak instead.

Claudia couldn't help but notice that the races which followed came as something of an anticlimax to those closest to the impromptu performance. Wheels might fall off, chariots overturn, drivers get thrown into the path of oncoming vehicles, but for those seated in the vicinity of Claudia Seferius, the antics of her sponsored actors had overshadowed anything the Circus organizers could hope to stage. Thanks to three well-upholstered females, there was enough gossip to see them through dinner parties for a month, and now it looked like war was being declared over who would sponsor the Spectaculars after Saturnalia.

'Dear lady, I cannot thank you enough,' Caspar glowed, as patrician fought merchant for the privilege of backing future performances. 'A more fortuititious meeting between our two parties I could not have envisaged and I praise the day our humblesome group was evicted from that fleapit tavern on Silversmith's Rise. The gods, I feel certain, smile on the Spectaculars.'

'Not nearly as much as they smile on my strongbox,' Claudia assured him. 'I'm on twenty per cent of the takings for six months. Or hadn't I mentioned that earlier?'

The feather in his turban reeled sideways. 'T–twenty?'

'All right, then, twenty-five.' She squeezed his plump little arm. 'After all, I *have* done all the groundwork.'

Once Caspar and his troupe had retired from the Circus – ostensibly to lick their moral wounds, but in practice because to linger would be to dilute the effect – Julia had forged her way through the crowds.

'No shame!' she hissed, plumping herself down on Claudia's cushion. 'None at all. Did you see what happened? No, of course you didn't, you weren't in your seat, but I saw the whole thing very clearly—' she pointed six rows up, to the left '—and I tell you, those women are nothing but *strumpets*.'

'It was hardly Erinna's fault that her tunic came off when Ion rushed to help.'

'Poor girl, of course it wasn't,' Julia agreed. 'But afterwards, did the wench exhibit a single sign of embarrassment? She did not, and I ask you, what kind of woman is more concerned with cuffing the culprit round the ear than covering her nakedness? If it wasn't for the decency of that nice chap with the shaved head, she would still be flashing her bazoomas round the amphitheatre and you want to watch yourself, sister-in-law, having floozies like that under your roof. You'll end up being tarred with the same brush.'

Claudia thought of twenty-five per cent of the takings and decided she very much liked the aroma of tar. 'Why didn't Flavia come to the races?' she asked.

'Don't be silly, I could hardly leave her mooning about the house, that child has gathered more wool than a whole crew of shearers lately. Of *course* I brought her along. Flavia? Come and say hello to—'

But when she turned her head, the seat beside her was empty. And that's when they both realized that Flavia had sloped off with the actors.

'Leave her,' Claudia said. 'Enjoy the chariot racing. She'll come to no harm with Caspar.'

Which was true. She would have come to no harm with Caspar. Only Flavia didn't stay with the maestro and his colourful troupe. According to Doris, while the troupe was still in the shadow of the Circus walls, Flavia slipped into the crumbling ruins of the old temple to Juventus. Which, by Claudia's reckoning, was between four and five hours ago.

'And she wasn't alone,' Doris had added, with a mischievous rattle of bangles.

Really? And what could a fifteen-year-old girl possibly have been up to that made her return home radiant with joy?

That didn't have three letters and end with an 'x'?

Claudia was sitting on the upper bunk, legs dangling, when Skyles breezed in through his bedroom doorway. She had counted it out in her head. One: drop Flavia at front entrance. Two: slip round to side. Three: flirt with a couple of the kitchen girls. Four: help self to something tasty off the griddle. A ham and onion rissole, from the smell of it.

He could, she thought, at least have feigned surprise at finding her in his room.

'My compliments to the chef,' he said, breaking off half the remains of the rissole and lobbing it over. 'Absolutely delicious.'

Ham and onion it was – with a smattering of chives, parsley and just a smidgen of garlic. Craggy eyes didn't leave hers. Not even when a strong arm reached behind him to pull the blue tapestry across the doorway. Curious how much sound was muffled by one piece of embroidered cloth. The clamour from the kitchens receded to a muffled hum. The rehearsals in the atrium to a distant drone.

Amazing how much light was blocked out from the torches that burned in the corridor, too. Plunged into sudden blackness, she heard him cross the tiny cupboard of a room without faltering. Felt the brush of air as his shoulder passed a whisker from her knees. Listened to him reach unhesitatingly for his tinderbox. *Fssst.* A small flame flickered on the rough wooden table between the two lower bunks as the tallow's wick caught light.

It might have been as though his eyes had never left her.

'Just so you know,' she said cheerfully. 'Any man who takes Flavia's virginity can expect to wear his testicles for earmuffs and warble higher notes than Periander could ever hope to aspire to. Are we clear on that?'

His long, low chuckle echoed round the little room. 'Doris wants to keep his mouth shut.'

He stripped off his tunic, leaned over the bowl on the table, splashed his face, neck and underarms and dried himself on the coarse linen towel hanging on an iron peg on the wall.

'But if it sets your pretty mind at rest, the only cherries that interest me are these.' He reached into a jar and tossed up one of the candied fruits he'd offered yesterday. 'Flavia's young enough to be my daughter.'

'Or old enough to be your wife.'

He pulled on a clean grey tunic emblazoned with purple and gold, poured two mugs of coarse red wine and bounced up on the bunk opposite. 'Then here's to fortune-hunters everywhere.'

Damn. And Drink-Me-Dry had acquired another chip since yesterday, too. 'Don't you ever stop acting?' she said.

'You ask a lot of questions for a woman alone with a man in the dark.'

'I'm sure you're used to questions in the bedroom, Skyles.' The women would all want to know the same things. Where did he get those scars on his back from? Did the wounds bleed much? Do they hurt? Can he feel it, when they do this . . . ?

He chuckled, a low dirty sound which came from deep in his throat. 'You're right, I am, but not to the type of questions you ask. Oh and, if you're interested, I always tell them the same thing when they get curious about how I acquired these.' He jerked his thumb over his shoulder to indicate the scars. 'From my last lover's husband, I say.'

Very funny, yes, and the women would laugh, but Claudia knew it wouldn't matter a damn to them, because they didn't care. They only wanted the salacious details. The pain, the blood, the humiliation. It was all part of the turn-on. They wouldn't want to know what he had done to receive such a lashing. Only that he'd passed out, to be brought round time and again, and tell me again how you'd bitten through the wood they put in your mouth. His conquests would be aroused sexually by the wheals, not roused to compassion. Who knows, maybe Skyles had deserved a good thrashing? But Claudia would not bet her house and her vineyards on that. No man would need to act round the clock, if he was all bad.

Or was that just another layer to the act?

Because hadn't she seen similar patterns on shoulder blades before? From a man who got sexual kicks from self-flagellation?

'Thanks for the wine,' she said, jumping down. 'Although you should be able to afford better quality now on the proceeds from Flavia's ring. Amethysts buy a jolly good vintage.'

Skyles leaned back on his elbows and stared at the dull, painted ceiling. 'The girl just needs to breathe, Claudia. Feel she's lived a bit, before she settles down and starts turning out babies like pots from a kiln.'

'I have no problem with Flavia breathing,' she said. 'Just bear in mind what I said about earmuffs.'

Dammit, Flavia's virginity was about the only bargaining power the family had left.

She was halfway back to the atrium when a deep voice called down the corridor after her.

'By the way, you don't have to worry about amethysts being wasted on the likes of me,' Skyles said. 'Flavia didn't give me that ring.' He timed his pause. 'She threw it down the disused well outside the Temple of Juventus. An offering to the god of youth.'

Sixteen

In his office covered with hunting trophies and memorabilia, Sextus Valerius Cotta looped his thumbs into his belt and stared across the peristyle, listening to the orchestral sounds made by the rain. The drumming as it landed on the large leaves of the castor oil plants. A tinkling as it hit the ivy on the trellis, the percussion as it bounced off fan palms and the lavender, the deeper plopping noises as it dripped from the bare branches of the pomegranate tree.

With space on the Palatine at a premium, his house was smaller than many of his colleagues', who preferred the grandeur of the Esquiline; the garden poky, if you like, in comparison. But prestige is measured in quality, rather than quantity, and Cotta's bronze discus thrower and rearing marble horses, like the furniture in his house, were prized antiques and the craftsmen he employed were the finest in Rome. The artists, for example, called every March to perforate the stems of that tinkling ivy to release a gummy sludge which they'd mix with wine and urine then boil to produce the blood-red pigment used to colour the walls of Cotta's office. There was, he decided, no substitute for detail. None whatsoever.

It was this attention to detail which had won him his victories in Cisalpine Gaul, among others, and had later honed his skills as a tactician in the Senate. He thought about the boar that had terrorized the Umbrian hills and whose head still snarled in defiance, only now it did so above his office chair. He recalled riding out across the

111

Syrian desert to spear the panther whose glistening pelt he wore home as a cloak, like Hercules, and whose fangs hung round the neck of his youngest son. He remembered the lion he took on single-handed and whose skin made a nice warm rug on his floor, its head a comfy footrest beneath his desk. Attention to detail. Without it, the boar would have sunk its tusks in his belly, gutted him like a sardine. Every victory, every triumph, from Gallic uprisings to the guile of the panther, had been engineered through painstaking plotting. Even in emergencies, Cotta hadn't rushed into anything, but had pored over the plans, rethinking, redevising, unafraid to scrap previous strategies and start again.

It would be the same when he blew up the Senate.

He opened the lime-wood box with an ornately carved hinged lid that sat on his desk. The box had belonged to his father, and Cotta had lost count of the number of times he'd praised the old man's good sense in keeping it in his bedroom rather than taking it to the west wing when he'd conducted his final experiment in the search for immortality.

Lined up side by side within the box, like dolls in a cot, lay several kid-skin pouches, separating the ingredients for the fabled elixir. Cotta untied the string from one of the pouches, dipped his finger in the ruby red powder and examined it in the light. Realgar. What the Arabs who fetched it up from the bowels of earth called *Fire of the Mine*. He sniffed carefully, but did not make the mistake of licking his finger, instead wiping it clean with a cloth. Realgar was a form of arsenic.

He retied the pouch, opened another and tipped out a series of opaque yellow crystals, each forming a perfect metallic cube. A third pouch contained crystals of a much brighter yellow. Needle-like, these crystals were sulphur, while yet another pouch kept separate the gritty, vermilion-coloured cinnabar, which the old man had insisted was essential. The final pouch contained the most precious ingredient of all. A substance known as Poseidon Powder.

Poseidon was the name the Greeks gave to the God of the Sea, who conjured up storms and cleaved the land with his trident, sending waves three storeys high to devastate the land after he'd shaken it. Fine and chalky, white as flour, Poseidon Powder was only found in a handful of secret places in the world, one of which lay close to the rose-red city of Petra in the Jordanian desert.

These nitre beds were formed from camel dung from the huge caravans that used to camp outside the city in the old days, before the sands – and the caravans – shifted. Over time, the dung reacted with the salty soil and the moisture in the air to form crystals that dissolved in rain then dried into a fine, white powder on the surface. To the Arabs who guarded these precious nitre beds, the powder was known as salt of Petra. Saltpetre.

For Cotta's father, this substance was the key to eternal life.

For Cotta, it was the key to releasing the eagle.

In its present form, the powder was not dangerous, but when mixed with other substances, it was – as his father discovered – highly combustible. What Cotta needed to know was the precise formula the old man had worked to.

Only one other person knew the answer. The servant who had helped the old man with his fatal experiment.

A servant who had apparently vanished into thin air.

Seventeen

Julia's husband, Marcellus, had no idea he was sitting a mere hundred paces from the Arch-Hawk of the Senate, and even if he had, he would have imagined the Senator's thoughts were concerned more with the burning of Dacian cities and the storming of Scythian fortresses than how a pinch of chalky powder would change the future of Rome. Every afternoon around this time Marcellus took himself off to the library. Not any old library, mind you, though heaven knows there were plenty to choose from. For Marcellus, there was only one library which mattered. The one adjacent to the Temple of Apollo on the Palatine.

The incentives were numerous. The view, for one. The vast spread of the city sprawled away below him, he could watch the ants bustling back and forth across the open plazas. Slaves doubled under the weight of barrels, beams and sacks, children scampering, donkeys plodding along with bulging panniers. He could see litters carrying the rich. Young men carrying the old. In fact, every stratum of humanity passed below him here, and if a man preferred a gentler pace on which to rest his eyes, he only had to gaze across to the rolling hills beyond, or watch the barges being hauled along the banks of the Tiber by patient oxen. On the other hand, if it was excitement that he craved, he could always crane his neck and watch the charioteers practising in the Circus Maximus below, leather chest protectors tied tight around their torsos and helmets to protect them when they fell. Not that Marcellus could see any of those things today. Low, grey clouds obscured the hills and released a relentless shrouding drizzle.

But if the view wasn't enough to lure a person up the Palatine's steep embankment, there was the sheer grandeur of the temple itself. The breathtaking colonnades of yellow Numidian marble. Exquisite frescoes, statues, marble busts, not to mention the Great Frieze depicting Augustus's victory over Antony and Cleopatra's fleet at Actium. Some of the finest paintings and sculptures the world had ever seen were on display here, many of them precious beyond price, being works by the old masters, but views and artistic splendours were not the motivation behind Marcellus's daily visits. He didn't give a hoot about the Greek and Latin archives, either, or the fact the ancient Sybilline Prophecies were stored at the base of Apollo's bravura statue.

Important men passed through this library. Senators, philosophers, landowners, merchants, shipbuilders, ship-owners, shipping magnates. One day might find Marcellus engaged in debate with a tribune, another day with a prefect for the roads. Sooner or later, he reasoned, one of them was bound to shove a commission his way.

There were few potential patrons in the library this after-noon, however. Rain invariably kept people indoors and now that the light was fading, there were even fewer. But Marcellus was determined to remain here to the very last, and he was happily whiling away his time on Plato's trea-tise on the—

'Janus Croesus, Claudia!' He picked himself up from where he'd been sent sprawling across the floor and looked around. 'Did you see what just happened? Some bastard sneaked up behind me and socked me clean off my stool.'

'You need a shave,' she said, sucking her knuckles.

'What did you do that for?' he asked.

'Pleasure,' she purred.

Marcellus never expected to figure out what went through women's heads, but come on. What the hell was wrong with Plato? 'Dammit, you've killed my reputation as an architect, you know that.'

'If your reputation had any sense of decorum, it would have committed suicide months ago,' she retorted. 'Outside.'

'But—'

'*Outside.*'

Trailing behind her, Marcellus wished he could have felt something other than a stirring in his loins, but by heaven, his sister-in-law was magnificent when roused. Her breasts heaved, her eyes flashed, a curl would spring loose from its hairpin, and although Marcellus would never have obeyed any other woman's orders, much less trot meekly after them, with Claudia he would jump off the Tarpeian Rock if she asked him.

'Would you mind telling me what that was all about?' he hissed outside. 'I'll be the laughing stock of the Apollo Library for months.'

A lie. He knew damn well they'd take her for a disgruntled mistress and that, if anything, his stock would soar.

'How long before it sinks into that thick skull of yours that prestigious patrons aren't placing contracts with you, Marcellus, because you spend too much time idling it away in this blessed library?'

'You've got the wrong end of the stick, love.' His patronizing would have made more impact, had he not had to break into a run to keep up with her. 'This is what's known in the business as "networking". Making contacts, sowing seeds—'

'Bollocks.' In the shade of the primrose marble portico, Claudia rounded on her brother-in-law. 'Has it never occurred to you, Marcellus, that if you were out supervising projects occasionally, these people might actually feel better disposed towards you? That they might see you then as a successful architect with a thriving business to run? Instead, you come over as a sad loser, hanging around hoping for work.'

116

'Well.' Marcellus's complexion turned the colour of porridge. 'That's pretty much the sum of it, isn't it?'

'The Emperor boasts that he's turned a city of brick into a city of marble in under seventeen years,' she replied. 'You must be the only architect in the whole bloody Empire without work, so ask yourself: What am I doing wrong?'

'Um—'

'That wasn't a question. Now then, I've been thinking.' They had reached the shrine in the portico that looked out over the city and, sheltered by the high walls from the wind and the rain, Claudia settled herself on the top step. 'Julia's told you I'm sponsoring the Halcyon Spectaculars?'

'Is it true the girls are going to strip nak—?'

Her glare cut him dead. 'By the time the curtain goes up, you will have put together a convincing portfolio of contracts that you've undertaken in – I don't know, Pisa, Florentia – places far enough away for people not to know the owners of the houses you are supposed to have built.'

'I specialize in warehouses,' he reminded her dolefully.

'Even better. Who cares who designed which depot where. That gives you three clear days to—'

'Three? I thought the first Spectacular was on the eighteenth?'

'By popular demand, the schedule's been brought forward to Saturnalia Eve, so you'll have to move fast, and you'll need a fistful of new proposals to flash around, too. That way, people will think you have a whole bank of overseers beavering away behind the scenes, earning you so many gold pieces that you're more than able to squander your valuable time in the library. I'll get one of my scribes to give you a list of who's attending and when, so you can tailor your pitch.'

'I say.' Marcellus's pitted cheeks glowed like a mulberry. 'This is dashed good of you, Claudia. I'll start drawing up that fictitious portfolio first thing in the morning, and don't worry about potential new projects. I have sheafs of proposals at home in my office.' He put his arm round her shoulder and squeezed. 'You know, Claudia, perhaps you and I—'

'In your dreams,' she snapped, flicking the hand off.

Marcellus couldn't believe it. He was going to be rich again. Rich. Just like the old days, when Gaius was alive!

'I don't know how to thank you,' he said. 'I'm a good architect, you have to believe that, it's just that I've never been hot on the sales side of the business. I'll either fumble my presentation, or drop the damn drawings and then I'll make the price sound too high or I'll oversell it. The long and the short of it is, I'm just not cut out to be a sales-man—'

If she heard one more 'I' from him, so help her, she'd black it.

'This is not about *you*, Marcellus. We both know that my husband secured all your contracts for you while he was alive, then after he died you relied on me baling you out. Well, I didn't mind you doing bugger all – for a while. Sooner or later, I reasoned, Marcellus is bound to stand on his own two feet.'

'I've been trying.'

'Exceedingly.'

Suddenly the impact of her words sunk in. 'You . . . You're not cutting my allowance? Think of little Flavia. You can't punish her because of me. And Julia. Think of Julia!'

'Unlike you, you selfish oaf, it's your bloody wife I'm thinking of.'

And before he could draw breath to protest, he was being lambasted by a list of the moth-eaten furs Julia had brought with her, of gowns two seasons old, of worn shoes.

'She turned up at my house without a single slave to attend her, and it took me a while to realize that it wasn't because she was penny-pinching. She's had to sell them to pay your household bills!'

'Times have been hard without contracts.'

'The ball's in your court, Marcellus. If you're no good at selling, hire an agent who is, because yes. As of now, your allowance is indeed severed.'

'B–b–ut how will we live?'

'Ah.' Marcellus had a bad feeling about the cat-like grin that she shot him. 'That's the next little problem we're going to solve,' Claudia said. 'Follow me.'

She didn't begrudge paying Marcellus an allowance. Hell, no. Far better to buy the Sponger Family a set of comfortable living standards than for them to contest Gaius's will, because god knows, if they dug hard enough, they'd find enough skeletons that the weight of them falling out of the closet would probably crush Julia and Marcellus to death. But comfort zones are one thing. The knowledge that the allowance was squandered on floozies quite another.

She snapped her fingers and a torch bearer came running to light their way across town. This went deeper than Julia not having clothes befitting her station, or being unable to heat her house properly, or even having a slave count that was going down and not up. Family values are the lynchpin upon which Roman society hangs. Claudia kicked a beetroot into the gutter. It went beyond Marcellus bejewelling his mistress at the expense of his family. Their social status was a reflection upon Claudia's social status, and she could hardly project herself as the epitome of wealth, success and prosperity if her sister-in-law went round wearing rags. Society would expect her to intercede. Which she was. Only not in the way Society might imagine!

'By the time I've finished with the gold-digging trollop who's had her hooks in you these past months,' she told Marcellus, 'you'll have enough to live on until March. After that, you're on your own.'

Untrue. She wouldn't let him. Couldn't afford to. But

119

there was no reason to let him know that, and you never know, the shock tactics might just work.

'You don't know what it's like, my marriage,' he bleated, as they navigated the tortuous stone steps of the Aventine. 'Whenever I felt frisky, Julia stiffened up and stared at a point over my shoulder, and no man can make love to a statue. I'm thirty-six years old, Claudia. I can't be expected to live without sex. It's unnatural.'

Darkness had cloaked the city and the drizzle had taken on an icy bite, but warm inside her furs and with their path illuminated by the bearer's torch, Claudia barely noticed as Marcellus grumbled his way along one winding alleyway after another. No one said Julia was in the right.

'I really love my little rosebud,' he said. 'The instant Flavia gets married, I'm divorcing that frigid cow. I've had it to here with her endless bloody carping and now I've been given a shot at happiness, I'd be a damn fool not to grab it.'

That was one way to look at it, Claudia supposed. She'd taken a rather different slant on the affair, and had a sneaking suspicion hers was the more accurate.

They had come to the apartment block that her body-guard had followed Marcellus to, to confirm Claudia's suspicions about her brother-in-law. Prime site on the Aventine Hill, with the Imperial Palace directly opposite and the Circus down below, establishments in this part of town rarely came more exclusive. Exquisite frescoes in the corridors reinforced the notion, as did the ornate carvings on the wooden stair rails, the painted stuccoed ceilings. The strong scent of elecampane burning in wall-mounted braziers emphasized the status this building carried, and not a single window had been sheeted out by heavy felt or skins. They were all protected by proper glass. Claudia contrasted this with the moths having such a field day in Julia's wardrobe.

'I don't know how I'm going to explain to my little

rosebud why I've brought you along,' Marcellus said, tipping the torchbearer.

'Leave the talking to me,' Claudia told him.

'She'll be surprised.' With every stair, his eyes glistened with emotion. 'I usually only pop in after I'm finished at the baths and before I visit the library.' His face took on a sheepish appearance. 'I, er, tell Julia I'm lunching with clients.'

By the time he rapped on the door, his face was flushed, his breathing shallow.

'Cherub?' he called softly. 'It's me.'

'Marcellus!' The door was opened a crack by a hard-faced woman in her twenties, whose hennaed hair was awry. Her tongue flicked apprehensively around her lips. 'Look, do you mind if I don't invite you in right now, darling? I'm really not feeling too well at the moment.'

'Nothing serious, rosebud?'

'Yes, I can see we've got you out of bed,' Claudia said cheerfully.

The rosebud pulled a shawl over her bare shoulder and ignored the woman at her lover's elbow. 'Come back in about an hour,' she cooed to Marcellus. 'I'm sure my headache will be gone by then.'

'Of course, darling.'

'Not bloody likely,' Claudia said.

'*Please, Claudia*,' Marcellus muttered under his breath. 'You're putting the poor girl in a very difficult position.'

'I'm sure she's used to that,' Claudia breezed. 'Aren't you, cherub?'

The love of Marcellus's life pulled her skimpy shawl tighter round her naked curves and glowered at her lover. 'Who's this cow?' she asked.

'Humour her, darling,' Marcellus whispered, his face turning scarlet with embarrassment as Claudia barged past him. 'She's um— um—'

'Your wife, is it?' Rosebud rolled her eyes in disgust.

'No wonder you're divorcing the old bitch.' She turned to Claudia, who was checking the rooms and even lifting the crumpled bedsheets to peer under the couch. 'I don't know what you're looking for, but you can bloody forget it. Marcellus. Get this old bag out of my flat.' Her voice changed to a wheedle. 'I told you, darling. I'm not feeling well.'

'You poor love, I—'

Claudia punched the wooden shutter opening on to the balcony. The woodwork winced. 'You can come out now,' she told the shutter. 'Besides. You must be freezing.'

A blanketed, cowering, shivering figure crawled sheepishly into the room. He could not be half as cold, Claudia thought, as the icicles which flashed from the cherub's eyes.

'I – don't understand,' Marcellus said. 'Who's this?'

'He's my brother, of course.' A hard kick landed on a shivering shin. *'Aren't you, Paulus?'*

'I think you and your brother had better start packing,' Claudia said.

Paulus didn't wait. He grabbed his clothes from the balcony and shot down the stairs, flinging them on as he went. Claudia didn't think lightning moved faster. Another married man, then. As for the rosebud, a few petals might have been knocked off, but the stem was holding firm. Without making any attempt to stop Claudia stuffing clothes into a trunk, she homed in on the weakest link, sidling up to Marcellus's chest and nibbling his earlobe.

'Now our relationship's no longer a secret, you can leave that old bag and move in with me. We can be happy here, just the two of us.'

Marcellus might be gullible, but he wasn't stupid. 'You've been screwing him all along, haven't you?'

The cherub blew in his ear. 'You're the only one I've been screwing, darling, and very nice it is, too. The old cow's just trying to drive a wedge between us. Paulus really *is* my brother.'

'Large family, is it?' Claudia trilled, emptying the jewels from the casket.

The cherub snorted. 'Don't let her wind you up, darling. She's just jealous, because I've won your heart in a way that she never could.'

Marcellus pushed her away. 'You even smell of him,' he said thickly.

With nothing left but her thorns, the rosebud pounced on the woman sorting through her bracelets and rings. 'You leave them alone,' she said, snatching the box back. 'They're mine. Marcellus gave them to me.'

'Which means legal title remains with the owner,' Claudia said smoothly.

Oh, goodie, there was an amethyst among the trinkets. Dear little Flavia might well have abandoned herself to impetuosity under Skyles' craggy, sex-drenched influence, but she was nothing if not her father's daughter. Come bedtime, that girl would be blubbing into her pillow for tossing a perfectly good amethyst down the well.

'You have until midnight,' Claudia informed the cherub, pocketing the keys of the apartment, 'before the bailiffs move in.'

Behind her, her brother-in-law's eyes were shiny with tears, there was a look of sheer agony on his pitted face.

'Come on, Marcellus,' she said softly. 'We're done here.'

The Digger dreamed. In the dream, the trees were clothed in their autumn riches. Golds, russets and amber. The air was warm, a stream bubbled nearby and butterflies filled the woodlands as they migrated south. In the dream, the Digger leaned on the spade and looked down at the newly covered grave.

Watched a hand rise up out of the soil.

As fast as the spade could shovel the leaf litter, the hand pushed, until it became an elbow, a whole arm, and suddenly the corpse was climbing noiselessly out of the hole. Black and crawling with maggots, it advanced, and over its face it wore an actor's mask.

'You think you can kill me, but I will never die,' it said through the hole in its temple. 'I will *never* die.'

Flesh fell away from the hand as it pulled off the mask, but there was a second mask underneath that, and a third. But when the corpse pulled off the grotesque grin of the comic, it was the face of the Digger that stared out from the decay.

And the body laughed. 'See?' it said. 'You cannot escape me.'

And the leaves fell from the trees, and it was winter again.

It is perpetually midwinter for killers.

Eighteen

'You know the best thing about December?' Claudia asked Drusilla, as they both stretched languorously in her bed. 'Festivities virtually every day of the month.'

Some, like the Festival of the Lambs, were sombre occasions, while others, like Faunus earlier in the month, were exactly the opposite. Indeed, if anything, Faunus verged a little too much on the rumbustious, with all that rough wine and ungainly clomping the rustics called dance, but it was good fun, this country festival, a mix of goat roasts, boar hunts and blessings-of-the-motherland, which was just an excuse for the locals to get drunk.

'Where would our advertisements for the Spectaculars be without these festivities?' Claudia murmured through a yawn.

'Mrrr.' Drusilla was less than impressed. Coming from Egypt, she hadn't taken to these cold, damp, miserable winters. No amount of gaiety could turn the streets of Rome into sun-baked oases of hot mice and crispy spiders.

'Fortune is smiling on us, poppet.'

The first commercial for the Halcyon Spectaculars took advantage of the Festival of the Lambs, the second capitalized on the Festival of the Seven Hills and now today, and without so much as a day off when people might forget, the gods had given Claudia yet a *third* chance to advertise her sponsorship!

'Not necessarily the finest,' she admitted, stroking Drusilla underneath blankets scented with chamomile. 'But

125

beggars can't be choosers, and the masses do tend to flock to the Festival of Ceres.'

More pious than most of the other winter festivities, and nowhere near on the scale of the goddess's bigger festival which took up such a large chunk of April with its theatres and games, this was still a day of happiness and rejoicing. Of giving back to this bountiful earth goddess some of the fruits of her labours, and the festival involved ceremonies and rituals in which even the lowliest plebeians and slaves could participate.

'Hrrow,' Drusilla growled, hearing the first excited shrieks from the kitchens below.

She had never quite forgiven her mistress for encouraging the children of the household slaves to make cakes of spelt and salt to sacrifice to Ceres today. Already the horrible little sods were squealing in delight as podgy hands mangled dough into bread snails and bread mice to be laid at the altar of the gentle goddess. Nor was Drusilla alone in her tingles of alarm. Since Claudia always laid on outdoor feasts of sticky honeycombs afterwards, the cooks and the flowerbeds also feared for their sanity. Someone's child, somewhere, would always be sick.

Wisely, Drusilla retreated beneath the covers and dreamed of hot sands and cold vermin in a land where it only rained moths. Claudia, dressed in white, the traditional colour for honouring Ceres, found her own escape from the bedlam was not quite as easy. Erinna was sprawled across the stairs tacking up the seams of the tunic Ion would later rip off at the Temple, singing softly to herself.

> '*One day a stranger*
> *Rode into our valley,*
> *Ravaged with scars of hard battles long past.*
> *His eyes, they were weary,*
> *He was tired of running,*
> *But the law was behind him and catching up fast.*'

126

The ballad wasn't one Claudia recognized from any of the plays.

> '*Long after the stranger*
> *Rode out of our valley,*
> *I bore him the daughter that he never knew.*
> *I know not what befell him,*
> *I hope he found freedom,*
> *But I'll always bear him a love that is true.*'

Erinna hadn't bothered pinning her hair into a bun, and today it hung down her back, a glorious cloak of glistening chestnut. No doubt about it. With her clear skin, big eyes and hauntingly beautiful voice, she was one of Caspar's finest assets.

'Sorry, I didn't see you there.'

She shuffled over to let Claudia past, and Claudia didn't say that she'd been there some time, wondering what it was about Erinna's voice that turned a few mediocre lines into something that made eyes prickle with tears.

Erinna bit off the thread with her teeth. 'If you want to make a real impact outside the Temple, all three of us girls could wear tacked costumes if you like?'

'No, no,' Claudia said hastily. 'That won't be necessary.'

There was more than enough flesh on display with Erinna. Three volumptuous beauties would blind the crowd for a week.

And in any case, there was a quality in Erinna that brought a special dimension to the farce. For a show based entirely around smut, the word sophisticated might sound paradoxical, yet there was a stylishness about her which was lacking in the other girls. Not that they lacked sex appeal. Far from it. Jemima in particular had it in spades. Proud of her outsize assets, Jemima was the type who'd tumble men at the drop of a hat and leave them laughing afterwards. But even Adah and Renata had that special appeal that comes from the sure and certain knowledge that they were both desirable and desired – and so what, there were girls out there who were prettier, more shapely, more intelligent? Caspar had chosen his volumptuous beauties with care. The girls in his troupe were *alive*. Vivacious, vibrant, independent and self-assured, they lived for the day and milked life for everything that it sent them and through the medium of farce, they were able to project this to the world. If that isn't sexy, what is?

The thing that set Erinna apart was her couldn't-care-less attitude, which emitted a different kind of sensuality, an effect that was all the more pronounced because Erinna was unaware of it. But none of this would have touched Claudia's consciousness, had it not been for Skyles.

Maybe, she thought, slipping into the thick, warm, woollen mantle Leonides held out at the foot of the stairs, she was mistaken about what she had seen . . .

Maybe she was reading too much into it . . .

The litter bearers dropped her outside Ceres's temple, just off the Cattle Market on the Aventine, in perfect timing for the start of the sacrifice. Adjacent to the shrine, in a great warehouse flanked by winches and cranes, stood the largest corn store in the city, and it was outside the Great Granary that the third, and final, advertisement for the Spectaculars was due to take place. Everyone, whether male or female, rich or poor, free or enslaved, wore white for the ceremony. Allowing Caspar's rainbow troupe to steal even greater attention!

A large crowd had accumulated and fragrant incense wafted on the breeze. Apart from the farmers, whose patron Ceres was, many slaves had also gathered. Should they ever need it, the temple gave them right of sanctuary – and only a fool would wait until the moment was upon them before propitiating the one goddess who was prepared to shelter them.

Not an obvious choice of audience to advertise the

Spectaculars, you might think. But you'd be wrong.

'Make way,' one of the temple acolytes shouted. 'Make way for the penitent! Make way for Meno the Coppersmith.'

Meno the Coppersmith had unwisely attacked a tribune over a long-standing grievance about rights of way past his premises, and the penalty for assaulting the elected representatives of the people was harsh. Meno was immediately stripped of his assets, which were sold off and now the proceeds of that humiliating public auction were being assigned to the Temple of Ceres. Penitent, indeed. One foolish punch had wiped out a lifetime of work.

But. Sad as it was for poor Meno, there's nothing quite like human tragedy to draw a crowd. Not only his fellow artisans were swelling the numbers, but like bees to a honeypot, businessmen were flocking to the precinct in droves. With his workshop sold and his stock liquidated, the only asset Meno had left was his talent. Like the good capitalists that they were, they came hoping to secure the coppersmith's skills on the cheap.

'O, Ceres, who first gave man bread,' the flamen intoned, as the sacrificial pig was carved up and laid on the fire. 'Who forced the first bulls to the yoke, that for the first time the upturned soil might behold the sun—'

Claudia's mind wandered. With the temple doors wide throughout the ceremony, the works of the Greek masters whose artistry embellished the interior showed none of the ravages of the fire which had threatened to destroy the temple nearly twenty years before. Its skilful restoration notwithstanding, however, Augustus rated Ceres important enough in the pantheon to want the exterior of her temple clad in white Parian marble. Not so much to reflect Ceres's purity, Claudia suspected, as Rome's superiority. How much more imposing would the temple look, had the sacred pine grove that used to surround the building still been casting softness and shade across the precinct. Unfortunately, the grove had been completely consumed by the fire and such was the demand for housing and storage, there was never any chance of the grove being replaced. Public latrines now rose from the site, alongside a slaughterhouse, a fish-curing factory and a statue of one of the Muses. How much kudos, Claudia wondered, would be attached if she donated a fountain with marble pine cones in commemoration of the sacred grove? What a poke in the eye for the Wine Merchants' Guild that would be!

'Ceres delights in peace,' the flamen was informing the yawning crowd, as flutes drowned out any evil spirits and libations of blood-red wine trickled across the stone altar. 'Ye who are husbandmen and ye who are not, give thanks with spelt and with salt, for Ceres is content with little, so long as what she receives is pure.'

Purity did not seem to be the issue, over where Jemima was peering through her chunky ankles and asking the crowd what did they think they were looking at. Ceres could stick her salt and spelt.

The house, she reflected, wouldn't be the same after Saturnalia. Sure, there'd be more oil in the jars, more charcoals in the store, and yes you'd be able to hear the fountain babbling in the atrium again, listen to the birds in the aviary, walk without fear of tripping over ratlines and actors sprawled out as they practised their lines. Felix the dancer would no longer make your jaw drop with manoeuvres usually only undertaken by eels. There'd be no Ugly Phils in furry leggings and horns camping it up as the Satyr. No masked actors leaping out of the alcoves to frighten the slaves. No 'plumptious' thighs, no 'volumptuous' wobbles, no Doris with eyes darkened by kohl and bracelets jangling softly as he let himself in and out at all hours. Ion wouldn't be found sitting alone in the kitchen at midnight with a tortured look on his handsome, bearded, god-like face and the boards on the gallery would not creak from the processions of female flesh which passed through Caspar's doorway. And, of course, there would be no bald Buffoons

tickling the kitchen girls and making them fall in love with
him . . .

The advertisement had reached the point where the
director had quite lost control over his quarrelsome crew
and insults were about to be exchanged for something more
physical. Even Meno the penitent was distracted.

'You never *said*,' a girlish voice whined in Claudia's ear.
'If I'd known *they* were going to be here, I'd have come
earlier.'

That was Flavia, whinge, whinge, whinge, and she hadn't
even had the common courtesy to wear white for the festival.
Suddenly, though, her spotty little face brightened as Adah
grabbed a handful of Jemima's red hair and yanked down-
wards.

'Look!' she goggled. 'There's a cat fight outside the
Granary.'

'Good heavens, so there is.' (Oh, come on. You'd hardly
let someone like Flavia in on the secret, now, would you?)

'They're *all* pitching in,' she said, her gasp lost among
a hundred others as Ion lunged to Erinna's aid and came
away with her tunic.

And there it was. The thing Claudia hoped she had been
mistaken about. What she'd prayed she'd read too much
into yesterday and the day before that. *Skyles*. During the
sacrifice of the ram outside the Temple of Janus, she
couldn't help but notice the way he'd been watching Erinna
from the corner of his eye. Saw how he'd kept his gaze
locked on her after the show. And, although Claudia had
seen that same scene repeated at the Circus, she was more
than prepared to give her other impressions the benefit of
the doubt.

Until now.

For a man who gave the word intensity a whole new
meaning, the expression on Skyles' craggy face as Erinna's
tunic came off in Ion's hands was completely blank. And
that was the problem. When Claudia had gone to his room

131

that first time and he'd offered her expensive cherries and cheap wine, it bore all the hallmarks of a seduction. Skyles throbbed with raw sex, yet all they did was sit on his bunk and sip wine from chipped cups in silence. Ditto yesterday. They had sat, widow and actor, alone in the semi-darkness of his bedroom, masculinity oozing from every pore. Yet on neither occasion had Claudia felt threatened. Felt anything other than under control. With Skyles, as she'd known from the outset, everything was an act. The monkey walk. The tripping over invisible objects. His riding imaginary horses round the garden to amuse the children. And if he wasn't clowning with the slaves or chasing the maids round the kitchens, he was flirting with Flavia, playing another role with Claudia, yet another as he imparted the lurid details of his sex life to Periander.

Act. Act. Act.

Pretend. Pretend. Pretend.

Beside the grain store, Skyles was whipping off his tunic to cover Erinna. Maybe it was what Flavia, like many others, perceived as a spontaneous act of chivalry that prompted the girl's lower lip to drop open, but Claudia wouldn't care to bet on it. Not the way Skyles was flexing his physique in a manner which appeared careless . . . yet highlighted every corded muscle, every thin, white scar!

Act. Act. Act.

Pretend. Pretend. Pretend.

As the farce ground to its conclusion, the Buffoon's gaze travelled round the crowd as though seeking someone, or something, out. When it alighted on Claudia, it stopped. Several seconds passed. Then he blinked, his intense expression relaxed, and he allowed his eyes to drop to the young girl at her side. Blushing to her roots because the great man winked at her, Flavia danced through the crowd to congratulate her hero on his gallantry. Skyles had made no effort to pull on the 'spare' tunic which Ion just happened to have at hand, even though the temperature down here by the river

was freezing. Claudia watched, and admired, his performance as he accepted the accolades from his tongue-tied
young female admirer. And noted that, even though his lips
were addressing Flavia, his attention was very much elsewhere. On Erinna. Just like before, his blank eyes followed
the girl who had not looked his way once.

Without waiting for the sacrificial pork to crackle to a
crisp or even remind the crowd who was sponsoring these
damned Spectaculars, Claudia shot round to her agent's
office behind the State Record Office on the Capitol. Her
agent was out, but she left him a note on a wax tablet.

'Find out everything you can about the actor called
Skyles,' the note read. 'And treat this as urgent.'

Up in Frascati, the woodsman's grisly find had caused quite
a stir.

'Who is she?' the townspeople clamoured. 'How was she
murdered? What shall we do with her? When did she die?'

The woodsman, who knew all about nature red in tooth
and claw, was able to provide some of the answers to the
crowd which had packed into the tavern at the crossroads.
From his experience with rotting remains, he pronounced
sombrely, the victim had been in the earth a month at least.
He did not add that his sole brush with buried corpses, as
opposed to wild animal remains, came from accidentally
digging up Xerxes's predecessor when he was planting his
cabbages. Instead, the woodsman allowed himself a refill
of unwatered wine on the house.

'The cause of death was definitely that spade we found
on top of the grave,' he added, wiping his callused hands
down his hide leggings as though wiping away the memory
of the hideous discovery. 'Someone really clobbered her
with it, too. Skull smashed like an eggshell.' The woodsman
pointed to the side of his head. 'Right here.'

'Poor cow,' said the barber. 'Let's hope it were quick and
she didn't see it coming.'

The woodsman found images of her long black hair and shattered face haunting his every waking hour and preventing him from sleeping. His wife said he must tell someone about what he had found, but who was there to tell? Frascati had no army barracks nearby, no resident magistrate, he could hardly post a notice on the wall of his house. *Found. One body. Please enquire within.* In the end, he had summoned his friends to help him.

'Spade, you said?' The ostler from the post house frowned. 'You know, now I thinks about it, some time around about the back end of October, I do believe some bugger stole one from right outside me stables.'

The ostler didn't know it yet, but his role in the girl's murder would haunt him for the rest of his life. Even though the post-house slaves dug carrots for the horses every day, he would come to think that he should have somehow ensured that the spade was locked safely away. Irrational and ridiculous, but the ostler would go to his grave feeling that he'd been responsible for the girl's death, never forgiving himself for leaving the murder weapon out in the open.

'Was she—' The fuller cleared his throat. 'Was she raped?'

A heavy silence fell over the tavern.

'She were naked, weren't she?' growled the blacksmith.

This time the silence was even heavier. No one touched their wine.

'At least we can rest easy that she weren't one of us,' the woodsman's wife piped up at last. 'I know it's a terrible thing to say, but it's better for the town that both the victim and the killer were strangers.'

Terrible to say, yes. But natural. A murmur of guilty agreement rippled round the tavern. Heads hung down. Feet shuffled.

'I suppose she *was* a stranger?' the fuller asked.

'Well, of course she was!' the barber replied. 'We'd have

noticed if one of our own women had gone missing, you daft oaf!'

'No, no, I didn't mean that. I was just remembering that time when one of Senator Cotta's slaves ran away. The one who screamed her bloody head off when they caught her.'

A different kind of silence gripped the tavern now.

'*She* had long, dark hair,' the fuller reminded everyone.

'So do lots of women,' the barber said carefully. But he, too, remembered her well from the fight she put up. Her screechings, kicks and protests had drawn a wagon-load of attention that afternoon. Which, for a town at the junction of three main roads to Rome and long accustomed to drama, had to be quite a show to draw a crowd, especially when it came so hot on the heels of the old man blowing himself up, although it was before Senator Cotta had gone swanning off to Cumae to consult with the Oracle.

'There was talk she'd run away a second time,' the potter said.

'So there was.'

Memories surfaced now. Of the Senator's men searching high and low for a girl who had effectively disappeared off the face of the earth. Now they knew why. The earth itself had claimed her—

'If she was that important to him, I'd best send word to the Senator,' the woodsman said. 'Tell him we've found her body.'

But he wasn't really concerned about how crucial the slave girl might or might not have been to Sextus Valerius Cotta.

The harrowing image of the hand plopping from his dog's mouth refused to leave him, and it wasn't much of a leap of the imagination to picture any number of pretty young women taking their last walk with this killer. A smooth operator, the woodsman thought, who could win a girl's trust so completely that she'd followed someone wielding

135

a spade meekly into the woods. What an actor that person must be!

What worried the woodsman more than the past, though, was the future.

That the killer had already marked out another victim. And was simply waiting for the right moment to strike.

Nineteen

Damp from the air mingled with the damp from the river, cloaking the city in a cold, dark blanket of grey. The tramontana might have relented, but the moist air it left in its wake carried sickness and disease disguised as a mantle of softness. Lungs would soon start to clog, just as surely as the damp would smuggle in fevers, rheumatics, colics and piles and steadfastly refuse to heal sores. At times like this, the Roman people looked to two sources to safeguard their health and that of their children.

One was religion. Money (from the rich), garlands (from the poor) would be left for Aesculapius at his temple on the island in the Tiber, for Aesculapius was the god of medicine and healing, and it was to him they looked if sickness descended. Carna's shrine up on the Caelian Hill would be inundated with cakes of fat bacon and beans in the hope that the goddess who watched over their vital organs might make them stronger, if she was propitiated accordingly. And they would pour solemn libations to their family gods with the prayer, 'Admit no plague or sickness into this household. If disease comes to our threshold, make it stay there.'

However, the populace was well aware that the Immortals would be rushed off their feet in times of crisis and, even though they'd hedged their bets three ways, it was still possible for their entreaties to slip through the divine net. Hence the second arm of the pincer.

Armed with potions and ointments, tablets and suppositories, the trickle of visitors from the herbalist's door was slow but steady as Orbilio and Dymas approached.

'Trust me, mate, we have to do this,' Dymas said, his hobnailed boots echoing dully on the timbers of the Sublician Bridge.

'The rape only took place yesterday morning.'

The people who visited the herbalist were not rich. Their coarse cloaks were patched, their sandals made from woven palm leaves rather than leather, and the men wore beards, since they were not in a position to afford barbers. Yet they were prepared to hand over what, to them, were vast sums of money for poultices and infusions, indemnity against the inevitable.

'I know, but you said yourself we don't have any fresh leads. Bloody fuck, mate, we need Deva's statement or we're screwed.'

Orbilio knew Dymas was right, but calling on the poor girl so soon after the attack felt like another assault. Unfortunately, time wasn't on Marcus's side. This morning another girl had fallen victim to the Halcyon Rapist. More lives had been destroyed by this monster. Panic was filling the streets. As much as it went against his personal and professional grain, he had caved in to his colleague's demands.

'We'll take it slowly,' he told him. 'See how it goes.'

The sneering allegation of his boss that Orbilio knew the victims had cut no ice. Whether he knew the girls directly, indirectly or not at all was irrelevant, but that was something he could sort out later, this vicious attempt to smear his reputation and character. Right now, all he cared about was that four young women had been brutalized. Four more young women violated *because of him*.

'Bloody fuck, mate!' Dymas had snorted with derision when Orbilio confided to him how he felt. 'You did everything you could, didn't you? Confession. Identification. Evidence. You got the bugger bang to rights, he paid the price, now quit beating yourself up. This is the work of a sick bastard copycat and don't you forget it.'

'What made you keep the records of this case, Dymas?' They were almost at the herbalist's door. 'I mean, if you didn't have reservations about the rapist yourself, then why bother?'

'Same reason I keep all the others,' the Greek said dryly. 'Insurance, mate.'

'Insurance?'

Dymas glanced up from his feet. 'Oh, fine for you. Midwife removed the silver spoon before she cut the umbilical bloody chord, didn't she?' The eyes dropped again. 'Me, I'm a foreigner. What you Romans very nicely call an alien, and a low-born blacksmith's son at that. If anything goes arse-over-tip, I don't have no poncy family to fall back on, do I? I'm in no position to bribe my way out of the shit, like some I might mention. Them case notes are my insurance policy.'

There it was, the old chip on the shoulder revealing itself to be half a pine tree. Another reason Marcus despised the surly Greek.

The herbalist opened the door to his knock and his eyes narrowed when he recognized his visitors.

'Have you caught him?'

Orbilio shook his head sadly. 'How's Deva?' he asked.

'How do you think?' the herbalist rasped back. Deep purple hollows surrounded his eyes and the skin on his face hung slack, like a person newly bereaved.

The house consisted of three tiny chambers. His workroom, the main room which served as living-area-cum-kitchen with wood-burning stove, plain, wooden furniture and functional clay plates and pots. And the sleeping chamber above, masked off by a makeshift screen that the herbalist had hastily thrown up and behind which Deva lay curled like a foetus, clutching her red Damascan shawl. The cottage smelled of balsam and fennel, horehound and sulphur, and sprigs of herbs hung from the joists on the ceiling. Thyme, hyssop, licebane and borage.

'We need to ask a few questions,' Marcus told the distraught herbalist under his breath. 'Any detail, no matter how small, how trivial it might seem, brings us one step closer towards putting this bastard where he belongs.'

'She hasn't uttered a word since it happened,' the man replied, 'and I haven't forced her. But— Well, if it's important, I'll see what I can do.'

'Of course it's bloody important,' Dymas snapped, making no effort to keep his voice low. 'If this is a repeat of last year's shenanigans, we're looking at ten more girls getting buggered and beaten, and if we don't nail the sick bastard this time, it'll be fourteen more next year, as well!'

The makeshift curtain was suddenly pulled back. Three heads jerked upwards in surprise. Her face battered and swollen, the skin beneath white as parchment, Deva stood looking down at the men. Her fingers clenched over the wooden rail.

'Deva! Darling—'

But before the herbalist could form one more word, the Damascan girl had launched herself into space.

It was late, nearly midnight, when Marcus retraced his steps. He was alone this time. His knock was soft. At first he did not think the herbalist had heard it, then the door opened. Without a word, he motioned Orbilio inside.

'I gave her a dose of poppy juice. Too much, probably, but . . .' His voice trailed off, crushed by horror, exhaustion and grief.

Indeed, the opiate dominated the other scents inside the small dwelling which the chill river air could not seem to penetrate. A single candle burned in the corner and Orbilio wondered if the herbalist had eaten since Deva had been brought home yesterday. Somehow he doubted it.

'You saved her life,' the herbalist said thickly. 'You can't imagine how grateful I am to you, Marcus.'

'I did not save her life.' Orbilio patted him reassuringly

on the shoulder. 'I saved her from breaking an arm or a
leg, that was all.'

When he saw Deva's fingers unclench from the rail,
caught the look of hopelessness and utter despair in her
eyes, the hairs on his neck had started to prickle. Almost
before her feet had left the landing, he had flung himself
forward to catch her.

The other man almost smiled. 'You're still a hero to me.'

'If I was a hero,' Orbilio replied wearily, 'Deva would
have gone to her mother's house yesterday, sold her honey
at market, then come home the same bubbly young woman
she was when she left.'

'Hm.' The herbalist led him into his workroom, lit an oil
lamp and reached for a jar on the shelf. 'I think we both
need some of this,' he said, pouring a thin, pale yellow
liquid into two cups.

The liquid was fire. It made Orbilio's eyes water, scalded
his throat, burned a hole from his stomach down to his toes.
Once he'd stopped coughing, he put his cup out for a refill.
'What *is* that?'

'In the mountainous regions of eastern Gaul, along the
Helvetican border, the natives brew up the yellow gentians
which grow wild on the hills and distil the juice. This, my
friend, is the result.'

'Then here's to barbarians everywhere,' Orbilio croaked.

He let the fire in his belly settle and used the time to
study the herbalist. Late-thirties, his red hair receding from
the temples and with the beginnings of a slight paunch, he
was not an obvious catch for a vibrant young woman with
a preference for bodices that showed off her midriff and
fringed skirts that swayed with her hips. But he could see
what had attracted Deva to him. His goodness, his gentle-
ness, his wanting to help those in need of it most. Orbilio
was wrong, he realized. The people who had trickled up to
this house for their potions and pills had not handed over
vast sums for their remedies. Deva and her man would not

be living in such humble conditions if he had charged them the going rate.

'I have a confession to make,' he said, twisting the cup in his hands. 'This is not an official call.'

Of all the times to seek a personal consultation, he could hardly have picked a worse one. The man was already a widower once, his first wife killed by falling masonry from one of the hundreds of renovation projects. Now Deva had been subjected to an ordeal that had driven her to the brink of suicide and the helplessness of it all was tearing the poor bugger to shreds. Yet here he was, in the early hours, being asked for his professional advice.

'Please don't feel obliged,' Orbilio said. 'I quite understand if you—'

'Marcus.' The herbalist motioned his visitor to sit. 'Other men would pick up a sword and go charging round the city to hunt down this beast. To my shame, I'm not other men. I do not know how to avenge her, I can only mend the wounds on her body.' His mouth twisted in self-revulsion. 'I do not even possess the ability to heal the wounds in her head.'

Orbilio wasn't sure about that, and he said so. He'd seen many victims of rape. Had seen how their ordeal was viewed as bringing disgrace on their families, seen their husbands reject them, even though the women were blameless. What all victims of rape needed was tenderness, patience and love. Qualities the herbalist possessed in abundance.

For several moments, the herbalist was unable to speak. Then he tossed down a third shot of the pale yellow liquor, grimaced, and his tortured eyes softened. 'That, if it's true—'

'It's true.'

'—makes me feel a whole lot better about what I was about to say,' he replied. 'Because I was going to tell you that the best thing you can do for me at the moment is give me something to work on. A problem which can occupy

142

my mind, even for the tiniest amount of time, affords me unimaginable relief from the pain.'

Orbilio leaned back in his chair. It was hard and uncomfortable, and far too small for his large frame, but he barely noticed. He knew, from his previous visit to discuss the attempts to poison the Emperor, that the herbalist was a man to be trusted to listen, understand, sympathize and not judge. And perhaps that was the most important role of any physician. That of confessor.

Which is how, at one o'clock in the morning, Marcus Cornelius Orbilio came to be telling a virtual stranger about the pixie. How he had met her at a friend's house when she was dancing. How they had got chatting and ended up at her house, too drunk to notice, too drunk to care, who satisfied his bodily urges. That, even when he took Angelina to a tavern to let her down gently over a meal, he found himself in exactly the same predicament the following morning. Furred tongue, lack of memory, those damned castanets clacking like crazy behind his eyes.

'My head wasn't the only thing that was throbbing when I woke up,' he admitted ruefully, explaining how he'd vowed never to touch another drop of wine so long as he lived. True to his word, he had gone to Angelina's house sober last night to break off the relationship but it was in her bed that he awoke, exhibiting the same muzzy symptoms, the same burning erection and, as previously, the day was more advanced than he would have wished.

'Hm.'

The herbalist laced his fingers together on the desk. Behind him, on the shelves, earthenware vessels lined up like soldiers, along with glass and ceramic pots, copper pots, tin pots, horn, silver and onyx containers. Bronze boxes, wooden boxes, flasks, scoops and balances stood to attention beside mortars and palettes, pestles and bottles, spatulas and bandages of varying widths. On the table beneath the shuttered window sat turnips, garlic bulbs, mustard and rue, and a small jar marked 'Cedar resin'.

'You suspect Angelina of drugging you?' he asked at length.

'Let's say the alternative worries me,' Orbilio replied.

Across the desk, the herbalist shifted. 'I have some good news and some bad news,' he said. 'The good news is that you aren't losing your mind and have indeed been the victim of drugs. A cyathus of mandrake, a scruple of henbane, one or two other bits and bobs and we have a sleeping draught which leaves a sledgehammer pounding between the eyes and a tongue that could pass for a rodent.'

'And the bad news?'

A muscle twitched at the side of the herbalist's mouth as he poured a shot of gentian liqueur for his visitor. 'The bad news, my friend, is that under a sedative of that strength, you could not possibly have managed anything more energetic than a snore.'

Despite the situation, Orbilio found himself laughing. 'Not the four times she said, then?'

The herbalist began laughing with him. 'Not even once,' he chuckled. 'Although.' He tapped the small jar at his elbow. 'I can, if you like, make you a potion that would help.'

Laughter was the trigger the herbalist needed. Within seconds, the first healing tears started to flow.

Orbilio and the herbalist weren't the only two whose problems kept them awake in the early hours.

In her office, Claudia was going through her accounts with a fine flea comb. Sending Butico those three thousand bronze sesterces had literally drained her coffers dry. How on earth was she supposed to fund her Saturnalia banquet now? There was no quick way to liquidate her assets. That brickworks on the Via Tiburtina wouldn't sell this close to Saturnalia. Rents on her properties could not be collected until New Year's Day. To be seen selling off the silver and gold plate would start alarm bells ringing.

It was enough that her fellow wine merchants had conspired with Butico and were, through him, turning the thumbscrews. She couldn't afford to have anyone else get wind of her financial troubles.

What a bloody mess.

She drained a glass of warm, spiced wine and went through the accounts again.

Julia's husband hadn't been able to face his scrawny, sour-faced wife after the scene in the apartment on the Aventine. Couldn't bear to hear another whine from her thin lips, another of her sanctimonious opinions. Pleading the necessity to work on his portfolio, he had returned to his own house and now, in the darkness and the cold, he had never felt more alone in his life.

His darling. His rosebud. His precious cherubkins.

My, how she must have laughed when he told her time and again that making love with her went beyond the mechanical release of bodily tensions.

'For the first time in my life,' Marcellus had confided, 'I know what it means to give someone my soul, my heart, my very being through the act of making love.'

He felt the prickle of salt behind his eyelids, felt the pillow dampen under his cheek. Trust him to have fallen in love with a whore. A cold-hearted whore, who had rented the most expensive flat on the Aventine, demanded it be furnished to the highest standard, redecorated, and all at Marcellus's expense. Claudia would have flayed him alive, had she realized that the stuff she'd repossessed was less than half what he'd given the slut. She'd been selling it on, salting away the proceeds like the good little whore that she was, but what hurt, what really hurt, was that she hadn't cared about him at all.

Another stab of pain ripped at Marcellus. She'd already

be latching on to another poor sap, flattering him with her weasel words, seducing him with her body (her beautiful, beautiful body), preparing to suck another man dry like the parasite that she was.

That Claudia, of all people, should have seen through her was the ultimate in humiliation. She hadn't pulled any punches, either. She'd exposed him to the truth in brutal fashion, emasculating him completely. She would never look him in the eye again. Jupiter's balls, was she blind? Couldn't she see that his beloved had been the image of her, with her bold, thrusting breasts and dark, flashing eyes? Did she not realize that his affair, at least in the beginning, had only taken off because he saw his mistress as a substitute for the real thing?

Another spurt of salt water squeezed between his eyelashes and dribbled its way down to his pillow. Now he was little more than a eunuch in Claudia's eyes. A middle-aged gullible fool. Even his rosebud would have forgotten him six months from now.

He thought about the things he had said to her. The words she had said in return. That's all they were, he thought bitterly. Words. *I love you, Marcellus.* The memory clawed at his heart, ripped it out with both hands. No one had ever said *I love you* to Marcellus in his life. Not his parents. Not his siblings. Not Flavia. Not even his wife.

His darling, his rosebud, his precious cherub.

He would have married her, too.

Sextus Valerius Cotta was not asleep. Beside him, in the wide double bed cast in solid bronze and covered with a damask counterpane scented with lilac, slept Phyllis. As beautiful and undemanding a mistress as he had ever taken. Skin the colour of cinnamon, the texture of silk, and with a laugh as soft as summer rain, she understood her status and behaved accordingly. Cotta was extremely fond of Phyllis. Much more so than his wife, in fact. His wife had the brains of a sheep. With his beautiful mistress, Cotta could indulge in his love of poetry, his passion for horseflesh. She sang as he strummed the lyre. More than any woman he'd known, Phyllis understood the complexities of politics, but Cotta was careful about what he disclosed. He didn't believe Phyllis was a spy, but a man could not be too careful these days. In any case, as an ex-general and military tactician of some standing, he was used to making decisions unaided.

Many considered leadership to be the loneliest job in the world, a sentiment Cotta neither shared nor understood. Patrician to his core, he appreciated the value of propitiating the gods, paying careful devotions to his family shrine of a day, pouring libations, intoning the prayers, leaving sacrifices of salt cakes and honey. With every success, whether political, military or domestic, Cotta followed up with a hefty donation to the temple of whichever divinity had looked after him and then offered sacrifices in the deity's honour. Look after the gods, and the gods look after you was his motto.

Despite what people thought, it was not the hand of Mars which guided the dashing Arch-Hawk. He was no warmongerer, regardless of what they might say. Cotta didn't relish Roman blood being spilled, or anyone else's, come to that. A simple look at the records would show that his tactic had always been to strike swiftly and to strike sharply. Catch the enemy when and where they least expected it to minimize casualties and maximize the Eagle's authority. Given that Cotta believed in justice as much as decisiveness, his protector was none other than the King of the Immortals, Jupiter himself.

Jupiter represented the honour and integrity that Cotta himself tried to live by. All he wanted – all he had ever wanted – was for Rome to fulfil her true potential. That her people should enjoy the riches that they deserved.

Sonofabitch, what the hell was wrong with that?

*   *   *

147

In a room littered with the paraphernalia of travelling players, the Digger also lay awake in the darkness, listening to the settlement creaks of the house, the soft snorts of sleeping companions. The house smelled of beeswax and venison, mulled wine and frankincense, with just a hint of fuller's earth from where the clothes had come back from the cleaner's. Homely smells. Homely sounds. Out in the street, carters geed up their mules and two tomcats squared up to each other up on the roof.

The killer was thinking about the scene in *The Cuckold*, where the Miser ambushes Cupid (played by Periander, now that the dwarf had decamped with the rival company), in a bid to force Cupid to make the Miser's Wife fall in love with her husband. It was a very funny scene. The point of Cupid's arrows is that, once they've hit their target, the victim will fall in love with the first person they see. Tricked by the Miser into firing off three arrows just to make sure his Wife gets the message, Cupid retaliates by closing his eyes as he shoots. Consequently, the flying arrows cause chaos. One lands on Jemima's bottom. Startled, she jumps up and who's the first person that she sees? The Miser's Wife. The Miser's Wife, meanwhile, gets the full force of an arrow in her back, which sends her sprawling into her lover's open arms. Whilst the third arrow ricochets off the wall on to the Miser, who has been watching developments in the mirror, so that the first person *he* sees is himself.

The audience would be in hysterics, the Digger thought. The kidnapped victim's hilarious revenge. But there was nothing comic about ambush—

Vulnerable people are easy to lure. They have so many mixed emotions swirling around inside their heads that they cannot think straight. Do not seek to question. Vulnerable people are easily led.

Easily led off the road.

Easily led into the woods. Fragile and emotional, they are susceptible to any old sob story going.

Staring up at the ceiling, listening to the rhythmic breathing of the others in the bedchamber, it seemed both yesterday and a lifetime ago that a young woman with a cloak of dark hair had run, laughing, down the embankment towards the stream at the bottom.

'Look at those beautiful butterflies!' she had gasped, using both hands to point to the profusion of painted ladies heading south. 'Don't they take your breath away, the way they dance through the trees?'

She could not have imagined that butterflies would not be the only thing to take her breath away.

And the young woman with a cloak of dark hair rose silently out of her grave.

'Why did you kill me?' she whispered. 'Why did I have to die? I, who had so much to live for?'

Entombed in the nightmare which would not end, the Digger shivered and cried.

Twenty

Gloomy and grey, daybreak brought with it an insidious damp to fill the vacuum left by the tramontana, chilling bones, wilting parchment and breeding mould on the walls and the bread.

'Leonides.' Claudia collared her steward on the landing. 'This damp's getting everywhere. I want the linens and blankets in the storerooms shaken then pegged out over the braziers, and when they're fully aired, I want them refolded with alecost.'

'Alecost?' Leonides wrinkled his long nose. 'Are you sure you want your clothes reeking of camphor, madam?'

'More than I want bugs and mould in them,' she retorted. 'And in any case it's a distinct improvement on the stinking hellebores which I notice you've strewn in the cellar to repel the vermin.'

She couldn't be sure. Leonides *might* have muttered something under his breath to the effect that if he was stretched any thinner, the mistress would be able to cover books with him, but then again it might have been his guttural Macedonian accent. She watched him barking orders at the underslaves and considered the changes she intended making to the house.

Stuff endowing the Temple of Ceres with a fountain to commemorate the stand of pines! Claudia wanted to get ahead in business, and the way to do it was not through ostentatious gifts to the city, but by establishing a sound rapport with her clients. Staging the Halcyon Spectaculars was a good start, her standing would rocket, and that would get up the Guild's noses. Like ghouls on a corpse, they'd hoped to pick over the cadaver of Seferius Wine after Gaius's death and now, believing they had tied her up like a kipper with the Moschus/Butico fraud, the ghouls were hovering again. Only this time they weren't waiting for the victim to die—

Claudia's survival hinged on greasing palms and schmoozing and given that the former was out of the question, she was stuck with the latter. Unfortunately, schmoozing at this level required more than simply entertaining on an epic scale. She could throw all the lavish parties she liked, but no matter how many peacocks strutted round her peristyle and no matter how many gilded gladiators she hired to slug it out during banquets, a woman in commerce was still anathema. Claudia Seferius needed an extra trick up her sleeve.

The merchants were accustomed to extravagance – tigers in cages, sinuous Spanish dancers – this was a buyer's market, where profligacy came with the territory and they expected every night to be a night to remember. They would certainly be wise to contracts being flashed in front of them while they were still merry. The point to grasp was that these were dyed-in-the-wool bigots she was trying to sell to, and the trick up Claudia's sleeve was to reel her fish in gently, without them knowing they were even on a line. The room at the end of her bedroom gallery was spacious enough to convert to a small, yet intimate, dining chamber and it was here that she planned to entertain a small, yet select, band of businessmen in style. The idea was to invite three or four firm supporters, plus one influential chauvinist who would be won over by good living and his peers. Softly, softly, catchee monkey. Hook them one at a time and—

'Erinna?'

Skyles' low rasp along the gallery cut short her schemings and Claudia realized that, standing behind the wooden support pillar, the actor hadn't noticed her. His watchful eyes were flickering down to the atrium, to where Caspar was supervising the rehearsals, checking that none of the troupe saw him slipping away. Claudia felt her shoulder blades tensing.

'Erinna?' he rasped again. He put his head round Caspar's bedroom door. 'Oh, there you are.'

'I'm making a new costume,' she said, and it was obvious to Claudia, and therefore to Skyles, that she had heard him calling her name. 'If I'm to play the Soldier's Mistress, I thought it would be fun if I wore a legionary's kilt and a bodice with stitching that resembled armour. Now the Soldier's Mistress comes on stage looking like another soldier, only with bosoms.'

'That,' Skyles said, 'is inspirational.'

From the shadows, Claudia expected him to make a bow or perform some extravagant comic gesture. Instead, she saw only a strained line round his jaw as he leaned against the door jamb watching her nimble fingers jab their needle at the fabric.

'What did you want?' she asked bluntly.

The strain stretched up his cheekbones to his eyes and he ran a hand over his smooth, shaven head. 'Tomorrow's the Festival of Consus. I was wondering if you'd like to go to the races with me? We could have a meal in that tavern on Tuscan Street, the one that always has a sheep roasting on a spit out on the pavement—'

'No.'

In the doorway, Skyles frowned. 'No, you don't want to go out? No, you don't like chariot racing? No, you don't want a meal? No, you don't like me? No, what?'

Clutching an armful of bright red fabric, Erinna squeezed past him on to the gallery. 'Sorry, Skyles, that was extremely rude of me.' She flashed him a radiant smile. 'What I should have said was, no thank you.'

* * *

Waste disposal was one of Rome's most illustrious achievements. What, not so many generations back, had been nothing more than a series of open, unconnected, stinking ditches had been converted into a network of jointed underground tunnels which were flushed with water from the aqueducts, and which were tall enough and wide enough to ride a hay cart through. Not that anyone had attempted such a feat, although from time to time bored schoolboys would take a boat inside to stick a river rat or two, egging each other on to see how far they could penetrate before the stench made them turn back.

The Great Sewer was their favoured choice, since it ran west below Tuscan Street then cut underneath the Forum, the current record holder claiming to have reached as far as the Julian Basilica, although the witnesses in this case were brothers aged no more than ten and could not be relied upon.

The shrine to the nymph who presided over this putrid underworld was round and built of Anio, a dull brown building stone, durable but ugly, and was capped by a marble rim. Since the structure lacked a roof and was thus open to the elements, many felt the shrine represented nothing more than a giant latrine and it was perhaps for that reason that Cloacina remained the most neglected deity in the pantheon.

Which is why the Halcyon Rapist had been able to subject his fifth victim to her ordeal in broad daylight.

No fear of interruption here.

He could take as much time as he liked.

Twenty-One

'**B**een shopping for Saturnalia presents, have we?' a familiar, husky voice called out breathlessly, and a pair of chiselled cheekbones thrust themselves under Claudia's nose.

'You know, you shouldn't be out on your own, kiddo.' He whisked the basket out of her hands. 'These streets aren't safe.'

Claudia could not tell him that shopping was a by-product of her excursion. That her real purpose had been to find out what her agent had learned about Skyles – and what did he mean, he couldn't find out one damn thing about the actor?

'*I doubt Skyles is his real name,*' her agent had said. '*But given that most strolling players are on the run from one thing or other, that doesn't surprise me. What bothers me more is that I've circulated his somewhat singular description among my sources and nothing's come back. Nothing,*' he added sinisterly, '*at all.*'

Which was odd, considering that network of scars.

'Keep looking,' Claudia had replied, reminding him that this was still urgent. Turning now to Doris, who was swinging the wicker basket through the crowds with nonchalant ease, she said, 'What's your real name?'

They had reached her front door, where a tantalizing smell of cooking greeted them, and Claudia could almost hear the rissoles sizzling on the open griddle and pullets turning on the spit. She'd spotted red mullet for sale in the Forum and hoped the Cook had seen them, too. Stuffed with soft cheese, prawns, parsley and chives and drizzled with garlic and olive oil, they were the sort of dish any hostess would be proud to serve to oleiculturists with a wealth of connections and an interest in her stepdaughter for a wife.

'My real name?'

Doris's hand froze as he returned her basket. An expression she hadn't seen before crossed his face. No longer the happy-go-lucky young fool, something feral flickered behind those cornflower-blue eyes.

'Do you really want to know?'

Claudia felt a chill in the air which wasn't down to the weather. 'Yes.'

'Then I'll tell you,' he whispered. 'But this is our secret. Yours and mine, understood?'

'Understood.'

Doris looked over his left shoulder, then his right, then checked the landings upstairs. 'Daphne,' he said and then, with a cluck of his tongue, the old expression was back and he was joining the Spectaculars with a series of athletic cartwheels.

Ask me no questions, I'll tell you no lies . . .

But before she could consider the implications of the sea change which had descended on Doris, Julia burst through the vestibule door behind her, rubbing her hands and tossing her mantle to a slave to dry off.

'Sister-in-law!' Either Julia was in the grip of chronic indigestion, or that was a smile on her face. 'I tried calling you in the street, but you didn't hear me. Isn't my oleiculturist simply *wonderful*?'

'I don't know, I haven't seen him.'

'Tch, poor fellow! Exhausted from travelling, I suppose, but he looked absolutely wretched when he arrived and I said to myself, that dear man is in no fit state to go courting our Flavia, so I *insisted* he went straight up to bed. Do you know, the darling boy had only been here ten minutes when

Marcellus came rushing in, gushing about all the contracts he'll be getting in the New Year. *Now* tell me the oleiculturist has no connections!'

'Did you just say "darling boy" . . . ?'

A thin claw grabbed Claudia's arm and drew her close. 'Forget what I said about Marcellus playing around. Nothing of the sort.'

'I suppose he's simply been working long hours?'

'Exactly, and last night, you should have seen him! Worn out with the strain, he was. Still.' Julia was quite unperturbed by her husband's apparent exhaustion. 'He made up for it by presenting me with this wonderful bracelet. Garnets, of all things, and my dear it's not Saturnalia for another three days. You know, he actually admitted he hadn't been paying me sufficient attention of late—'

'Apologized that he'd been preoccupied with his work?'

'Absolutely.' Marcellus ought to apply to Caspar for a job. He'd learned his script off pat.

'And he gave me this *sweet* little scent bottle. Look, he's even put some perfume in for me.'

Claudia dutifully sniffed the floozy's overblown scent. Typical Marcellus, though. Hadn't even bothered to have it filled up to the stopper, but what the hell. The main thing is, Julia's happy, the allowance is going where it ought to be going and Marcellus, with luck, might actually be earning his own supper for a change. If Julia felt that was all down to some washed-out olive-oil man, who cares? Claudia made a mental note to up the schmoozing stakes over dinner. Get him to sign up Flavia for a wife and Claudia need never see her in-laws again!

So heady was the prospect that she barely noticed Caspar bearing down on them. No mean feat, considering the little man was decked out in orange, blue and yellow and with a dark-green bejewelled turban bouncing sideways on his head.

'Dear lady.' He performed an elaborate bow at Claudia's

feet and remained there. 'We have reached the point in our Spectaculars where we are ready to put on a full dress rehearsal. Would you, madam, be so gracious therefore as to honour us with your presence, both as critic and spectator this evening?'

I would have hoped for nothing less. 'I would be delighted,' she replied.

Caspar rose to his feet, miming a comical stiffening of the joints, and turned to Julia. 'And you, ma'am, if I may be so brash, look younger and more fair with each hour that passes underneath this roof.'

'Oh. Well. Well, I—' Blushing to her roots, Julia blinked coyly. '*Heavens!*'

Caspar seized her hand, pressed his rosebud lips to the skin and kissed it passionately. 'Such fragrance,' he sighed, inhaling the floozy's perfume that Julia had dabbed on her wrist. 'Oh, such splendiferous fragrance!'

'Dear me.' Julia fanned herself after he'd gone. 'Such a gallant fellow, what? So terribly earnest that one can almost overlook his night-time philanderings.' She lowered her voice to a girlish whisper. 'You wouldn't believe how many times his bedroom door creaks open and shut, and my word, at the strangest of hours.'

'I'll get the hinges greased.'

'I tell you, sister-in-law, that oleiculturist has really brought me and Marcellus good luck,' Julia trilled. 'How delightful, if some of it were to rub off on you.'

In her bedroom, Claudia ran a tortoiseshell comb through her curls, formed her pillow into a representation of Julia's face and punched it till its feathers flew. Take that, you ungrateful, ill-mannered, selfish, toffee-nosed bitch. Sometimes, she thought, moving her attack to the bolster, she wondered why she bothered with Gaius's revolting family. Marcellus was too lazy to put himself out to get work. Julia was so absorbed with her upturn in fortunes, in bracelets and perfume and overblown flattery, not to mention the olive grower's illustrious connections, that she hadn't even *noticed* that Flavia was welded to Skyles like a boil. If they had feelings for anyone other than themselves, this couple, a surgical probe was required to locate them.

Feeling better for venting her anger and frustration, Claudia slipped into a cherry-pink linen gown and, with snowflakes of swansdown still drifting on the air, set off to consider the conversion of her guest room into an intimate dining chamber. She could almost picture the finished result. Gilded stucco on the ceiling. Scenes from the vine harvest inlaid on every couch. Bacchus frescoes painted on the walls. A tad wine-laden, perhaps, but all's fair in love and commerce, and although the merchants would be coming here ostensibly to pass a cosy social evening, never underestimate the effect of subliminal messages. The bastards would sign up one way or another.

She eased open the door. With the shutters closed, the room came across as gloomy and depressing, but light, she decided, would be a feature of this upstairs dining chamber. Holes could be knocked in the wall to enlarge the current windows, a new one opening up on the far wall, the balcony extended by stone corbel supports to—

'Room service is improving,' the bed said.

Typical Julia, reallocating the accommodation and dammit, she might at least have told Claudia she'd moved the oleiculturist into here. 'Terribly sorry,' she said. 'I didn't realize— *You!*'

The tousled head which appeared over the top of the coverlet nodded. 'Me,' it confirmed, and there was a flash of white teeth in the shadows.

'You told Julia you were an olive merchant!'

'Oleiculturist,' Orbilio corrected mildly. 'Your sister-in-law has a penchant for long words.'

'She is under the impression that you intend to put a lot of business her way.'

158

'Really? I wonder where she got that idea from.'

'The same place she got the idea that you're courting Flavia.'

'In passing, I may have mentioned how charming I'd found the child.'

'You only met her once and disliked her with a fervour, as I recall.'

'She was suffering from an unfortunate bout of BO.'

'Then, as her ardent suitor, you'll be delighted to know that consistency is one of Flavia's strong points. Stand downwind and even skunks peg their noses.'

'Is that a feather in your hair?' he asked. 'Because if so, there's another on your shoulder and two more sticking to your skirt.'

'I've been playing Daedalus and Icarus, learning how to fly. Why don't you give it a whirl? It's really simple. You just hold a feather in each hand and then jump out the window.'

'Sounds too easy,' he said. 'I prefer something with a bit of a challenge.'

'Then jump from the Tarpeian Rock, I'm not proud.'

There were enough bristles on his chin to engage a hedgehog's mating instinct, Claudia noticed, and his eyes matched the pink of her gown. Julia may have got most ends of the oleiculturist stick wrong, but she was right when she said he looked ghastly.

'Exactly what were you drinking last night, Marcus?'

'Something the Gauls on the Helvetican border brew from fire, sulphur, acid and bleach. It's actually rather good.'

A thought occurred to her. She drummed her fingers gently against the bedstead. 'When did you last eat?'

'Can't remember.'

'Then I'll send for something. Porridge, perhaps?' Despite the paucity of light in the guest room, it was still possible to watch his face turn from ashen to a rather subtle shade of green. 'Or would you prefer a nice dish of curds?'

'I know you're mad at me,' Marcus began, urging his rising gorge to ignore pictures of lumpy white milk curds.

'Me? Cross? Perish the thought.'

'Then why are you bending over the bed with your teeth bared?'

'You know my motto, Orbilio. Start every day with a smile,' she breezed. 'And get it over with.'

The noise from his throat was like water gurgling its way down a storm drain. It was the best laugh he could muster through the hangover.

'Claudia, I'm serious. I apologize for the subterfuge, I really do, but I need to talk to you—'

'I'm listening,' she said, flinging wide the pinewood shutters.

Like salt on a slug, Orbilio recoiled at this sudden surge of light and by the time the black and orange zigzags had ceased to blind him, Claudia was already halfway down the street and humming.

The blind beggar on the corner could not believe his luck. Bronze? After all these years, the Widow Seferius, who normally snorted in derision when she passed, had actually dropped *bronze* in his begging bowl?

So amazing was the miracle, the beggar couldn't help untying the bandages round his eyes to make sure.

Twenty-Two

One hundred and forty miles to the south, in the caverns beneath the fortified coastal town of Cumae in Campania, the High Priest unwrapped a package. Inside a soft cloth protected with oiled goatskins was a bowl. It had been fashioned from solid gold, engraved with horses and warriors, inlaid with silver, and weighed a bloody ton.

'Let me see, let me see!'

Yanking off the wrinkled mask with one hand and reaching out for the bowl with the other, the Sibyl whooped with delight. Far from the old crone her clientele mistook her for, the Oracle was a handsome woman in her thirty-eighth year, who saw no reason why she and her brother shouldn't keep this scam going for many more years before he retired to the estate he fancied in the country, she to a palace a long way from Campania, where she could retain a harem of girls well versed in the art of pleasing women.

'Who's it from?' she asked, leaning back to maximize the light from the tall candelabra behind her throne as she studied the bowl.

'Sextus Valerius Cotta, estate owner, senator and gullible fool.'

How they fell for it, she'd never know. You'd think someone would twig that the ghosts they met were not floating on air, but on wooden platforms manipulated by black painted ropes. It never ceased to amaze her by what miracle these so-called Seekers of Destiny uniformly accepted that the faces of their loved ones had been rendered unrecognizable by death, not by a thick coating of chalk! Even more incredibly, no one had questioned the necessity of the heads of their ancestors being veiled in the Underworld. They didn't think that maybe long, flowing robes and an abundance of thick, swirling mist might be to disguise physical dissimilarities between the originals and the facsimiles!

Of course, it wasn't all smoke and mirrors and a cast of bad actors. To maintain her credibility, the Oracle needed to have her facts right, so she and her brother arranged for the Seekers of Destiny to be drugged, disorientated then left alone in a darkened antechamber to stew for a while. During this time they were able to compile a dossier on the Seeker's nearest and dearest from the masses of files which were housed in these tunnels. Given that only the very, very, very, very, very, very rich could afford the exorbitant entrance fee to the theme park that was Hades, the Oracle and her brother could easily afford to have these files constantly updated by a whole team of scribes working round the clock on data gathered by a network of inform-ants. It was from the secret libraries beneath Cumae that the scenes for the re-enactment were rehearsed and put together.

'Is the Arch-Hawk planning a return trip?' she asked hopefully. The work on this bowl was quite splendid.

'He doesn't say.' The priest turned the note over. 'Nope. It would appear this is simply a token of his gratitude.'

'Pity others aren't as grateful,' the Oracle muttered.

'We don't do badly out of the deal, little sister.'

'It's an expensive business, the special effects, the inform-ants, the huge number of staff, the elaborate costumes—'

'Get away with you.' The priest laughed. 'We earn enough to give this bowl to the dogs to eat off!'

Ah, but they were good howlers, those hounds. Mournful buggers, whose baying travelled for miles through those underground echo chambers.

'Buying silence doesn't come cheap,' the Sibyl reminded him tartly.

Only last year, the wife of a well-known politician became lost in the catacombs and fell down a shaft. Her pitiful wailing had only added to the atmosphere, but by the time the team had located her, she was so badly injured that she'd died before they could get her up to the surface. Then, and rather more recently, there was one of the Sibyl's lovers, who, when discarded, had threatened to expose to the Emperor the hokum they practised and unfortunately had had to be strangled.

'Not so expensive,' the priest corrected. 'Remember, an awful lot don't come out anyway.'

He'd lost track of the poor sods who were so keen to speak to their ancestors that they'd tried swimming what they thought was the Styx, only to drown as the underground river sucked them under before disappearing in swirls back into the rock. Or those who came here for the express purpose of joining their loved ones. Once they were convinced there really *was* life after death, they'd stab themselves, fall on their swords, slash their wrists – and in such quantities that each Seeker of Destiny was now searched for concealed weaponry.

Death, however, accounted for only a small percentage of mishaps. Far more visitors became so traumatized by the experience, succumbing to claustrophobia and worse, that they suffered a complete mental collapse. Many more fell victim to the effects of ingesting a cocktail of henbane, belladonna, hellebore and poppy seeds which was fed them. Consulting the Oracle was a dangerous business.

None of which, the priest reflected cheerfully, led to adverse publicity! Disappearances and breakdowns only added to Cumae's mystique, corroborating the Sibyl's power to summon the dead. After all, it wouldn't do for Hades to become a place which was not to be feared.

All that gold the Seekers laid out, just to watch a few

actors wailing away on a plank suspended in mid-air by ropes! Throw in a spurt of fake blood from the loved one's 'fatal' wound. Gloss over tough questions with a moan or a groan. Ward off misgivings by having the weary ghost being called back to the Elysian Fields. Money for nothing.

But what the Sibyl and the priest could not get their heads round – and had frankly given up trying – was that every single Seeker of Destiny went away happy with their few lines of inscrutable gibberish! The Sibyl did not feel in any way responsible for her actions. Did not see how she shaped anyone's destiny, other than her own and her brother's. Even though she had an idea of what Cotta was planning, so what? I have no influence here, she would plead. Fate is fate, I cannot change it. We simply let the punters see what they want to see, let them hear what they want to hear.

'Right,' the Sibyl sighed, replacing her wrinkled mask. 'Back to business.'

Business was greed. Business was god. Their minds had been closed to morality a long time ago. Brother and sister ceased to take interest in the ambitions of their clients, even when that client was the Arch-Hawk of the Senate and his plans threatened to undermine the whole Roman Empire.

The High Priest tossed more sticky beads of Arabian incense on the fire, turned down the lights, then beckoned the next disorientated visitor forward.

'Who's there?' the ancient crone on her gold throne cackled. 'Who comes to consult the Oracle?'

Twenty-Three

One of the less noble consequences of a quarter of a century of peace was gluttony. As the Empire stabilized, it grew increasingly fat on its victories, and since fat had become synonymous with affluence, wastage with wealth, it was a sign of true prosperity that a person could stuff themselves until they were sick, then start again.

Whether her Saturnalia guests might be so inclined or not (and the johnny-come-lately merchant classes definitely showed a tendency to keep abreast of fashion!) Claudia had no intention of allowing anyone at her tables to progress to such disgusting extremes. For a start, no one was stinking her house out with their nauseating practices, thank you very much, and secondly, if they wanted to throw up, they could bloody well bring their own slaves to hold the goddamned bowls. Outside!

On the other hand, certain social standards had to be maintained and this was where cooks became unwitting conscripts in the ferocious social war being waged among the equestrian and patrician classes. For as the rich grew richer, the pressure was on to keep coming up with more and more innovative menus, which – roughly translated – meant more and more outlandish delicacies were served up at banquets.

In this, cooks were aided by the influx of exotic creatures as the boundaries of the Empire continued to expand. Wild beasts were already being captured for the arena, why not ship over ostriches, gazelles and porcupines for the dinner table? Very quickly it became a benchmark of status that a man could afford to have peacocks despatched from farms on Samos in the Aegean at the same time as a delivery of lampreys arrived from Spain for the same banquet.

Unfortunately, as Claudia was rapidly discovering, bear cutlets and antelope steaks were no longer singular enough to satisfy the jaded taste buds of the Roman glitterati. Which meant that, now the novelty value of Syrian hazel hens and specially fattened dormice was wearing increasingly thin, the burden was falling upon the holder of the banquet to come up with further culinary refinements, with the emphasis shifting away from content towards ostentatious presentation. In a nutshell, then: the more complicated the meal and the more elaborate the preparation, the more impressed the guests – and thus the more amenable they would become to engaging in trade with Gaius's alluring widow.

Hence her idea of a zodiac theme for Saturnalia.

That she couldn't actually afford to *buy* the food was neither here nor there.

'Da zodiac vill be a real talking point,' her cook boomed when she outlined her proposal. 'A real talking point!'

Behind her back, Claudia carefully uncrossed her fingers. With twenty Spectaculars sprung upon him without warning, the cook had not been in the best of tempers lately. Naturally he would carry out whatever commands the mistress ordered, but far better to have the big man on her side.

'Bugger stuffed sow udders and pickled goat wombs dat the nobility are demanding,' he expounded in his loud Teutonic roar. 'Give people proper food on dere plates, dat's vot I say. Give dem things dat makes da mouth vorter.'

By the time he'd finished outlining his ideas for twelve substantial, unpretentious and wholesome dishes to correspond with the signs of the zodiac, Claudia's mouth was already vortering and she left him rubbing his hands as he went off to plan the banquet, oblivious of any conflict in the Roman ethos that nothing divides society quite like food, even though he was enslaved himself. Going well, she thought happily. Now she'd got him hooked, it would be so much easier when he went to buy the food to find that he'd also have to negotiate credit terms.

'*How dare you barge in here like this,*' a female voice shrieked from upstairs, '*then have the bare-faced cheek to—*'

Taking the steps two at a time, Claudia thought, that bloody Marcellus! The old, old story no doubt. How his guilt preyed on his conscience and now he wants to make a clean breast of it, blah, blah, blah. Men! She raced along the gallery. When will they ever learn that adultery shared is not adultery halved? But when she flung wide Julia's door, it was Flavia on the receiving end of Julia's tongue, not Marcellus.

'You won't believe what this little bitch has done now,' Julia hissed, slamming the door behind Claudia, as though no one in the house had heard her voice rattling the nails in the roof tiles.

'I'm not ashamed of it—' Flavia countered, but her aunt's strident tones drowned the girl out.

'She's only insisting on marrying that . . . that *gigolo* of an actor!'

'I love Skyles, so there,' Flavia said sulkily.

'And what about the oleiculturist?'

'I think you can forget that angle,' Claudia interjected.

'After all I've done to get you hooked up with him,' Julia continued, ignoring her. 'He's handsome, rich, extremely well-connected—'

'I don't care if living with Skyles means living in poverty,' Flavia said. 'At least I'll be happy.'

'*Happy?*' Julia, of course, had never understood the word, what chance of projecting it on to a third party now? 'For gods' sake, the man's old enough to be your father. He's a sexual predator on an Olympic scale and heaven *knows* what unspeakable disease he spreads with his alleycat morals. Tell her, Claudia. The only reason that vile little man plays the stage is because it gives him the opportunity to screw anything with a pulse—'

'I love him,' Flavia screamed. 'And I'm going with him when the troupe leaves.'

'And what happens when he discards you? Do you really think men like Skyles *like* women? His type are misogynists, girl, they loathe women. That's why they use them so freely and so cheaply. They want to defile them, exploit them—'

'Skyles loves me, I know it, and in any case, you keep telling me I'm old enough to make my own decisions, well I've made one. I'm going to make my career in musical farce, and so what if it means taking my clothes off in public? Anything's better than being stuck in this shit hole for the rest of—'

The slap was so hard, it sent both Julia and Flavia reeling with its ferocity. For two stunned seconds, Flavia could not believe that her aunt had actually struck her. Then her cheek started to burn and before Julia could stop her, she was storming out of the room, calling her aunt all the names under the sun, although 'bitch' figured more frequently in her tirade than most.

Julia rounded on Claudia. 'I *warned* you what it would be like, inviting that vulgar tribe into your house. That beast has not only corrupted my baby, he's manipulating the child. I tell you he's only after her money—'

What is it with this family? Can't *any* of them see past the end of their elbow? 'Leave it with me, Julia.'

'—the scandal won't just taint Flavia, it will sully the whole family name and everything my dear brother worked for will be washed down the drain because of his stupid, self-centred daughter—'

'She's not going to marry Skyles, now calm down. I'll sort this out.'

'Doesn't that girl have *any* concept of the word responsibility? Doesn't she stop, just for an instant, to think what impact the scandal would have on Marcellus and me? We, who brought the poor child up, when her father wanted nothing to do with her—'

'*Julia!*'

Claudia's tone stopped the older woman in her tracks. Julia blinked, regrouped, then poked a bony finger into Claudia's flesh.

'This is your fault,' she snarled. 'You got us into this mess, Claudia Seferius, you can bloody well sort it out.' And in a swirl of green linen she was gone, slamming the door in her wake.

Claudia rubbed at her temples. Dear Diana. To think Caspar actually wrote a script for his farce.

All across the city, women walked the streets in fear. Official proclamations had been posted. No journey to be undertaken unless it was absolutely essential, and on those journeys, women should be accompanied wherever possible. Fine for the rich, but there remained a large sub-section of the female population who had no option, other than to risk it. And these women trembled.

Opinion on the rapist was divided. Either the wrong man had been executed last time round, or else this was a copycat. Either way, they could not afford to take chances.

The rapist *might* only snatch one victim a day. Then again, he might not.

Women all across the city prayed. To Jupiter, to cast his thunderbolt of justice on the rapist. To Nemesis, that retribution would be harsh.

Any doubts Claudia might have harboured about the Halcyon Spectaculars not hitting the professional standards she'd been hoping for were dispelled the instant Caspar appeared in full stage regalia to lead her to her seat. For the two hours building up to this dress rehearsal, there had been no activity whatsoever in the atrium, not even from the labourers. Just a loud, empty silence, reminding Claudia what it would be like when the troupe packed up and moved on, only without the gaudy canvas backdrop for company. Hell, so what?

(a) she enjoyed living alone,

(b) it afforded her all manner of freedoms unavailable to most Roman women,

(c) she was accountable to no one and nothing,

and so on and so on went her list of counted blessings until she reached the letter *m* in the alphabet.

(m) *M is for Marcus Cornelius*, a little voice said, so she quickly skipped *m* and continued the list of reasons why alone is best, with:

(n) being that she had a wide double bed all to herself and

(o)—

(o) is for a man who smells of sandalwood with a faint hint of the rosemary in which his clothes had been rinsed, and whose baritone is as evocative as any actor's and – and – oh,

(p) off, she told the voice.

And because Claudia comprised the entire audience for this dress rehearsal, she felt it would not do for the critic not to meet the same exacting standards required of the cast. For that reason, and not because of any Security Policemen roaming round the house, good heavens no, she took extra care in dressing. The gown of midnight blue and trimmed with gold that showed off her breasts to best advantage. The little brooch shaped like a leaping dolphin, her favourite. The gold chain round her left ankle, which led the eye towards a flash of shapely leg. Why should that be affected by tall, dark investigators on the loose?

'Dear lady, you positively snatch the breath from my body,' Caspar said, having called at her bedroom to escort her to her seat.

'The feeling is mutual,' she replied honestly.

Colourful at the best of times, his costume as Narrator was prism combined with rainbow then mixed with a very big paddle. It took a moment or two before it registered that the spots before her eyes were, in fact, a collage of stylized fabric fruits sewn on to a plain-apple green robe. Figs, melons, apricots, mulberries, cherries, raspberries and grapes proliferated round his ample form.

'You approve?'

'I certainly do.' Claudia linked her arm with his. Any man who goes to such lengths to impress the punters is all right by me, she thought cheerfully, reflecting on her own plans for the Saturnalia banquet.

It did not cross her mind that Caspar's, or indeed anyone else's equally dazzling costume, might be a distraction. That it was eye-catching for that very reason. To catch the eye – and thus draw attention from the face.

Killers like to observe. Not to be observed.

In the end, Claudia had not been able to get the quiet word in Skyles' ear that she had hoped. During dressing for the rehearsals, the company's quarters had been off limits to anyone not part of the production, and that, apparently, included the mistress of the house in which they were staying.

'Time is so of the essence on these occasions,' Caspar had explained, adding that he most truly hoped the dear lady would not be offended, but the schedule needed to be timed to the same accurate perfection as the water clock in the atrium, which, incidentally, he had moved, because although its drips did not interfere with the show's timings, alas the same could not be said of the whistle and ping which marked each passing hour.

Fine. There was no hurry to speak to Skyles. In fact, the longer Flavia stewed in her own stupidity, the longer she had to reflect. Sadly, with most girls fifteen is mature. More than old enough to know their own minds, choose their own husbands, run their own households, plan their own babies. Thanks to Julia's coddling, Flavia couldn't plan her own wardrobe, although immaturity in itself wasn't a problem. Girls grow up fast. Fact of life. Flavia's problem lay in that, caught between the rock of her father not wanting her and the hard place of being fostered on an aunt who wasn't given the option, she'd developed selfishness to an art form. She neither noticed nor cared that image was the diet on which Julia, the daughter of a lowly road builder, had grown strong. That image was the yardstick by which Julia measured her life. Or, therefore, that image was the one thing that could destroy her—

Right in the middle of Felix's balletic miming of the Judgement of Paris, and just as Claudia was wondering how to bring Flavia to her senses and make her realize that Skyles wasn't remotely interested in the stupid little cow, she caught a faint whiff of sandalwood.

'One simply cannot get the staff these days,' a baritone murmured, easing itself into the seat beside her. His chin no longer resembled a hedgehog, and his dark eyes were clear. 'Would you believe I found my trunk outside on the pavement? Fully packed, too? Tch. And when I'd left strict instructions for it to be unpacked, as well.'

'It's probably homesick, trying to make its way back by itself. Why don't you humour it?'

'You know, anyone would think I'm not welcome here.' He winced as Felix performed the splits.

'Yes,' she agreed, clapping. 'Anyone would.'

If, in rehearsal, Felix had been magnificent, in costume he was sublime. Considering he was playing four characters with only soft cloth masks to differentiate the roles, and considering that three of the characters were female, it was amazing. Felix was more than capable of earning his living by going solo with just a flautist to set the mood of each scene. He didn't even need the young castrato to sing the story. But there was comfort in group companionship, she supposed. As well as emotional security.

'What do you know about these people?' Orbilio whispered, applauding loudly as Felix retired from the stage. Quite a few of the slaves had slipped in to watch, Claudia noticed. Leonides, the cook, several of the boiler-house boys, half a dozen of the kitchen girls (to swoon over Skyles, most likely), plus a small contingent of the cleaning staff, too.

'What's to know?' she replied as Skyles, dressed as Augustus in imperial purple and with a laurel crown over a cropped wig, strode on to the stage with Doris, as the Emperor's lushly adorned wife, on his arm. Her agent's report echoed in her head. There is nothing on this man at all, he insisted. He is self-made in every sense of the word.

'*What do I do all day?*' Skyles boomed, and dammit he even sounded like Augustus. '*Livia, darling, haven't you seen the giraffes I've brought back from the African plains? The black bulls from Spain? The lions from the Syrian desert?*'

'*Exactly. All you do is play zoo—*'

That was it. Chip-chip-chip at the political scene. Nothing too contentious, just a gentle poking of fun at the expansion of the Empire, and fingers crossed Livia won't take offence or we'll all be facing lions from the Syrian desert. Seated on the floor with her back to the pillar, Flavia applauded Skyles's every word and movement, funny or otherwise.

'*You men are all the same,*' Doris-as-Livia said. '*I suppose you think it's easy, being a woman, while you're out potting Germans and Gauls all day long?*'

Beside her, Orbilio stared at his thumbnail. 'I apologize for the subterfuge, but I felt it was necessary, because of the Halcyon Rapist.'

'I do have a bodyguard,' she reminded him sweetly. 'Or is one Security Policeman better than six lowly slaves?'

'... *Livia, darling, last year I built eight-two temples. All you did was weave me this shirt ...*'

Claudia clapped, not so much because it was a funny line (indeed the humour came not from the script but in the fact that the scene was set inside a humble thatched cottage, another dig at the Emperor's asceticism), but because she didn't want Caspar to think his satire was so poor that it made her attention drift. Beside her, Orbilio understood and said nothing until Jemima, Hermione and Adah came on to perform the first of three song-and-dance routines. Since they weren't acting, the girls weren't obliged to wear veils for this part and, versatility being the name of the game, they played their own percussion instruments. Hermione's lisp was unnoticeable when she sang.

Orbilio leaned sideways in his seat. 'It occurs to me that the rapist might be an actor,' he said.

Claudia swallowed. 'Because of the mask?'

'Not entirely.' He gave a broad beam of encouragement to the girls, but the smile didn't extend to his eyes. 'The rapist only strikes during the winter solstice, which just happens to be when most strolling players are in Rome. He's also a man with a pathological hatred of women, who has the ability to stalk his victims without arousing suspicion.'

'He could be any one of several entertainers, not just actors,' she said. 'An itinerant musician, an acrobat, a juggler, a rope walker.'

'I'm sure he is.' He turned round to face her. 'I'm just not prepared to take any chances.'

'Well, he's not one of the Spectaculars, that's for sure.'

Jemima, Adah and Hermione left the stage, and Erinna and Fenja took their place, but Claudia barely registered the change.

'After all, I think I'd know if I was harbouring a monster under my roof.'

A muscle tweaked at the side of his mouth. 'You didn't know I was here.'

'Oh, you're like a draught. You sneak in anywhere.'

'Thanks. It makes a change from being told I'm a load of hot air. But the point is, Claudia, I'm worried.'

'Orbilio, I'm a big girl. I can take care of myself.'

'If you were able to take care of yourself,' he countered mildly, 'you wouldn't be so wary of the Security Police. But shabby as it is to admit to such base needs, it's not just you I'm thinking of.' He drew a deep breath and held it. 'There's been a shift in policy at Headquarters. My boss insists it's purely political, but whatever the reason, he's handed the case over to Dymas.'

'Then let Dymas have the headache of solving it.'

'I can't,' Marcus rasped, and suddenly he looked ten years older. 'Because of me, an innocent man went to the lions. I have to make that right.'

Claudia pleated the folds of her dress. That's the trouble when you keep saving the world, Marcus. After a while, the world comes to expect it.

'Silly question,' she said, 'but you have spoken to last year's victims?'

'Some.' He rose to his feet and called for an encore, but she could see his mind was elsewhere. 'Unfortunately, so deep was the trauma that it's virtually impossible to draw the girls out.'

He spiked his hands through his hair. As a member of the same sex as the beast who'd perpetrated those brutalities, how could he explain how it felt when he saw the victims recoil physically – and sometimes violently – when he and Dymas had knocked on their doors?

'All we're doing is forcing the victims to relive the agony,' he said thickly. 'They don't deserve that.'

One had trembled and started to whimper. Another curled herself into a ball and howled like a wolf. One screamed her lungs out. One clawed at her own flesh, drawing blood. Worst of all, one, like the Damascan girl Deva, had even tried to commit suicide. Only that poor bitch had more success.

'What makes you so certain you didn't put the culprit on trial last time?'

'That's the trouble. I *was* sure.'

He waited until the intermission between the second and final routine before outlining the evidence that had nailed the man he and Dymas believed to be the Halcyon Rapist. Information through street contacts that led them to a suspect. The mask beneath the suspect's bed, which tallied with the description the victims had given. The strong smell of aniseed on his clothes.

'Crucially, of course, the suspect signed a confession.'

'Wouldn't you, under torture?' Claudia countered.

'He was a citizen,' Orbilio replied with the ghost of a grin. 'Not Captain Moschus. He was never put to the torture. And anyway, it was immaterial. Three of the victims identified him.'

As Fenja and Erinna wound up their routine, Claudia digested the information. Well, if those were the facts, those were the facts. Unless . . .

Unless—

She thought of the mask and the creeping around, the rapist's ability to merge with his surroundings, the mentality of the man who committed such visceral crimes. Secrets, secrets, so many secrets.

Then, suddenly, as though a lamp had been lit, everything fell into place.

'Master Orbilio?' The messenger nodded apologetically to Claudia. 'Sorry, sir, but the steward says you're to come home as a matter of urgency.'

Jupiter, Juno and Mars, should she tell him now, Claudia wondered. Or think it through first? Later, she decided. She'd tell him about her suspicions later, because Mr Upright-Conscientious-and-Thorough had made what he believed was one terrible mistake on this case. He'd need to be one hundred and ten per cent convinced next time round.

The arrival of the messenger provided the very breathing space that she needed. Yes, of course, she thought she was right. But far preferable to jumping to conclusions and forcing the pieces of the puzzle to fit, wasn't it better to lay the evidence out in her own mind first? Check any cracks in her theory?

Claudia watched Marcus go. And prayed to Jupiter that her hunch was wrong.

'The lady is in your bedroom, sir,' Orbilio's steward announced.

'Lady?' he queried. 'What lady?'

But he might have known. Angelina lay sprawled across his wide double couch in a diaphanous silver gown.

'I think we should paint these walls green,' she purred, 'and have clouds on the ceiling, so we can pretend we're making love outdoors, under the open sky.'

'Define we,' he said, bundling up her belongings.

'We could get a couple of dogs, too. They'll be company for me while you're out at work—'

'The only thing that's going out, Angelina, is you. Right this minute.'

'—and in the evenings we can walk them in the public parks and—'

'Mother of Tarquin, woman, there is no "we", there never was, so let's hit this thing dead here and now.'

'I'll have to give up dancing, of course—'

'Did you hear one bloody word? I want you out of my house, Angelina, and out of my life. *Now.*'

The pixie drew a little-girl-lost circle on the coverlet with her forefinger. 'Don't tease me, Marcus,' she pouted. 'I know how much you love me, I can tell by the way you make love to me.'

'I never made love to you, Angelina. You drugged me, god knows why, but—'

'Don't! Don't say such horrible things!' She sat up, her hands over her ears. 'I would never do anything so mean and so horrible. I love you, just the same as you love me.'

'Is it money you want?'

'Look, I know you've been working hard lately, Marcus, but please don't be bloody. You know the only thing I want is you. I adore you, Marcus. I'd give you the world if I could.' She patted the couch. 'Come to bed now. Pretty please?'

Croesus, the woman was absolutely barking! Well, no point in employing rational argument with a lunatic. Orbilio hauled her off the bed, dragged her screaming across the atrium and threw her bodily into the street, tossing her clothes and her baggage behind her and slamming the door as hard as he could.

Cruel, humiliating, and it made him feel a right bastard, but there was no other way to get his message across.

Stalkers not welcome.

Twenty-Four

In her bedroom, Claudia snuffed the flames of her oil lamps. Too bright. Far too bright. Instead, a single beeswax candle notched with the hour burned in the corner, its flame flickering in the reflection of the enamel inlays of her jewellery boxes, bringing the gold and silver engravings to life. A fawn with its mother. A trio of geese. A dog chasing its tail. Claudia sighed. Sat on the bed with her knees drawn up to her chest. Beside her, curled into a ball, her blue-eyed, cross-eyed, dark Egyptian cat slept peacefully, dreaming of crunchy voles and crispy sparrows and biding her time until the street mice felt safe enough to venture out of their holes.

Time passed, the candle burned lower, and Claudia Seferius stared into space.

Orbilio hadn't returned and within a matter of hours, another girl would be pulled off the streets—

The responsibility pressed down on Claudia's chest like a weight, stifled the air in her lungs. If she took action herself and her hunch turned out to be wrong, the fall-out would be horrendous. To accuse an innocent man of being a rapist was tantamount to destroying him. Was she prepared to condemn someone on a mere hunch? On the basis of stringing a few ill-thought-out conclusions together? The hell she was. She would need proof. Concrete evidence. A cast-iron case to present.

All the same, in a few hours, another innocent victim would be walking along minding her own business—

Drusilla's paws twitched in her sleep, dark whiskers flicked back and forth. She barely stirred when her mistress swung her legs off the bed and wrapped herself in her furs. Like snowflakes in a blizzard, the same thoughts kept going round and round in her head, getting nowhere, and out on her balcony Claudia forced the Halcyon Rapist out of her mind. There was nothing she could do until she spoke to Orbilio. What was keeping him?

The hour was late. Approaching midnight. The shops had long since ceased trading. Artisans' workshops had fallen silent. The scaffoldings round half-built structures were abandoned and eerie. But the bustle of day had been replaced by the bustle of night. Delivery wagons rumbled past, bringing everything from tanned calf skins to bricks into the city, and with just two days before Saturnalia, the drivers were homogenously jolly. Even their mules seemed more perky as they kicked and brayed their way down the thoroughfares. Claudia listened to the song of the street, and found herself humming another tune under her breath.

> '*One day a stranger*
> *Rode into our valley,*
> *Ravaged with scars of hard battles long past.*
> *His eyes, they were weary,*
> *He was tired of running,*
> *But the law was behind him and catching up fast.*'

Her thoughts turned to her stepdaughter's latest crush on unsuitable types, but if there was one thing to be salvaged out of this whole bloody mess, it was that the problem of Flavia, at least, could be solved. Live in poverty and strip for a living? Hades would take day trippers first! The scheming little minx had no intention of running off to join any circus. She was working towards getting her foster parents to buy him off, providing the loving couple with sufficient capital to set up home together, happy ever after.

Claudia shook her head in disbelief. How badly can you misread someone, she thought. But if it had been Flavia's intention to mention this gem of an idea to her beloved, she wouldn't have had much opportunity. The instant the curtain went down on *The Cuckold*, the cast had disappeared into a scrum, thrashing out the weaknesses in the plot, shoring up the holes, playing up the laughs and, judging by the babble coming up from below, they were still hard at work on their rewrite.

In any case, Claudia had pre-empted the situation by calling her bluff. *Congratulations on your betrothal*, read the note she'd left in Flavia's room, *you will make a wonderful bride.* On her bed, she'd laid a wreath of greenery weaved with hellebores, the closest she could get this time of year to orange blossom. Ha. You want to run away with a penniless actor? Be my guest!

> '*Long after the stranger*
> *Rode out of our village,*
> *I bore him the daughter that he never knew.*
> *I know not what befell him,*
> *I hope he found freedom,*
> *But I'll always bear him a love that is true.*'

Dammit, the song wouldn't go out of her head.

Across the gallery, Caspar's eyes opened. Easing one arm from where it had become trapped under Jemima's hip, he climbed gently over Adah and tiptoed across the thick woven rugs. There was no light in the room, but Caspar was used to feeling his way around in the dark. He discarded his nightshift and slipped into his best rose-red embroidered robe. As he belted it, he noticed that both hands were shaking as though they had minds of their own.

His mouth was dry, too.

His breath shallow.

For a second, he faltered. He didn't *have* to do this. He could pull back. Stop right now— He swallowed. Wrung clammy hands together. Wished there was another way.

But there wasn't.

Familiar now with which boards creaked and which didn't, Caspar eased open the finely carved cypress-wood door and padded along the gallery on feet that were surprisingly light.

The herald in the street was calling the sixth hour when the entrance to the slaves' quarters was unbolted. The figure was tall and bearded, with black hair that fell to his shoulders, and his handsome face was still flushed from the accolades his fellow thespians had showered upon him for his role as King of the Gods.

From the alcove where the wood for the oven was stored, Claudia had a perfect view of the door. She did not want to believe that the Spectaculars were anything other than they appeared on the surface. But want didn't enter into the equation. This was real life, not fairy tales. In real life, people got hurt.

Sometimes they died.

Secrets, secrets, so many secrets—

Pulling his cloak high round his neck to cover the lower half of his face, Ion glanced to the left, then to the right, and then, with the agility for which actors were renowned, melted into the swarm of farmers heading for market.

Very little time passed before Claudia heard another sound in the hallway. With the faintest of jangles, Doris snaked his way past the tables and the shelving, checking over his shoulder as he eased the door shut behind him. It could, of course, be simply an assignation. Then she recalled that look in his eyes earlier. That dangerous, feral expression.

In the alcove, Claudia shivered.

She attributed it to the young man with chiselled cheekbones who'd just made his exit.

In fact, it was the draught from the front door. As another member of the cast slipped silently into the crowd.

Skyles hadn't seen Claudia in the kitchen, but he had smelled her. That rich, Judean perfume was unmistakable, and he had hovered in the doorway for a minute or two, waiting for the scent to dissipate, as it surely would if she'd just been passing through. But the scent lingered, which meant she was waiting. Hidden some place, and watching.

Skyles slipped out through the vestibule instead. Past the porter, whose sleeping mouth was still curved upwards from laughing so much during the show.

Dawn was poking a bony finger through the darkness as the Digger breakfasted on warm bread and smoked liver sausage from a street vendor. Like the rest of the cast, the Digger was on something of a high still, the dress rehearsal having sent a rush of adrenalin coursing through everyone's veins, a combination of excitement, pride, fear of failure, supreme confidence and stage fright.

Performing *The Cuckold* in 'real' time, as opposed to rehearsal, this sense of achievement had acted like a rivet, uniting every member of the team and turning them into one cohesive unit as invincible as any Roman legion.

No one in the troupe underestimated this feat. Two months ago, they were a band of strangers brought together by circumstance and held together by chance. Some were old hands at the performing arts. Some, like the Digger, were new to the challenge, but had taken to it like widgeon to water.

But in those two turbulent months, they had united to become Caspar's Spectaculars in the truest sense of the word. And, just like the human tortoise made when legionaries overlapped their shields and advanced upon a besieged fortress, so the company had united, several individual pieces forming a single unified body.

Indestructible and proud.

But killers are like leopards, they can't wash off their spots. Dawn might be breaking, the streets might be a crush of barrows piled high with cabbages, live fowl, flowers and carcases, but the Digger's mind remained trapped in the rich russet shades of autumn.

In a world where the leaves hung permanently limp in the warm, humid air and the proliferation of butterflies never moved on. The smell of moist, Frascati earth remained for ever in the Digger's nostrils, and the rut of the stags and the yaffle of a woodpecker were a relentless echo in the Digger's brain. *As was the grunt of surprise, when spade crashed down upon skull.*

This time, however, the woman in the shallow grave said nothing. She merely pointed a skeletal finger at the blood on the spade. The same hot, red blood which had splattered her murderer's face.

Warm bread and smoked liver sausage turned to ash in the Digger's mouth.

Twenty-Five

'Won't be long, sweetie.'

The young woman planted a kiss on her baby's cheek, soft and flushed with sleep, and combed his silky hair with her fingers.

'Be a good boy while Mummy's gone.'

With luck, the little 'un wouldn't stir until she got home, and whilst she didn't like leaving him on his own, it wouldn't be for long. But today was the Festival of Consus, another public holiday, and she had chores which would not keep. He ought to sleep through for another hour yet.

Striding out along the Via Sacra, she noticed that there were very few people around at this time of the day. As dawn clawed its way through the heavy grey sky, the last of the delivery carts would be rumbling out of the city, the gates closing behind them, and there were no farmers this morning to set up for market.

Public holidays meant very little to this young mother. As the wife of a hot-food vendor, there was just as much work servicing the needs of the crowds who flocked to the Circus Maximus as there was meeting the daily demands of their regulars. No more work, but certainly no less, and that's exactly how she liked it.

Predictable income + predictable outgoings = domestic serenity!

Turning off the Via Sacra opposite the Regia, she thought she noticed someone hesitate at the entrance to the narrow passageway. She smiled grimly to herself, well aware that she fitted the pattern of the rapist's victims. She was young – twenty-two in a range of ages varying from sixteen to twenty-four – and she came from a respectable, though hardly wealthy, background. Those same attributes, however, applied to several hundred other women all around the city. Why should he pick her? Nevertheless, the vendor's wife had chosen a route this morning where, should anyone be following her, she'd quickly know about it and be able to thwart him with evasive action.

Emerging from the passageway, she checked left then right before setting a brisk pace between the high-rise tenements which dominated this commercial quarter of the city. Secure in the district's respectability, the young woman finalized her plans for Saturnalia. Four days with no work, just Shorty and her and the baby, was nothing short of a dream come true, and although the baby was too young to understand the garlands and the gifts, she and Shorty would take great pleasure in watching the little 'un's face light with pleasure at the sculpted candles and painted clay dolls. Shorty had carved him a wooden donkey on wheels to pull along on a rope and—

She stopped. Glanced back over her shoulder. Nothing out of the ordinary. Just an old man coming out of a doorway and hobbling away down the hill.

Ridiculous! Whatever would Shorty say, the mother of his child being spooked by an old man! She marched on up the Esquiline, planning her Saturnalia party, just the three of them, with them all wearing funny felt hats, green for her, blue for Shorty and a mustard-yellow miniature one for the baby that would tie beneath his fat, dimpled chin. Engrossed in the games they would play, she did not notice that the old man had straightened up, turned round and become someone else altogether as he followed her cracking pace up the hill.

Twenty-Six

The baths were just opening when Sextus Valerius Cotta arrived. Divesting their master of his heavy striped toga, his luxurious woollen tunic, his soft undershirt and helping him into thick-soled wooden sandals so his feet would not burn on the hot mosaic floors, his slaves then handed over his valuables to the attendants for safe-keeping and took themselves off to the gymnasium.

'You'll be the only one in the sweat room, Senator,' the usher apologized, leading the way through the thick, swirling steam.

'Good.'

The handsome mouth of the Arch-Hawk pursed in approval. He couldn't cope with chit-chat and gossip today. His mind was reeling from the devastating news he'd received from Frascati. Choosing a seat in the corner, he leaned his elbows on his knees and buried his head in his hands.

Dead? Sonofabitch, she couldn't be dead! Not the girl who knew the formula to make saltpetre explode!

'Boy!' He snapped his fingers and an attendant materialized out of nowhere. 'Hot room.'

The baths were filling up fast. Vaulted halls rang with grunts of massaged pleasure, the slap-slap-slap of pummelled flesh, the clomp of wooden clogs as attendants puttered back and forth with linen towels and strigils, scented massage oils and tweezers for plucking eyebrows and unwanted hair. Along the lofty promenade, lined with

187

works of art looted from Greek temples, a group of youths had organized a raucous competition rolling iron hoops with hooked sticks round the twenty-foot-high marble statues, first one past the Minotaur is the winner.

'Will you be wanting a shave after the massage, sir?'

'What?' His mind was still in Frascati. Had somebody killed her for the secret of the saltpetre? 'Oh, shave. Yes, and I'll have bergamot in the rub.' Bergamot oil was renowned for its uplifting properties and Jupiter alone knows, he needed a boost at the moment. Had it really all come to nothing?

The Arch-Hawk closed his eyes as the attendant scraped his back with the bronze strigil. He might not have the backing of the Senate, but for many months, he'd been cultivating support among the plebeian community. With the working classes and the gods behind him, he had truly expected to see the eagle soaring to its true heights. But now . . . ?

Cotta flipped over to lie on his back. Tense, he was no better than useless. He needed to clear his mind. Think. Rethink. Then think again. As the massage relaxed the knots in his muscles, his mind drifted back to his visit to Cumae.

Had he been ruthlessly conned by that shrivelled old crone sitting on her throne in the half dark surrounded by swirls of evil-smelling smoke? Or had he really looked into Hades? Spoken with the shades of his ancestors?

In truth, he hadn't held out much hope when he set out after the funeral, but hope was all he had left. The servant girl who had the formula for the explosion had run away and this time the Senator's men couldn't find her. Now, of course, he knew why. Some bastard had caved her skull in with a shovel. But he hadn't known that at the time, and in any case it didn't make a scrap of difference. What mattered was that he had the chemicals and no formula and desperate times require desperate measures.

Cotta knew he had to try everything in his power – everything – to get his hands on the formula, and he'd heard the Oracle put people in touch with their ancestors. Ludicrous? Maybe. But the Arch-Hawk had nothing to lose.

Had the priest added drugs to the smoke, or slipped them in the wine he had given him? Cotta didn't know, but with music coming from nowhere then fading again, he had felt strangely disconnected from reality when the white-robed acolytes guided him along the eerie corridor of light and shadow that led to the Sibyl's dark lair. Black eyes glittered from the ancient face as she considered his request. Finally she agreed, and huge sums of gold were handed over before he was led outside, blindfolded, and taken on a short overland chariot drive to the black mouth of a tunnel.

'This way,' lisped the priest, removing the blindfold.

Cotta was still cynical at this stage. Wary of theatricals and vast sums of money. But it was so bitterly cold inside the rock, and the tunnel was blacker than jet and after four hundred paces of stumbling behind the priest in a hillside that resonated with sighs and moans, and following a sharp bend in the tunnel, which suddenly dropped a hundred, maybe two hundred feet, to a great chamber through which oily waters gurgled and swirled, Cotta's doubts vanished. There was no uncertainty at all in his mind that what he was looking at here was the River Styx.

'Do not be afraid,' the priest intoned solemnly, and his voice was brushed by a thousand whispering echoes.

Fear was not an emotion the Arch-Hawk recognized, yet the skin on his scalp prickled.

'You must wait in the Hall of Destiny,' the High Priest announced, 'while we appease the shades with the blood of bullocks, oxen and lambs.' Black-hooded acolytes magicked out of the shadows. Holding boughs of mistletoe over his blond head, they led him through a door into a decorated chamber.

'Once the Oracle has summoned the shades of your ancestors, we shall return,' the priest said.

Minutes passed like hours, days like weeks, and all Cotta had to live on was bread, herbs and some strange-tasting wine. Bizarre paintings on the walls of the chamber depicted men and women in the throes of terrible disease, and for a time he feared he was going insane. When he tried to escape, it was to find the door had been locked, and the only sound inside the chamber was the babble of distant water – and whispers. Soft, sibilant whispers that came and went without warning.

Eventually the door opened, the black-hooded priests chanting as they led him through the tunnels to where a coracle bobbed on the water. Cotta could not see the Ferryman's face, but from one long, tattered sleeve, a skeletal finger crooked in a gesture of beckoning.

'Come,' the Ferryman rasped, and goose pimples rose on the Senator's skin. 'There are those who wait to greet you.'

'You will need this.' An acolyte handed him the mistletoe branch, a gift for the Queen of the Underworld. 'And this,' he added, placing a coin on the Senator's tongue. In the distance, three dogs started barking. Or, rather, one dog with three heads. Cerberus, the guardian of Hades. The Hound of Hell.

At surprising speed, the coracle was swept downriver and the temperature grew warmer. Steam rose from the water in places, which bubbled wildly in others. Finally, the little boat put into the side.

Wordlessly, the Ferryman held out his hand for his fee.

Struggling out of the bobbing boat, Cotta handed over the coin then laid the mistletoe in a special niche for Persephone. When he turned, the coracle had gone, though the sound of baying still echoed through the dark caverns. His mouth was dry. He had crossed the Styx and paid the Ferryman. Was there any way back? Spluttering torches cast strange shadows on the rock face, and a lyre was strummed by invisible fingers.

He waited, unsure what to expect. Then his brother appeared. Veiled, but still in full dress uniform, he floated in and out of Cotta's vision on the far bank of the river, the wound which killed him still gushing blood. A female voice called across the hot underground springs.

'Greyhound, is that you?'

'Mother?'

It was the nickname she'd given him as a child, because even as a small boy, he could run like the wind. But as much as he loved his mother, he didn't know how long he'd have and it was imperative he spoke to his father. He called him. Heard the hammering of his own heart. Suppose he had come all this way, paid all that gold, for the old man not to appear? But the old man did appear. Not quite as tottery on his legs, but still bent and needing the help of another veiled ghost to lean on.

'Father.' He could scarcely breathe. 'I must know the formula of the potion you mixed.'

A harsh laugh floated across the bubbling waters of the River Styx. 'I am dead, my son. I hardly achieved the immortality I sought for so long.'

'I know.' Cotta had to guard against impatience. If he offended the shade of his father, the old man would never return and Rome's expansion would be set back for years, maybe for ever. He bent his fair head in reverence. 'You don't know how sorry I am, sir. We're all sorry. Shocked that it happened like that, too.'

'It was a quick end, son. I didn't suffer, if that's what you wanted to know.'

It wasn't. Although he was glad. 'The formula, father. I need to know what adjustments you made to the elixir when you – when it exploded.'

There was a long pause, and a rustle as though pages of notes were being scrolled through out of sight. Whisperings.

'My box survived the fire,' the quavering voice replied at last. 'You possess all the ingredients for the Elixir of Immortality.'

'Yes, sir,' Cotta said patiently. 'But I'm not seeking immortality. The west wing blew up. *I need to know how you did it.*'

This time the silence was longer, the rustlings more intense, the whisperings harsher.

'Father, please. I need your help.'

The ghost supporting the old man muttered something in his ear. The old man nodded. 'You don't need my help, son,' he replied. 'The gods smile on your destiny.'

'They do?' Cotta blinked. 'You mean . . . on the whole expansion programme? Including my plans to blow up the Senate?'

'Of course, my boy! Jupiter, King of the Immortals and Bringer of Justice, gives you his blessing in all your endeavours. Success, my son, will be yours.' And in a sudden swirl of smoke, they were gone. All of them. His brother, his mother, his father – even the whispering voices fell silent.

Now, in the bathhouse, as the barber rinsed off the last of his whiskers and rubbed balm of Gilead into his chin, that rare and precious oil that the Queen of Sheba presented to Solomon, Cotta regrouped.

Not all facts could be taken at face value, but he had no doubts whatsoever that he had sailed the River Styx, stood at the mouth of the Underworld, spoken with the shades of his kinfolk. By default, then, if he believed in the Oracle's powers, he must also accept his father's assurances that Jupiter himself blessed Cotta's plans. Sonofabitch, one way or another, that Senate House was going to blow.

Twenty-Seven

The morning air was chill, but for the first time in days, chinks of brightness penetrated the gloom and, if the farmers' forecasts were to be believed, Rome might actually see blue skies and sunshine for Saturnalia. Until last night, in fact right up until this morning, the holiday forecast had been uppermost in everyone's thoughts. With so many celebrations taking place out of doors, fine weather made all the difference. But today on the streets, there was only one topic of conversation. The Halcyon Rapist.

And the news was electric.

'Did you hear? The victim got away!'

'It's true, you know. I heard it from the rope maker, who heard it from the silversmith, who heard it from the hot-food vendor himself!'

'She wounded him, apparently. Don't know where she got him, or even how badly the bugger was hurt, but by Jupiter, she got one over on the dirty bastard. He won't be so hard to hunt down now.'

'Grabbed him by the balls, the hot-food vendor said, then stabbed him with her knife and ran home.'

'A bloody heroine, that woman. The Emperor ought to give her a medal.'

Orbilio had still not returned, and Claudia was elated by the news. It was like Atlas taking the weight of the world from her shoulders, giving her a reprieve when she didn't deserve it. And an appetite to match. She was taking breakfast in her

193

office, working on the schedule for Saturnalia with Leonides, when Skyles burst into the garden. He was wheezing and holding his side, as though he'd been running, and sharp eyes searched the courtyard and peristyle. Whoever he was expecting to see wasn't there and he arranged himself with carefully constructed nonchalance against one of the marble pillars.

'There are no eggs with my breakfast, Leonides.'

The steward tilted his head on one side. In all these years, the mistress had never asked for eggs with her breakfast. Fruit, yes. Bread, yes. Cheeses, cold meats, salt fish, grilled chicken, goose liver, omelettes and walnuts, yes. But—

'*Eggs*, madam?'

'Little ovally things. Often speckled. You find them in nests.'

'And . . . you'd like some right now?'

'Hard-boiled,' she replied.

'Naturally,' Leonides murmured, and dammit she'd sack him if he wasn't enslaved. Well, now. Hard-boiling a few eggs must take a good while, she calculated, moving behind the tall bust on the podium where she could look out into the peristyle but not be seen in return.

> '*One day a stranger*
> *Rode into our village,*'

a clear voice sang.

> '*Ravaged with scars of hard battles long past.*'

'Adah told me you wanted to see me,' Erinna said.

'I have something for you.' Still propped against the pillar, Skyles dangled a perfect circlet of flowers from his outstretched finger.

Erinna looked at the chaplet then at the flower beds. 'Does our hostess know you've been raiding her garden?'

'If you're asking, does this constitute receiving stolen goods, then the answer is "probably".'

The clown. Always the clown.

'But with the courts closed and the jails full to over-flowing, I don't think they'll clap you in irons, Mistress Erinna.'

'I think you're missing the point,' Erinna said.

'What? That I didn't actually buy you the flowers? Well, no. But I wove them myself.'

'That's not what I meant and you know it.'

Claudia could only see the back of Erinna's head, but she could see all of Skyles. Especially the dark intensity burning holes in his eye sockets. 'I'm an arsehole at times,' he said equably.

'Aren't you.' There was a smile, though, in Erinna's reply.

'Good, because if we agree on that, we at least have *some* common ground.'

'You're incorrigible,' she replied, and of course, it being Skyles, Erinna couldn't help laughing.

Very slowly, very gently, he positioned the chaplet of crocus and hellebores. They were a perfect fit over Erinna's tight chestnut bun. 'I don't suppose you've changed your mind about going to the Circus and having dinner with me?'

'No.'

Skyles stared at his feet. 'Mind if I ask why?'

'You can ask, but I'll only lie to you, Skyles. Now if you'll excuse me, I need to rehearse my lines, now that Caspar's got me playing the Virgin as well.'

A hand fell on her arm. 'Then let me ask you something else.'

'No.'

Whatever else followed, Claudia would never know. Julia chose that moment to come flapping into the office, her hair spiked in a dozen different directions as though she'd been taking lessons in coiffure from Hermione.

'She's gone!' she cried. 'Flavia's run off with that gigolo just like she threatened.'

'Calm down.' Emerging from behind the podium as though it was the most natural place in the world to be standing, Claudia pushed her sister-in-law into a chair and forced a glass of vintage Chian wine down her throat. 'No one's run off with Skyles, Julia. See for yourself. The gigolo is outside in the garden.'

'Then where is she? Her bed's not been slept in and—' Bony hands bunched into fists. 'That little cow's playing me up again, isn't she? When I get hold of her, I swear I'll—' She broke off as a thought suddenly occurred to her. 'What am I saying?' she laughed. 'Once Flavia meets our handsome oleiculturist, she'll soon forget about penniless actors!'

'You do realize that his sexual preferences swing the other way?'

'What?' Julia reeled in her seat. 'My divine Marcus?'

'Keeps a harem of little black boys in his house on the Esquiline and another at his estate at the seaside.'

'Oh, my!' Julia fanned herself with her hand. 'So many shocks, one on top of the other, that I've come over all—'

'Queer?'

'Faint.'

She rose to her feet and made some effort to pull herself together.

'So much has happened, that I nearly forgot,' she said primly. 'Sister-in-law, I shall expect you to have bolts fitted to my bedroom door by tonight, and I would advise you, my girl, to have them fitted to yours.'

'Bolts?'

'This house,' Julia hissed, 'is turning into a *brothel*.'

With that, she swept out through the door, knocking Leonides aside.

'Four hard-boiled eggs, milady,' he said, laying down a covered silver platter.

'Eggs?' Claudia scowled as she lifted the lid. *'Eggs?* Oh, for gods' sake, Leonides, take them away. You know I can't stand the bloody things.'

Unlike other divinities, the Shrine of Consus was sited underground, below the first turn in the Circus Maximus. In a mirror image of the August festival, when a bowl of earth was removed from its place as centrepiece of the altar, in December a bowl of freshly turned soil was positioned in the empty slot. The gesture was purely symbolic. The August bowl represented the tired soil in which the harvest had been grown. The December bowl symbolized the rich, fertile earth for the new seeds, the idea being to bless the god of the store bin, for in theory without wheat, Rome would starve.

Theory be damned. Since Augustus took the helm, the provinces of Egypt, Pannonia and Sicily had been turned into the Empire's wheatfields, with fleets of four-hundred-tonne cargo ships, known as ten-thousanders after the number of sacks that they carried, doing the Puteoli–Alexandria run in under twelve days. Rome would never be brought to her knees again, held to ransom over her need for grain. But it was important not to forget these things. Remind citizens of how it used to be, before the Eagle's shadow covered the earth, and for that reason Augustus had restored the much larger temple to Consus on the Aventine. It was here, in the main temple, that the sacrificial offerings were burnt before being taken in festive procession down the hill to his underground shrine, but it was in the Circus where the real entertainment took place.

In full Imperial regalia, Augustus himself would ride a circuit in his war chariot. This would be followed by a procession of some of the finest horseflesh in Rome, then the consecration of offerings to Consus. After that, it became a free-for-all of mule races, donkey derbies, athletes racing on foot, before the festivities culminated in a series of full-blooded chariot races, and all this with the six most mysterious women in Rome in attendance at the Emperor's side, the Vestal Virgins. Something for everyone, then, on this lively public holiday.

Everyone, apparently, except Claudia Seferius.

'If you're going to make a habit of inviting men into your bedroom,' Orbilio said, warming his hands briskly over the brazier, 'you'll have to get your pitch in a lot faster. Jemima's already offered me a knee-trembler, thank you.'

'Be grateful it wasn't Hermione. Thecks in the thellar for thickthpenth,' Claudia mimicked.

'I was more worried about Fenja. I have nightmares about her catching me in the hallway and jolly well helping herself.'

Ah, yes. The more urbane, the more dangerous . . .

Claudia shifted her weight to the other foot and thought about the reason she'd invited him into her room. Frankly, she wasn't sure how to play this. Whichever way, it wasn't going to be easy—

'Last year's victims,' she began.

The dancing light in his eyes vanished. 'You're talking about the rapist?'

She nodded. Ran her tongue over her lips. 'Could you write down the addresses of the three women who identified their attacker?'

'For gods' sake, Claudia, if you know who—'

'I don't.'

That much was true. It was still only a hunch. Images swirled like a kaleidoscope inside her head. Of Ion, handsome and rugged, but never happy, sneaking out as the herald called the sixth hour. Of Doris, slipping out after him. Of a draught from the front door. Of Caspar, sneaking along the gallery in the dark. Blood thundered at her temples, and there was a pain at the back of her eyes.

'Claudia,' he said, warningly, and there was no trace on his face of the unimaginable relief that had swamped him when he heard about the hot-food vendor's wife. 'This is too dangerous a game to mess with. The man's a monster and if you have even the tiniest suspicion, you have *got* to tell me. I'm serious, now who is it?'

'I have absolutely no idea.'

'It's within my authority to have this house searched top to bottom,' he said. 'If I find one of your actors is injured—'

'Very well, if you must know.' She smiled, although the smile did not seem to reassure him. 'I got to thinking last night that, well . . . Maybe a word, woman to woman, might coax one or two details out of the victims that they hadn't liked to discuss in front of a man.'

Scepticism stretched the air. Silence stretched into infinity.

'I don't know what the hell you're up to,' he growled at last, spiking his hands through his hair. 'But I don't believe you'd cover up for this bastard, or that your talking to these girls can be worse than a pair of flatfoots trampling their fragile emotional progress.' He reached for a quill and the inkwell.

Claudia's eyes narrowed. 'Last night you said you wouldn't – *couldn't* – put the victims through that torture again.'

'Nor would I,' Orbilio said tiredly. 'You have to remember that I'm no longer in charge of this investigation.'

Both horns of Claudia's dilemma prodded her at once. Bugger.

If she told Orbilio who she suspected was responsible, he would arrest him at once. That would be fine, provided, of course, she was right. But it was possible, more than possible in fact, that her suspicions were way off course – and there would be no way back for Marcus Cornelius after that.

Of course, a disgraced Security Policeman was a Security Policeman off Claudia's back and, with Orbilio's career in shreds, she would no longer be facing a lonely and penniless exile for fraud. But was she really prepared to jeopardize the career of a passionate investigator, who spat in the face of family convention to fight murderers, assassins and rapists? Especially when it had become a personal crusade between him and the monster terrorizing the streets? Being wrong twice would destroy him—

The horns started to hurt.

'Dymas is adamant we interview the victims again,' Marcus said, 'and has it in his head to start with Deva, to ask her the questions we didn't have a chance to put yesterday, and although I can see his logic, that girl's sanity is already stretched to the wire.'

'Then stop him,' she said brusquely.

'I can't. The Head of the Security Police backs him all the way on this, but . . .'

His voice trailed off into a tortured silence and, with his eyes glued to a point in the corner, he explained how Deva had tried to jump from the mezzanine. How he'd caught her, felt her bones quake uncontrollably in his arms, read the hopelessness in her eyes. He talked about what Deva had been like before the attack. Vivacious and vibrant, with her pretty pert bodices and Damascan fringed skirts.

'A happy young woman with her whole life ahead of her, until that bastard destroyed her.'

Then, fixing his gaze on the door jamb, he explained how the herbalist had been driven to the last resort of drugging her into oblivion with poppy juice, even though the risks of addiction were perilously high.

'The herbalist seems a good man,' Claudia said softly.

'One of the best,' Marcus replied, and, maybe because it was cold and he hadn't slept last night, maybe he was in confessional mood, or perhaps it was simply because he was lonely, demoted and utterly demoralized, fearing the drops of the water clock were moving too fast and that soon, far too soon, there would be another victim to add to the list, he also told her the reason why he'd gone back to the little house by the river.

'That was why my steward summoned me home,' he explained. 'Angelina had moved lock, stock and barrel into my house—'

But when he glanced up, it was to find Claudia and the three addresses had gone.

Which was a pity, Marcus felt, because he hadn't got round to telling her that Captain Moschus had escaped from jail.

But then he had a feeling she already knew about that.

Twenty-Eight

'Who are you?' A hatchet-faced woman with permanently pinched lips peered through a slot in the woodwork. 'What d'you want?'

Claudia told her.

'So?' the dragon barked back. 'What's it to you?'

Claudia told her that, too.

'Hmmm.' Shrewd eyes bored into shrewd eyes. 'Well, you'd best come on in, then. Before the neighbours start gawping.'

The woman, who introduced herself as the victim's aunt, relieved her of her mantle in a pleasant hallway from which four equally pleasant rooms led off. Fragrant oils burned in a niche, and the hall was decked with holly and yew. A white cat snoozed on a tasselled cushion on a chair.

'In there.'

The aunt beckoned her into a light, spacious living area with rich tapestries hanging on the walls and bearskin rugs on the floor. The seating was padded and comfortable, apple logs crackled and spat in the hearth, filling the air with their scent.

A year on and the poor girl was still jumpy, and was it any wonder, Claudia thought. Her bastard husband had thrown her out after the rape, proclaiming her an unfit mother for their children, an unfit wife as a result of her subsequent breakdown. Now she was reduced to living off a divorced aunt, and the only good thing to come out of that was at least the aunt was comfortably off. For a year, now, the girl had refused to set foot outdoors, the aunt said, could not be left alone, was terrified of strangers, especially men.

'I've spent twelve months nursing her,' she warned under her breath. 'You be careful.'

It was like walking on butterflies' wings. Round and round the questions went, gradually creeping closer to the target, every moment more painful than the last.

'He pushed me in the middens,' the girl said at last, and it might have been an automaton talking, a wooden dummy from whose mouth the ventriloquist projected his voice. *"Filth"*, he said. *"All of you, nothing but filth,"* and he put his foot on my neck and pushed me under, knowing I couldn't breathe and I'd have to swallow the muck. *"Go back to the filth where you belong,"* that's what he said.'

And that was it. The ultimate violation. The one that preyed on the victims' consciousness and remained there. That he had made them dirty. Dirt, from which there could never be any cleansing . . .

'How could you identify him, if he was masked?' Claudia asked gently.

The girl tensed, glanced at her aunt. 'Same as I told the Tribunal. From the smell of aniseed, the way he held himself, his voice, the shape of his hands. Why?' Her jaw tightened, her knuckles clenched white. 'He *is* dead, isn't he?' She turned to her aunt, her face stark with horror. 'You said he was executed. You swore—'

'Yes, he's dead,' Claudia assured her, and caught an imperceptible nod of relief from the aunt. 'I watched the execution myself. Lions. Very nasty.'

The girl relaxed, but only a fraction. 'Then why all the questions?'

'The Emperor,' Claudia lied. 'He was so concerned for the daughters of Rome, that he asked me to, uh— counsel the victims and help them talk it out of their systems.'

'Did he send money?' the aunt asked.

* * *

At home, the revisions to *The Cuckold* were going well. Which, roughly translated, meant that the group hadn't actually killed each other – at least, not yet. But the amendments were testing the company's cohesion to the limit. Adrenalin had finally ceased to pump. Last night's dress rehearsal seemed aeons ago and now they were tired, scratchy, anxious and vulnerable. A perfect breeding ground for egos.

'No, no, *no*,' Ugly Phil protested. 'The Virgin *has* to come on first, so I can walk around the edge of the stage leering at her. It isn't funny otherwise.'

'It isn't funny either way,' the Virgin protested, amazed that her chaplet was still fast round her bun after the energetic rerun of scenes. 'Ogling is what perverts do.'

'Erinna'th right,' Hermione said. 'The Thatyr ith thuppothed to be a comic figure.'

'All right, then. Suppose I creep behind the Virgin on tiptoes?'

'Creepings are not funny,' Fenja boomed. 'Make you look like pervert with bunion.'

Everyone laughed, save Ugly Phil. Hermione tried to force her unruly frizz into the pins. Fenja adjusted Periander's Cupid wings, which had gone crooked in the melee. The Virgin and the Satyr tried again.

'Iss worser,' Fenja said and even Renata, who liked to keep the peace wherever possible, could not disagree.

'Oi, Skyles!' Jemima called across. 'Show Ugly Phil how it's done, willya?'

But Skyles seemed lost in space, so she tossed her slipper across the atrium to attract his attention. 'There,' she crowed triumphantly. '*That's* clowning, Master Satyr. Look how he pretended to wince when it hit him, how his breath came out in a hiss, and it's only an old felt shoe. Soft as lard.'

'How did you do that?' Ugly Phil asked Skyles. 'How d'you make yourself turn pale like that?'

'Can't you see he iss hurt, you damn fool?' Fenja snapped. 'Skyles, let uss look, huh?'

'It's nothing, I'm fine,' Skyles rasped. 'Just a touch of cramp.' But his colour still hadn't come back. His face was as white as Renata's. 'Look, this is how I'd play the scene,' he said, and instead of hobbling round the set leering at the Virgin as Ugly Phil had been doing, the Buffoon cracked his knuckles, licked his lips and with a wink at his audience, set to caressing Erinna's voluptuous shadow. The more they laughed, the more he put a finger to his lips to silence the chortles, and so the more the audience laughed, and as the Virgin turned, so did Skyles and her shadow, so that the Virgin appeared to be the only person not in on the secret.

'I still don't see why I can't play the Virgin,' Adah whined. 'Now Erinna's got *two* parts in the play, as the Soldier's Mistress and the Virgin, and me, I've only got a brief walk-on.'

'Swings and roundabouts, kiddo,' Doris said, buffing his fine oval nails. 'I'm sure Caspar will write you a bigger role next time, although—' He leaned back and peered at her backside. 'Some might say you've a big enough roll already.'

'Up yours,' she retorted, but there was no sting in the rebuke.

In fact, Adah was happy with the part she'd been given. It was at the beginning, when the Miser mistakes the Neighbour's Wife for his own spouse and rips off her gown, thinking he's about to make love to his wife. As a result of her full-frontal exposure so early in the proceedings, Adah was assured of the audience's unwavering interest, and therefore she was guaranteed to be the centre of attention in all subsequent scenes, even though the Neighbour's Wife merely stood in the background wagging a censorious finger. What more can *any* actress ask?

'One more time, then,' Ugly Phil said. 'From where I

come on, up to the bit where my horns get stuck in the Virgin's robe and— here! How about her frock comes off when I pull away?'

'No!' Adah squealed. It was too early to introduce further nudity, it would take away the effect of her scenes. 'The point is to make the Satyr look stupid, stupid.'

'Hey.' Jemima paused from combing her red hair through her fingers. 'Suppose, instead of creeping in, the Satyr comes down on Jupiter's platform as though he's descending straight from Olympus?'

'Jem, you're a star,' Skyles said, his hand still clamped over his side.

'I still think we ought to check with Caspar first,' Adah cut in.

'But he's not here,' Ugly Phil said, 'so I vote we incorporate it straight into the act.'

'Where is he?' Renata asked, rouging her cheeks with wine lees. 'Not like him to miss a rehearsal, considering we're opening tomorrow night.'

'Never mind Caspar,' Ugly Phil said, eager to keep his comic profile raised. 'Let's get cracking.'

Doris indicated the stairs with an eloquent roll of the eyes. 'In bed, lovey,' he told Renata. 'Catching up after a rough night,' he said.

'Not from me, he bloody didn't!' Jemima let out an infectious giggle. 'Come on, own up, you lot. Which one of you buggers gave him that shiner?'

'Not guilty,' Ugly Phil said.

'I wouldn't put it past him to hit himself with a broom handle,' Skyles said, 'just so the colour of his eye can match his kaftan.'

'I hope he'th all right,' Hermione said sombrely. 'Only when I thaw him earlier, he wath limping quite badly.'

'So would you, kiddo, if you'd shared a bed with Jemima all night.'

'Pig.' Jemima stuck her tongue out at Doris. 'Anyway,

he wasn't with me all night, was he, Adah?'

Adah shook her head. 'Randy old sod sloped off in the early hours. Thought we wouldn't notice.'

'Yeah, and the next I see of him,' Jemima said, 'he's asking Erinna to sew him a bleedin' eye patch.'

'So vere did he get his black eye and a limp?' Fenja wanted to know.

'Search me.' Jemima shrugged.

'Yes, but can you imagine how he'll bill the show?' Erinna stood up and spread her arms in a perfect imitation of the maestro. '*Ladies! Gentlemen! All you majestical creatures who have flocked to see our beautifious entertainment!*' She performed the impresario's deep bow. '*Allow me to present Caspar's – Halcyon – SPECTACULARS.*' She raised a mock eye patch. '*The only show in the Empire guaranteed to knock your eyes out!*'

Their sides aching and their bruised egos massaged at last, the troupe resumed their positions on stage. It was in everyone's interests to be scene-perfect for tomorrow's opening night.

'From the top, then,' Skyles said.

Adah said, 'I really think we ought to insert an extra scene where Jupiter soothes the Neighbour's Wife—'

She was shouted down by everyone, including Periander.

'Even if we wanted to,' Renata pointed out, the voice of reason as usual, 'we can't do it without Jupiter, and since no one's seen hide nor hair of Ion this morning, I suggest we move on. Now, then. Should I be playing the same tune, now the Satyr descends from Olympus?'

'No!' The cast was unanimous. The revision called for a boisterous horn, not a creeping-around flute.

'Here, will someone please give us a hand with this bleedin' pulley?' Jemima puffed, trying to haul the Satyr up to Olympus. 'It's too heavy for me on me own.'

'Coming right over,' Skyles said, making annotations on the script in ink.

'Like *now*!' Jemima wheezed, since no one had moved to help.

'Sorry.' Doris shrugged in apology. 'Can't help, kiddo. Pulled a muscle in my side, didn't I, swinging down from the gallery? Daren't risk making it worse before the performance.'

'Well, one of you buggers had better hurry,' she snapped. 'Me arm's coming out of its socket!'

'Ach, giff it here.'

Fenja marched over and, with one Nordic yank, the platform shot upwards, flinging the Satyr on to his backside, his cloven hoofs flailing into the Olympian heights.

'Put that in the script, too,' Erinna said.

Twenty-Nine

Sitting in the VIP section of the Circus Maximus, Sextus Valerius Cotta cheered the charioteers as though he hadn't a care in the world. To a skilled military tactician, it was vital no signs of uneasiness should be transmitted to the troops and if acting was part of a general's role, then so be it.

As two hundred thousand people stamped and whistled as the winner thundered past the post, his chariot wheels smoking, Cotta was acutely conscious that time was running through the sandglass at an alarming rate. In three months, the new campaign season got underway and it had been his intention to have the new regime in place by then. He had allies in six of the ten newly elected tribunes. Had the backing of the plebeians. Knew which generals and naval commanders he could trust. Had plans to deal with dissenters.

The winning charioteer drew his team up in front of the Imperial box to receive his victory palm. Blowing up the Senate and assassinating the Emperor would not have been Cotta's first choice. (Naturally.) But for Rome to achieve her true potential, hard pruning was the only solution. New shoots could not flourish without cutting away the dead wood.

Down in the tunnel, lots were already being cast for who got which starting box for the next race, the Novice Crown, and a swarm of broom boys were out sweeping the sand with their besoms. This time of year, when it got dark so early, there was no time to lose between contests, and under

Augustus, the number of races had increased dramatically.

'A people that yawns, Cotta, is a people ripe for revolt.'

It was one of the Emperor's favourite sayings.

As the magistrate signalled with a drop of his handker-chief for the Novice Crown to begin, the trumpet sounded and Cotta marvelled at the arrogance of his fellow Senators who sat so comfortably on their cushions beside him, believing nothing, and no one, could displace them. Secure in their cocoons of wealth and their positions of authority, they had ceased to ask: never mind us patricians, are the *plebeians* content? They didn't question whether erecting a temple of marble was more important than rebuilding death-trap tenement slums. Had stopped caring whether the funds would be better invested in schooling, housing and policing the streets.

The novices thundered by, kicking up clouds of sand with their hoofs. Suddenly, one of the drivers veered too close to the central stone spine and his competitors crowded him into the wall, overturning the chariot. The two outside stal-lions thrashed in their traces, their eyes rolling with fear, while mechanics rushed to free the two terrified mares who were trapped in the shaft before they became trampled in the next lap.

Augustus wasn't a bad man, Cotta reflected, glancing across to the Imperial Box, where the great man sat in gold crown and purple robes beside the Vestal Virgins. He'd introduced many worthy elements into Roman society, including free games, free public baths, the dole and, of course, his complete overhaul of the army, right down to equipping it with surgeons and vets. Augustus was objec-tive and rational, wily and just, making Cotta more than willing to throw his lot in with this man instead of Mark Antony. (Especially once everyone realized how far that bloodsucking Egyptian bitch, Cleopatra, had got her hooks into him, weakling that he was.) But seventeen years at the helm was taking its toll.

210

Augustus might only be thirty-seven years old, but he was softening.

The eagle was relaxing its grip.

The Empire was growing flabby and lax.

Dole tablets didn't prevent fires from sweeping through the tenements every night and taking a score of lives with them. No amount of Games could heal the diseases that ravaged the slums and made the inhabitants' lives a perpetual torment. With the contents of his father's box, though, Cotta could reverse that slide.

Realgar. The form of arsenic known by the Arabs as *Fire of the Mines.*

Sulphur. Produced by roasting fool's gold and recrystallizing the vapour.

Honey. Binding the ingredients and rendering the mixture volatile.

Poseidon Powder. That fine, floury, combustible substance that would change the history of Rome for ever.

Sonofabitch, who could have predicted it would all come to nought with a body found in the woods? And yet— Cotta shouted encouragement to his team as they passed. And yet— The ghost of his father was in no doubt that Mighty Jupiter himself blessed his plans . . .

'Note for you, sir.'

A reverent tap on his shoulder, and a roll of parchment was passed to him by a messenger wearing the Senator's own livery of amber and green. He broke the seal and read the note carefully. It was from his steward in Frascati, and Cotta read the note again to make sure.

'*Yes!*' he said, punching the air, as his team passed the post two lengths ahead of the field.

Thirty

'**O**rbilio?' Claudia rapped on the door of the guest room and, when there was no answer, swept in. 'Marcus?'

Dammit, now that she had all the proof that she needed, where were the Security Police when you need them?

'Off playing with his harem of little black boys, I shouldn't wonder,' Julia sniffed across the other gallery. 'Pervert! Anyway, sister-in-law, I need to talk with you about Flavia.'

'Not now, Julia.'

'She still hasn't come home, and as I said at breakfast, her bed wasn't slept in—'

'Not *now*, Julia!' Sweet Jupiter, he could be anywhere. But she had to find him. Quickly. Tell him he was right about the Halcyon Rapist. That he—

'—but that's not the worst part.'

'*Goddammit, Julia, this isn't the time!*'

'The worst part is that, according to that awful boy with the eyeliner, she went to a hotel last night. With a man.'

Give me strength. 'Doris is winding you up,' Claudia said. 'Now I've a hundred urgent things to do, and trust me, Flavia's fine.'

'You don't know that, and you don't care either, you heartless creature.' Julia got out a handkerchief and dabbed at her eyes. 'What my dear, kind brother saw in a gold-digger like you, I shall never know.' She blew noisily into the linen. 'You've never liked us, couldn't care a fig what happens to us, *any* of us—'

Good grief, any more honks and you'd think there were geese on the gallery. 'Julia, go and lie down. There's absolutely no reason why Flavia would go swanning off to hotels with strange men—'

Oh. Sweet Juno. Since when had Doris started telling lies?

'Yes, you just relax, Julia. Close your eyes for an hour or two. Then, you'll see, everything will be fine.'

Lies, lies, it wouldn't be fine. There was only one reason why Flavia would go swanning off to hotels. Skyles. And Claudia Seferius had paved the way with her stupid imitation wedding bouquet! Shit. Far from calling her bluff, Flavia had interpreted the gesture as a genuine endorsement and I don't care what anybody says. Give a man with Skyles' reputation a young virgin on a plate, and he's hardly going to refuse.

Goddammit, Skyles. I hope it's going to be a bitter, bitter winter. Because you'll need those bloody earmuffs when I've finished with you!

'You really think Flavia's playing another trick?' Julia asked.

Claudia dredged up the kind of smile any self-respecting conman would be proud of. 'Positive.'

Shit, shit, shit. *Now* who was going to take Flavia off their hands? Her only remaining asset squandered in a sordid hotel encounter. It would cost a *fortune* in dowries after this! And suppose the silly bitch got herself pregnant . . . ? The only consolation was that Skyles might not have done the dastardly deed yet. If he had, Flavia would be home by now, crowing like a wretched rooster. Which meant if Claudia could get to her first—

'Madam.' Leonides materialized at his mistress's side.

'Not *now*, Leonides.' There was a grinding of teeth, and they were probably hers. Doesn't anybody listen around here?

'But madam—'

'Leonides. My sister-in-law is deaf, Skyles is about to

213

be, I'm perfectly happy to make it a hat-trick.'

Her steward retreated one pace out of range, but no more. 'The package you were expecting has been delivered,' he said staunchly. 'It's waiting for you in the storeroom.'

'What?' Of all the stupid timing— 'Moschus?'

Leonides nodded mournfully. Call it his Macedonian upbringing, but harbouring escaped jailbirds just before Saturnalia didn't seem to be his idea of a treat and suddenly there were any number of urgent needs pressing on Claudia. She went through a quick checklist in her head. Skyles, Felix, Caspar and the others were downstairs. Flavia's virginity could afford to stay on ice a little longer. Orbilio could be anywhere. Fine. Claudia was in just the right mood to scatter Moschus's ribs from Naples to Messina.

The Spectaculars had just one evening and whatever time they could squeeze out of tomorrow to perfect their perform-ances. Felix was pretty confident about his. To dance four different roles, three of them female, he wore a tight, white, figure-hugging costume, offsetting its neutrality with four flexible cloth masks. Each mask was painted with a different facial expression and was sown to a wig differing in both style and colour. It took exactly seven seconds to remove one mask and replace it with another, provided he had help from the wings. There could be no mistaking Venus from Helen of Troy in his mime, but he continued to practise differentiating Helen's passionate high kicks from the goddess of love's tranquil slides.

Renata, who took her cues from the bleached blond, rather than the other way around, was too experienced a flautist to rehearse further. Instead, she filled her time experimenting with the vast range of cosmetics in her box, ending up with a thicker mask than the dancer's. And hers took considerably more than seven seconds to remove.

Ugly Phil was complaining that the furry leggings made him itch since they'd been washed, had someone put soda in the water, and why is it one of his horns kept going limp?

'Don't fret, kiddo, these things happen to every chap sooner or later,' Doris said seriously.

'I prefer it,' Caspar said, flapping his hands like little fat kippers. 'It adds greatly to the humouritiousness of the scene. Miser, can you just lead in from where you catch your Wife with the Poet? Oh, and Cupid, suppose we suspend you from a rope so you swing through the air?'

'Isn't the poor little sod's voice high enough?' Jemima said, adjusting her veil up and her décolletage down. With that amount of bosom on show, she ought to do quite nicely for her old age out of this run.

'I don't suppose you've changed your mind about dinner?' Skyles asked Erinna under his breath, since the scene required neither Virgin, Soldier's Mistress nor Buffoon. 'I mean, I don't have to wear this.' He tapped the wooden phallus strapped to his groin. 'Well.' He grinned. 'Not unless you want me to.'

Erinna couldn't help laughing. 'No, Skyles. I haven't changed my mind.' She picked up a lyre and began to strum.

> '*One day a stranger*
> *Rode into our valley,*
> *Ravaged with scars of hard battles long past.*'

'You wrote that song, didn't you?'

'I did.'

'And I know who you wrote it about.'

The string snapped with a twang. 'Really?'

Skyles glanced round the Spectaculars. Made sure their collective attention was occupied. Shifted his weight on to his other foot. 'If you don't want to eat, there are sword swallowers in the Forum. Fire-eaters, snake charmers, dancing monkeys, even some trick where a boy climbs up a rope and disappears.'

'No means no, Skyles.

His eyes, they were weary,
He was tired of running,
But the law was behind him and catching up fast.'

Being a string short didn't seem to deter her.

'I'm persistent, Erinna.'

'Pissed, you mean.'

'Nowhere near enough.' He stroked his jaw. 'Look, if it's the women after the shows—'

'Oh, for heaven's sakes, Skyles, I know they're just conquests and don't mean a damn thing.'

Anger flushed his craggy face. 'Is that what you think? That I shag 'em to prove myself to the lads?'

'What, then?' she asked, but she was talking to herself. Stiff with anger, the Buffoon had stormed off.

Claudia, who had been observing the exchange from the gallery, swept down the stairs.

'My compliments on your black eye,' she told Caspar. 'In fact, I think it's the best shiner I've seen since my cook's wife caught him in bed with her sister.'

'My motto, dear lady, is that if one has something, one should have only the very best.' He leaned forward and lowered his voice to a conspiratorial whisper. 'I also possess a magnificentious bruise on my hip bone, if only you would care to verify the matter?'

'Thanks, but it would only get me overexcited and compromise my widowed status.' Claudia brushed away the feather of his turban from where it was tickling her ear. 'Is Ion back yet?'

'Misfortunately, madam, he is,' the little man intoned solemnly. 'Jupiter returned two hours ago in the highest of dudgeon and the lowest of temper, and is growling like a bear with two sore heads. My advice, dear lady, is not to approach the grizzly for a while.' He affected a mock injury. 'Those of us who tried have been severely mauled.'

'What's eating the moody sod, anyway?' Jemima asked.

'He'th thulked before, but never like thith,' Hcrmione said.

'One can only pray he comes out of it in the next hour,' Caspar added miserably. 'Before our talented company launches into a full – and I might add final – dress rehearsal.'

'He normally comes out of his sulks quickly, then?' Claudia asked.

The company exchanged glances among each other and shrugged. 'We've no idea,' Periander said. 'Most of us only met up in Frascati. Ion joined us then, too.'

Frascati was of no interest to Claudia. She had business waiting down in the storeroom. But as she ducked under Jupiter's platform to Olympus, she could hear Skyles apologizing to Erinna under the stairs.

'About those conquests,' he said. 'I know you'll think I've spent the last ten minutes trying to come up with a better explanation—'

For the first time since she arrived in this house, Erinna's expression hardened. 'You don't know one damn thing about what I think,' she snapped.

Catching Claudia's eye as she stomped off, Skyles winked. She thought it was probably the hardest bit of acting he'd done in his life.

'Leonides.' Claudia beckoned her steward over. 'Post my bodyguard at both exits,' she said, 'and have two of the biggest, burliest slaves stand guard beside them.'

'Now, madam?'

Claudia nodded. 'Until further notice, no one leaves this house without my permission.'

'But suppose you're not here?'

'Then, Leonides, they don't leave at all.'

With so many things happening at once, there was one crucial factor that Claudia had overlooked. Captain

Moschus's personal hygiene. Dear Diana, if anything was guaranteed to turn the olive oil in the storeroom sour, it was three days in an overcrowded jail. Rancid wasn't the word.

He was sitting on a three-legged wooden stool with his hands tied behind his back and his boots removed to ensure he couldn't run far, even if he tried to make a break for it. Looking at his filthy feet, Claudia suspected his boots could outrun him, in any case.

'*You?*' Moschus jumped to his feet. A hand on his shoulder from Claudia's bodyguard reseated him firmly.

'Really, Captain, that's no way to greet the woman who broke you out of jail.'

'If you'd been doing me a favour, I wouldn't be trussed up like a bleedin' chicken. What d'yer want?'

'I see you're prepared to dispense with the small talk,' Claudia said. 'A man after my own heart.' Indeed, judging by the snarl on his face, he'd like to claw it out with his bare hands, given the chance. 'But since you ask, I thought it was obvious. I want my five thousand back.'

'I ain't got yer five—'

'Before you say anything you might regret—' Claudia snapped her fingers and three men entered the storeroom. 'I'd like to introduce you to Beno.'

She beckoned forward a rugged individual whose left socket was sewn over. Unlike Philip of Macedon, Beno hadn't lost his in battle when it got pierced by an arrow. He'd fallen down drunk and hit his head on the corner of a stone step, and he was no warrior, either. He stoked the fires in Claudia's boiler house, although she saw no reason to draw Moschus's attention to that.

'His friend, Atticus—' She waved forward a giant, six feet six, broad as a barn, with a grin as wide as the Caspian Sea. '—is better known as Hatchet Atti,' she said blithely, forgetting to add that Atticus had the mind of a nine-year-old. 'And the third member of the trio is Tiro. You might

218

know him by his nickname? The Butcher of Brindisi?'

Tiro curled half a lip and Moschus recoiled on his chair. He hadn't heard of any Butcher of Brindisi, but he didn't like the look of those dark red, rusty stains round the hilt of Tiro's knife.

'Right then.' Claudia rubbed her hands briskly. 'What was it you were going to tell me about my five thousand sesterces?'

Marcus Cornelius Orbilio had had a brainwave.

Although he could see the logic of Dymas's argument, that the more they talked to the victims the more they might learn about the rapist, he would have preferred to divert resources into questioning witnesses. People who lived or worked near where the attacks had taken place and who might have seen something, even though they hadn't necessarily understood its significance at the time. Talking to the victims' neighbours and friends, asking whether they had noticed anything unusual, because the rapist had clearly stalked his victims. Knew enough about their movements to know when, and where, to strike. Had it been him in charge, he would be talking to the hot-food vendor's wife and her family.

More than merely channelling resources in different directions, though, Marcus felt it was morally reprehensible to pressurize Deva by questioning her again so soon. Had he honestly thought it would advance the investigation, he would have had no hesitation, but forcing answers from a girl who'd retreated into herself would severely damage her chance of recovery.

But Orbilio's methods were not Dymas's methods and, if nothing else, these last few days had shown him that the surly Greek was far more ambitious than he'd given him credit for. Today he'd shown no signs of wanting input from his patrician colleague, and if that was how he wanted to play it, going solo and getting all the credit, then so be it.

Just remember that two can play at that game!

Conspiring against the Security Police wasn't exactly the career move Marcus had envisaged, but either a man had principles or he hadn't. They could drum him out of the force and he would still bring this bastard to justice and so, without a word to anyone, Orbilio had arranged for Claudia's house to be put under twenty-four-hour surveillance. If the rapist was one of the Spectaculars (as he was beginning to suspect, given Claudia's strange behaviour), then by heaven the monster had claimed his very last victim. Marcus was lucky enough in that he could afford to hire private surveillance teams, but thwarting the rapist wasn't the source of his brainwave.

Demotion meant there was nothing he could do to prevent Dymas from questioning Deva. *Providing Dymas could find her.*

'This is strictly between ourselves,' he told the herbalist. 'I'll send a covered litter to collect you. You can stay at my house for as long as you like.'

Deva and the herbalist might as well make use of the servants, enjoy full central heating, an indoor sunken bath, good food and vintage wines. Hardly the Saturnalia the Damascan girl would have wanted, he knew, but at least she could recover at her own pace and he had left strict instructions with his steward not to let Dymas inside.

'This is extremely kind of you,' the herbalist said thickly.

Kind? Marcus felt a lump form in his throat. Had it not been for his incompetence, Deva wouldn't be in this state. Neither would four other girls—

'I don't know how to thank you.'

'I do,' Marcus said, smiling. 'Appoint me godfather of your first child.'

Thirty-One

Orbilio had still not returned home, but coincidentally several large muscular types had appeared in Claudia's street and stationed themselves on various corners, trying for all the world to blend in as locals and ending up looking – well, like large muscular types. It could be the linen merchant was taking no chances with his money box for Saturnalia. Then again, Claudia wouldn't bet her life on it.

Moschus had gone. Very soon he would realize that he'd been conned, but at the time he was too terrified to do more than answer Claudia's questions. Jail for a sailor used to wide-open seas was the ultimate terror. Especially for one who had, as Orbilio very conveniently pointed out, a low threshold of pain. Put the two together and Moschus had been putty in Claudia's hands.

Getting her five thousand sesterces back was easy. After leaving Claudia in the Temple of Portunus, Moschus had merely transferred the funds within the temple depository, with a view to collecting them later and with his misfortune of being picked up by the Security Police within hours, he'd had no chance to return. Moschus had been a tad reluctant when it came to disclosing the precise location of the receipts which would redeem her money, but then the Butcher of Brindisi began to strop his blood-encrusted knife, and of course Moschus didn't know the blood came from skinning rabbits for the stewpot. After that, he became very accommodating, because Claudia had needed more from the good captain than her money back.

Moschus and Butico had to be partners in this shipwreck scam, and you could bet your bottom quadran that Claudia wasn't the first person they'd conned. No doubt the deal was that Moschus got to keep the profits of the fraudulent wreck, while Butico made his money from his extortionate thirty-two per cent interest, knowing only desperation would drive people to embark upon a criminal course in the first place. After that, he'd have them for life, sucking them drier and drier until they shrivelled like raisins. Bastard.

Conclusive proof of their collaboration, were it needed, was the involvement by the Guild of Wine Merchants. Clearly one of their members knew about the scam and passed the information on to his brothers, knowing that if penury didn't force Claudia Seferius out of business, then exile on some scrubby island would. She really, really hoped they'd paid Butico a humungous amount of money for this. As much as she despised the moneylender, she despised the Guild even more. How sublime, that moment when they realized that they'd shelled out huge sums for nothing!

And so, for that reason, Claudia had needed more from Captain Moschus than her five thousand bronze sesterces. She'd pumped him for details of all his previous transactions with Butico and he, of course, with three goons standing over him, sang like a lark over a wheatfield.

A small matter, then, of paying Butico a visit.

'The deal is straightforward,' she told him. 'One, you forget you've ever seen me. Two, you give me your solemn oath that my body won't be found in some dark alleyway with its throat cut, because if anything nasty happens to me, there's a box that goes straight to the Security Police containing Moschus's confession. And three, I shall, of course, require the name of the wine merchant who hired you.'

From his considerable height, Butico stared down at her for several seconds and this time she returned his gaze quite steadily.

'The Guild were foolish to underestimate you, my dear,' and maybe it was the lamplight, but Claudia could have sworn she caught a slight twinkle in his cold, implacable stare. 'As, I'm beginning to think, was I.'

Which was nothing to what Moschus was thinking. Butico had undoubtedly ridden rougher seas than these, although it was unlikely the captain would, once Butico caught up with him. His chilling words floated back to her. *No one gets away from me*, he had said. *No one*. The seas might be closed, but one ship would certainly try battling them this winter and the *Artemis* would have to change more than her name and the colour of her canvas this time.

'There's one final piece of information I need from you, Butico. The addresses of your two burly henchmen.'

Revenge on the scum from the slum was Claudia's Saturnalia present to herself!

It was dark, but not late, when Orbilio wove his way through the crush and up the Esquiline to check on Deva. More than any of the others, he felt personal anguish for the young Damascan girl. Perhaps it was because the attack had happened on her seventeenth birthday, perhaps it was because he had struck up an acquaintanceship with the herbalist last summer, just when he and Deva had moved in together. Marcus didn't know. All that mattered was that they got through this ordeal. Somehow.

Mid-December, of course, there was inevitably a bite in the air, but the drizzle had gone and although clouds still hung low over the hills, they were altogether much lighter, brighter and whiter. The kind that, one never knows, might suddenly part to admit blue skies and sunshine. The wind had gone, too. And with tomorrow being Saturnalia Eve, the whole city resounded with laughter and joy. So much holly and fir was decking the houses, it was a wonder there was any greenery left in the forest, and down on the Colonnade of the Argonauts, the Saturnalia market buzzed like a beehive as people shopped for gifts of candles and dolls, sipping spiced wine from street vendors as they browsed, munching on hot sausages and slices of wild boar hot from the spit roast.

Orbilio hadn't eaten, and the smells from the taverns made his stomach growl, although he was unaware of the rumbles. It frustrated him that, thanks to Dymas diverting him away from the rapes to sort out that domestic killing down in the Subura and rounding up the counterfeit dole gang, he was no closer to getting this beast off the streets. His head pounded. It made him physically sick that another girl would soon be enduring the worst ordeal imaginable and that her life would be ruined because of him cocking up and sending the wrong man to die for a crime he hadn't committed—

Evil. Many times Marcus had pondered the meaning of the word. Many times he had seen it made flesh. But the Halcyon Rapist's savage depravity brought a new dimension to the word.

A pain stabbed at him behind the eyes.

When he chose to forgo a lucrative career in law in favour of the dark underbelly of society, he'd realized it would mean shouldering a huge responsibility. Like the judiciary, he knew he wouldn't be able to win every case, but, until now, he hadn't realized how big a burden he would have to carry. Or that he would be shouldering it for the rest of his life . . .

The acrid smell of smoke prickled his nostrils. Shouts in the next street. Another fire, he thought wearily. More families with no roof over their heads, salvaging whatever possessions they could. At least up here, in the patrician quarter of the city, it would be an isolated fire. An artisan's workshop, perhaps, or a bookseller's premises. Down in the populous areas, such as the Subura, where he'd just come from, where families were crowded together in six-storey apartment blocks, or packed into the slums, the fire would be far more damaging.

He turned the corner, saw buckets of water being fetched in a line. His own street. Orbilio clucked his tongue in sympathy. He couldn't help this time. Unfortunate if a neighbour had been burned out at Saturnalia, but he had promised the herbalist that Deva could stay as long as she liked and she had to have privacy. The consolation, he supposed, was that at least people around here could afford to rebuild and repair. Those poor creatures in the slums and the artisan quarters were all but ruined. Darting between two slopping leather buckets, it was at the back of his mind that he was glad there was no wind tonight to fan the flames. Why, they were so close, it could well have been his house that—

It was his house.

Breaking into a run, he barged through the crowd that had gathered to gawp. Mother of Tarquin, his atrium! It was blacker than Hades, and swimming with a viscous black sludge. Choking black smoke streamed out of every doorway, oily and sour, and he could hardly see his own hand in front of his face. Damping his handkerchief in what was left of the atrium pool, he covered his nose and mouth.

'Sir? Is that you, sir?' The voice of his steward, hoarse from the smoke, called from somewhere in front. He realized that, in his white toga, he must stand out like a barn owl.

'What happened?' he asked. 'Is anyone hurt?'

Janus. *Deva!* How much more could the girl take? As the last of the flames were extinguished, he flung open whatever doors and windows he could to distribute the smoke into the night.

'No, sir, no casualties.' But the steward's lungs were in such a state from breathing the acrid air that, when he wasn't wheezing like a pair of rusty bellows, he was wracking his ribs with the cough. Orbilio immediately sent him outside. If he wanted to help, better that he thanked the fire chain who had rushed to their rescue. It took him a moment or two before he realized that there was someone else stumbling around in the blackness, helping to fling open the shutters.

'You lead an interesting life,' the herbalist said.

'This is only Saturnalia. You should see what happens when we celebrate birthdays,' Orbilio said. 'How's Deva?'

'I think it's no exaggeration to say the fire was a distraction.'

'Is that why you started it?'

There was a flash of a grin from the corner. 'Had I thought it would have worked, I'd have burned down the city, but no. I'm afraid I didn't pay the young lady.'

'Excuse me?' Orbilio found a candle and lit it.

'Little blonde thing. Very pretty, as far as tornadoes go. Your toga is ruined, by the way.'

'And your face is blacker than a Nubian's arse. What blonde— oh shit.'

Angelina! The candle began shaking in Marcus's hand, so the herbalist took it.

'If you want my professional opinion,' he said, 'your pixie is two strigils short of a bathhouse.'

He and Deva had only been here three hours, he explained. Three good hours at that. The opiate was already wearing off when they arrived and rather than tell her the blunt truth of why they had decamped to this exquisite house on the Esquiline Hill, the herbalist had explained this was the Emperor's treat.

'I'm sorry about that,' he said miserably. 'I'll own up when she's better. Make sure you take the credit—'

Orbilio grinned. 'Yes, I can see how that will impress her. Telling her you lied when she was at her most vulnerable!'

The herbalist smiled back. 'Oh, well. Since you put it like that ... Anyway, I wouldn't say she was perky, but coming here was a turning point. Deva suddenly realized that she wasn't alone in her torment.' His voice became ragged, and not from the smoke. 'That other people, rich, influential people, acknowledged the seriousness of the crime – and felt compassion.'

He had even got her to eat something. A few delicacies. Things she'd only seen from afar, that they'd never been able to afford.

'I sat with her until she fell asleep.' He pointed to what had been the master bedroom. 'I— I just needed some air, you know?'

It haunted him that he should have walked round the courtyard, rather than leave, but god knows, he had needed some space to himself. So he'd taken himself off to the public gardens, to think and to mourn, to rage and to grieve, and when he came back, a young woman with a froth of honey-coloured curls was throwing oil at flaming drapes. The herbalist cast a wry glance at his host.

'I am, of course, assuming this *was* Miss Four-Times-A-Night you referred to the other evening?'

'No, I have this effect on all women.'

The smile on the herbalist's lips froze. He wiped a sooty face with a sooty hand and shook his head. 'I'm responsible for your lovely home being destroyed,' he said. 'If I'd been here—'

'Then Angelina would have come back some other time.'

'Perhaps.' He shrugged, unconvinced, as Orbilio took the candle back and held it high to inspect the pixie's handi-work. It was a mess, certainly. But nothing that could not be put right.

'No structural damage, thank heavens,' Marcus said, adding, 'Hell hath no fury like a woman scorned.'

'That's the trouble with delusions,' the herbalist sighed. 'That's all they are. The only way your pixie can protect herself from a complete mental breakdown when the fantasy is exposed is to eradicate the source. Once it no longer exists, you see, it is as though it never happened. She has wiped it clean from her mind.'

'She thought I'd supplanted you,' a female voice said.

227

Both men spun round. In the doorway to the garden, shivering from the cold, Deva stood in her night robe. Orbilio thrust his toga round her shoulders, the herbalist rubbed her warm.

'Darling, I told you to stay in the kitchens. You're freezing.'

'Am I?' She hadn't noticed. Her eyes were scanning the destruction.

'I'll take you home,' he said gently.

'You will not!' Deva pulled the wool tight around her. 'The Emperor said I could stay here for Saturnalia, and stay here I damn well will!'

Behind her back, both men exchanged smiles. There was no sign of the red shawl.

She scowled at the walls, the floor, the ceiling. 'She's not getting away with it,' she spat. 'She can't just barge in here and overturn the oil lamps then walk away.'

Angry eyes turned on Marcus.

'She has to be made to understand! She can't go around spoiling things out of spite. It's not right, leaving people's lives in ruins and not paying the price.'

She swung round to face her man. 'I'm not going home. I'm going to wash these walls and scrub these floors until they sparkle like new.' She picked up a marble statuette and polished it on Orbilio's toga. 'That bitch is not going to beat me,' she hissed.

With a tingle running the length of his backbone, Marcus realized that her tirade wasn't aimed at Angelina. This was Deva's way of getting back at the rapist. Of telling him that he could do what he liked with her body but her spirit could not be broken. The herbalist's woman was fighting back, she was saying. *And she would win—*

Replacing the statuette on the table, which she had also wiped clean on Orbilio's toga, she turned to the herbalist.

'Why on earth are you crying?' she asked. 'It's only a bit of wool, love. It'll bleach out.'

Thirty-Two

'Skyles! A word!'

The dress rehearsal was already underway, but Claudia didn't care. What she wanted to say couldn't wait, and in any case it shouldn't take longer than Felix's balletic mime.

'Shut the door.'

He made an exaggerated show of closing the door to her office, but she was sick of the act-act-act, pretend-pretend-pretend style of this actor with no name and no past.

'Flavia,' she said crisply.

'You weren't kidding when you said you only wanted one word.'

It would have been easier, this conversation, if he'd been dressed in the Buffoon's brightly coloured patchwork, a razzle-dazzle juxtaposition of reds and yellows, oranges and blues. Instead, his first skit was impersonating the Emperor and he remained in character. Dignified and majestic in purple, with a cropped wig and laurel crown, he took a seat in a high-backed upholstered chair, crossing one stately leg over the other.

'You took her to a hotel,' Claudia said.

One noble eyebrow rose languidly. 'As I said before, Livia wants to keep his mouth shut.'

'If it hadn't been for Doris, you irresponsible bastard, we'd have been out of our minds looking for Flavia! Where did you take her?'

One imperial shoulder shrugged. 'How could I afford

hotels?' he asked. 'Me, who hasn't two copper quadrans to rub together, and you can search me, if you don't believe me.'

'I didn't ask how much.' Typical. She even pays to lose her virginity! 'I asked where? Hold on a moment—' She flung open the office door. 'Leonides, did I just hear someone come in?'

'No, madam. That was a cask falling over in the kitchen.'

'Orbilio isn't back yet?'

Leonides shook his head. Damn. She'd left strict instructions at his house to call here as a matter of urgency. She'd even said it was concerning the rapist. Which meant he hadn't called there, either. Double damn.

'The instant he sets foot indoors, then?' she reminded Leonides.

Across the atrium, Helen of Troy was doing her utmost to convince Paris that *she* was the most beautiful woman in the world and worthy of the prized golden apple. Time to cut to the chase.

'How much do you want?' she asked Skyles.

The intensity in his eyes darkened. 'I thought I'd made that point clear. I never take money from ladies.'

'I'm no lady. How much will it cost to keep you away from Flavia?'

Puzzlement swept his face. Claudia didn't think he was a good enough actor to fake it. 'Are you serious?' he asked, his eyes narrowing. 'Is she really missing?'

The word 'missing' made Claudia's heart skip a beat.

'Her bed wasn't slept in and she hasn't been seen since the dress rehearsal last night, when she sat gooey-eyed following your every movement.'

Another time and he would have smiled and said, '*Every* movement?' Now he swore, a four-letter word rhyming with duck, and the Imperial impersonation popped like a bubble.

He didn't like to say anything, he said, because he hadn't wanted to get the poor kid into trouble. But last night, after the rehearsal, Flavia had rushed up to him, told him in an excited whisper that she'd booked them a room in a hotel near the Capena Gate, that she'd wait for him there, and that she loved him and was going to marry him and have his babies.

'I had no idea,' he said, spreading his hands. 'I mean, I wanted the kid to have a good time. I took her to a few grown-up places, a cock fight, stuff like that, and I made her laugh, flirted a bit—'

'A *bit*?'

'All right, more than a bit, but come on, you've seen her parents. No wonder she's mixed-up and repressed.' He ran his hand over his shaven head. 'That kid's not like Jemima or Adah, who eat because they enjoy food and thus life. Flavia's fat because the food she stuffs in her mouth is a substitute for love and affection.'

Claudia felt a pang of something that might have been guilt.

'I admit I opened her eyes to another world, showed her a side of life that was shocking and exciting to someone her age, but never in a million years did I think she'd read so much into one afternoon touring the fleshpots of Rome plus a few odd winks on the side.'

Flashes of imitation wedding bouquets flashed through Claudia's mind. Of Flavia pouncing on this blessing of her engagement to Skyles. 'What happened?' she asked.

Outside, Periander was singing about Paris's dilemma. Which of the three should receive the apple engraved 'To the Fairest'?

'I told her I couldn't *go* to the hotel. I explained about the script conference and the rewrites that were necessary after rehearsals and thought, hell, that would be that. "But you have to sleep some time," she said. "And it doesn't matter what time, day or night, you come to me, I'll be waiting." Oh.' He flashed her a grin. 'I think she called me "darling" as well.'

Outside, Paris had made his judgment. He'd awarded the apple to Venus and now, in angelic soprano, Periander sang of the irony of that decision. How Venus would make Helen of Troy fall in love with him, starting the war to end all wars . . .

Claudia waited.

'In the end, I realized I had no choice. I had to go to the tavern and tell the poor kid the truth.'

'What is the truth, Skyles?'

'That she's too young. Obviously.'

'Yes, and she's too fat, and she's spotty, and awkward, and silly, but Flavia will grow into herself, and her age isn't the reason you didn't sleep with her.'

'Hey, I don't go around deflowering virgins—'

'I know. You go for married women with no strings attached, you shallow bastard.' She leaned forward into his face. 'You'll take sex, provided it comes without emotion.'

'What I do is my business.'

'Not where my stepdaughter's concerned.'

The last haunting notes of Renata's flute died away.

'I have to go,' Skyles said.

He covered the room in three strides, a blur of imperial purple, and as he did, other images flashed through Claudia's mind. A bald Buffoon chasing the kitchen girls, riding make-believe horses round the garden to amuse the children, slapping his head like an ape, tripping over imaginary ropes, caressing Erinna's shadow, mimicking Leonides, the cook and anyone else. Act, act, act. Pretend, pretend, pretend. But running through this round-the-clock performance ran the constant thread of the entertainer. A man who wants to make people like him. Tell me, are those the actions of a man who is shallow?

'One more thing. That wound on your side.'

'Cramp.'

Yes, and I'm Pegasus and I can fly. 'How did you get it?'

The intensity of his eyes burned through to the back of

her skull. 'That's also my business,' he rasped.

The draught from the slamming of the door was reminiscent of the draught from the front door in the early hours. Skyles might have sneaked out this morning, Claudia thought. But Juno be praised, neither he, nor anyone else, would be sneaking out for a while. Her bodyguards had the house sealed.

Dammit, Orbilio, where the hell are you? I can't cope with this by myself.

In a grim little room in an overcrowded hostelry close to the Capena Gate, Flavia snivelled into her pillow. Unlike the pillows at home, it wasn't stuffed with soft swansdown, it was lumpy and dirty and she could swear she'd seen something move. She hated this horrible place. She hated Skyles, and her aunt, and her uncle, she hated them all.

No, she didn't. She loved Skyles.

No, she didn't. She hated him. It was spiteful and cruel to lead her on, pretend he'd fallen in love with her.

No, he hadn't. He hadn't said or done anything. It was her.

No, it wasn't. It was Julia, the frigid old cow. She never let Flavia out of her sight. Never let her have any fun. Only Claudia understood how she felt. She'd sent her blessing for the marriage with Skyles.

No, she hadn't. Bitch. It was sarcasm, that's what it was. She didn't mean a bloody word. That was Claudia being horrid, as usual.

No, she wasn't. Claudia didn't sit at home, like other women, dependent on men. She stuck two fingers up to convention, forged her own path through life, and stuff anyone else.

Flavia turned the soggy pillow over and sobbed some more. She couldn't go home for the shame, and she couldn't stay here, and it was Saturnalia Eve tomorrow, and she hadn't bought any presents.

And that *was* something black wriggling around under the bolster.

Having confronted the brutal truth, that she had been violated and abused and that it was for real, Deva's body collapsed as quickly as her mind had done, when it had tried to block the attack out. The herbalist's tears had triggered a series of cold sweats and uncontrollable shaking, a reaction her man had strangely pronounced to Orbilio to be a good sign.

'These are symptoms I can treat,' he said confidently.

Between them, they carried her to the remaining habitable guest room, where the herbalist covered her with blankets and raised her feet. 'And no poppy juice,' he told Marcus firmly, adding that he felt bad that it had taken an arsonist to bring Deva out of her trance.

'A small price to pay,' Orbilio told him, and meant it.

Aired, warmed and scented with lavender, you wouldn't know there had been a fire in this room. The gilded stucco on the ceiling glittered in the light of the flickering lamp stand, and the frescoes on the wall might have been painted last week. On the bronze couch, under a pile of soft blankets and with a pale green damascene coverlet on top, Deva looked twelve years old. The herbalist ran the back of his finger lovingly down her cheek. His own face and his clothes were still black with soot and he left a dark smudge on her skin.

Marcus watched the rapid rise and fall of the covers. Stared at the white, waxy face on the pillow. The fringe plastered to her forehead with sweat. And thought of the cordon around Claudia's house.

'If you need me, my steward knows where to find me,' he said, but that only led to another problem.

'Oh, no!' The steward buried his head in his hands when his master passed on the instructions. 'With the fire, I completely forgot, sir. Mistress Seferius.'

'What about her?' Orbilio asked.

'She sent word that you were to go to her house imme-diately. She had urgent news about the Halcyon Rapist.'

Shit. 'When was this?'

The steward stared at his sludge-sodden boots. 'Four hours ago,' he said dully.

Orbilio didn't have time to change. He didn't have a clean toga to change into, even if he'd wanted. His clothes chests were ruined, the contents contaminated, in the end he'd had to scrounge a cloak from the porter. Nor did he care that his face was streaked black or that his hair was thick with soot as he sliced his way through the crowds of Saturnalia revellers. He wondered what she'd found that was so urgent. What she would think, another girl he'd let down—

He was barely two hundred yards from his house when a small figure darted out of the shadows.

'How dare you be unfaithful!' Angelina hissed. 'You belong with *me*, no one else.'

Two strigils short of a bathhouse, the herbalist had pronounced. That had to be the understatement of the decade. The girl was nuts. Pistachio, pine, hazel and walnut, every kind you could imagine. He drew a deep breath and turned to face her.

'It does me no credit to admit this, Angelina.' He drew her by the elbow into the doorway of a shuttered silver-smith's shop, out of the main thoroughfare. 'The only reason I approached you after that dinner party was because I was drunk and thought it might lead to sex, and that, I'm afraid, is the truth.'

'Who cares how relationships start—'

'Angelina, listen to me. I'm really sorry, but you have to accept the fact, even if you hadn't drugged me, it would never have been more than a one-night stand.'

How could he ever have thought of this demented vixen as a pixie?

'Just because I'm lowborn and you're an aristocrat doesn't mean we can't see each other, Marcus. I don't expect you to marry me, darling—'

'*Marry* you? Angelina, I don't know you, I don't like you, I don't want anything to do with you. How much clearer can I make this?'

'But you will, Marcus. Given time, I know you'll fall in love with me!'

'Mother of Tarquin, woman, you burn my house down, endanger the lives of a lot of good people and then expect me to fall in love with you? Exactly which part of the word "no" don't you understand?'

As he spun round to leave, he saw a flash of bright steel in her hand. It was something he hadn't expected. Hadn't been prepared for. Although it was, he realized too late, inevitable.

The only way she can protect herself from a complete mental breakdown is to eradicate the source of the fantasy. Once it no longer exists, it is as though it never happened.

What a fool. What an absolute fool. Orbilio was the fantasy. Not the house.

Even as he understood, he felt the blade plunge into his flesh. Heard a strange ripping sound. Felt a burning pain shoot down his side.

'Angelina—'

As he slipped down on to the cobbles, his vision started to blur. His hands were covered in something hot and sticky and he thought, Croesus. Now Callisunus really *will* think I'm the Halcyon Rapist. I've got the bloody knife wound to prove it.

As the blackness finally swallowed him up, it occurred to Marcus Cornelius that he knew now who the rapist was. What a ridiculous time to find out.

For a farce that hadn't been born a week before, Caspar had created a tour de force with *The Cuckold*. True, it was a patchwork of old scripts and ancient gags set to a back-drop of familiar songs and set pieces, but there was a fresh-ness about the way the play had been cobbled together that gave it a vitality all of its own.

Doris made a surprisingly good Miser. Thin and sinuous, he was perfect for all that agonized hand-wringing and coin-counting, and his throwing in the odd feminine gesture when the Soldier came on only added to the humour.

Ugly Phil hadn't been warned that his cloven hoofs had been greased to make him slip, but the thick wad of furry padding broke his fall. The only injuries there, Claudia thought, would come from tomorrow's audience splitting their sides.

Caspar's eye patch glittered in fierce competition with his dazzling kaftan and bejewelled feathered turban, and no one could ever accuse the Narrator of blending in with the background. Half his lines he made up as he went along, a complete switch from last night's performance, but the cast fitted in with his ad-libbing, their confusion only adding to the hilarity.

Whether Ion remained in a foul mood or not, Claudia couldn't tell. Ever the professional, he put personal issues aside and boomed out his Jupiter to comic perfection, looking handsome and god-like and every inch the show's heartthrob.

He wasn't, of course. The bald-headed Buffoon stole every scene as well as every heart.

The girls were terrific. Jemima, that arch-exhibitionist, decided to lift her robe to examine the mark where Cupid's arrow had hit her bottom and Adah, despite her whingeing, made a lasting impression on the audience, being the first nude of the show. She wasn't the last. Fenja performed a statuesque striptease for the man she believed was the Poet, but who turned out to be the Satyr wearing a mask, and the point in the play where it fell off was one of the funniest, especially since he had one limp horn.

Not that Claudia could concentrate. She'd staged the Spectaculars to suck up to buyers and steal a march on the Guild. How petty and irrelevant that all seemed now. Yet tomorrow, the first of many potential clients would be taking their seats in this hall and she must smile and laugh and be witty, she must look ravishing and desirable, the perfect hostess, and they must leave thrilled, sated and won over.

Never before had she had so much respect for actors for whom the show, above everything, must go on . . .

Eventually, though, the confusion about the identical twins was resolved. Cupid's arrows hit their targets, albeit wrong ones, and Periander even threw in an ad-lib himself by firing one at the Narrator. Happy endings all round, clap, clap, clap. The Wife had run off with her Lover and got to keep all the money. The Miser fell in love with himself. The Virgin remained virginal. Jupiter duly went back up to Olympus, removing Hermione's clothes as the platform was winched up.

Claudia shook her head. Impossible that any member of this troupe could be a monster. Quite impossible.

In a gesture reminiscent of the incident in the Alban Hills, the Digger mopped up the sweat with a cloth. Everyone was laughing, the Digger included. The rush of adrenaline after a show, especially when it went well, was amazing. Indescribable. The feeling of unity among the company closer than family ties.

The Digger knew this euphoria could not last.

That this feeling of contentment was a mirage.

Soon, there would be more blood spilled. Very soon.

The Digger prayed to Hercules for the strength to put off the inevitability for as long as humanly possible.

Thirty-Three

Butico's two henchmen, Balven and Armenius, lodged in adjoining rooms over a tavern in what could only be described as a rough part of town. Stabbings in this dock-side quarter were routine. For money, for vengeance, for fun, who the hell knows? Bodies regularly rolled into the Tiber, no questions asked.

The tavern itself was long overdue demolition, the air round it rancid with river smells, rotting refuse, stale urine, vomit and smoke. Raddled whores lifted their skirts against the wall for no more than a goblet of cheap wine while, inside, the stench of long-unwashed bodies mingled with the smell of the greasy grey stew that bubbled away in the cauldron, and drunken laughter rattled the beams.

Claudia's revenge on the scum from the slum had been easy and quick to arrange, requiring just one call on her old friend, Lulu. Sweeter still was the speed with which her plan was able to swing into effect.

'Hello?' The door to the rowdy tavern opened tentatively, and a pouting youth wearing rouge on his cheeks and kohl round his eyes popped his head through. 'Is Armenius here?'

He was not, of course. Claudia had had Butico call his henchman away as part of the deal.

'No?' The boy put one long finger to unnaturally red lips. 'Oh.' He minced into a room which had fallen silent in shock and pouted some more. 'Well, look. When he comes back, can you give him a message? Tell him I won't be able to meet him at Lulu's tonight after all.'

Lulu was a six-foot-two retired gladiator, famous for his double thrust and parries in the arena, and for running a string of pretty rent boys near the Forum. He also ran an infamous male brothel off Tuscan Street that specialized in sado-masochism.

'I've got to visit my auntie, she's sick,' he said, adding brightly, 'But you can tell him I'll be there tomorrow, as usual.'

He blew a kiss to his astonished audience and departed, chucking a burly stevedore under the chin as he passed. Another time and they'd have had a field day with the lad. Tonight they couldn't believe it.

'*Armenius?*'

'It's a wind-up,' someone with a scar said. 'Innit?'

They weren't sure. Hadn't Armenius come home nursing a head wound the other day, and refused to say how he got it?

'Nah.' After an hour's discussion, they dismissed it. A wind-up. Someone having a joke.

But the next stranger was neither effeminate nor pretty, and he had to duck to get under the lintel. 'Where is he, the fat bastard?' He strode across to the stairs. 'Oi, Balven! You up there?'

He grabbed the tavern keeper by his tunic and glowered into his face. In a world where might is undeniably right, a lot of drinkers noticed how easily he lifted the tavern keeper off the ground and decided to make themselves scarce. If they wanted trouble, they made it themselves.

Besides, his face looked kind of familiar . . .

'Where's Balven, you little shit?'

'Out.'

'Yeah?' The giant shook the tavern keeper like a doll. 'Where?'

'I d–don't know. He doesn't t–tell me where he goes.'

The giant dropped his charge.

'Well, tell him when he comes back, he owes me money.' He pulled a shining scimitar out of its sheath and held it against the tavern keeper's throat. 'And you can remind him what happens when Lulu doesn't get paid.'

Lulu! The gladiator with the string of pretty rent boys who runs the bawdy house off Tuscan Street!

'You c–can rely on me,' the tavern keeper croaked. 'G–gods' honour.'

'Good.' Lulu sheathed his scimitar. 'Oh, yeah. One other thing.'

He drew out a floaty female undergarment from inside his jerkin.

'Remind the scatterbrained berk not to leave his knickers behind next time.'

'Leonides.'

Claudia thought she'd wear out the mosaic in her office from pacing.

'Leonides, when Orbilio comes back, give him this.'

She'd toyed with the idea of summarizing on parchment her visits to the three victims who had been able to irrefutably identify the rapist. Precis the main points as to why she'd come to the conclusion she had, and the evidence she had to support it. In the end, she wrote just one word on the wax tablet. The bastard's name.

'Immediately,' she added.

'I understand, madam.'

Leonides would not let her down. Never had. But to be on the safe side, she'd left another note in Orbilio's room and sent a messenger to his house. There was nothing more she could do, and she had gnawed her fingernails to her elbows wondering where he could have got to. Suppose he'd arrested another false suspect? It would destroy him. What if Deva, or one of the other victims, had been pushed over the edge by further interrogation? That would destroy him, as well.

Marcus, Marcus, where the devil are you? Why don't you come home?

Home?

The word brought a pain to her stomach. This wasn't his home. Never would be. He might have made himself *at home* here, but that would be part of the softening process, using the rapist as a pretext for another case, two birds with one criminal stone. Originally, he'd used her as bait to hook Butico, but with his star witness mysteriously missing, a fraud was a fraud was a fraud. Never underestimate the power of results when a man wants a seat in the Senate. Seeing Cupid's arrows hit all the wrong targets had done nothing to make her feel better.

'Are you wise to go out this late, madam?' Leonides asked mildly, even though he knew he was wasting his breath. Wisdom and Claudia were not soulmates. But as he raised his hand to summon his mistress's bodyguard, Claudia stopped him.

'They stay where they are,' she insisted. 'Inside, guarding the exits.'

The colour drained from her steward's face. 'You can't go out *alone*.'

'Silly me, Leonides. I thought I was the one who decided who could and who couldn't do what in this house. Hand me my wrap.' She waited. And waited a little bit longer. 'Leonides,' she warned.

Besides. She wouldn't be alone. Unless she missed her guess, a couple of large muscular types would prise themselves away from the walls where they were pretending to blend in with their surroundings and would follow. That was one good thing about the Security Police, she reflected, pulling her furs tight round her chin. You can always rely on one or the other of them to be on your tail.

'Mind if I walk part of the way with you?' Erinna asked. 'Only since we're performing on Saturnalia Eve, I'd like to soak up at least some of the festive atmosphere.'

Claudia was glad of the company. She had no particular destination in mind. Just felt caged indoors, waiting for footsteps that didn't come, knowing that merely a few hours stood between now and daybreak, and – if her conclusions were wrong – another young woman's life ruined. Beside her, Erinna said nothing and Claudia wasn't surprised. Performances like that were utterly draining.

Sure enough, as they left, two strapping ex-army veterans down the street exchanged glances and casually ambled their way down the hill behind the two women, pausing, as they paused, to watch pantalooned fire-eaters perform on the corner. Stopping, as they stopped, while Persian acrobats tumbled and twisted their way down the thoroughfare, skirting riders on horseback and hoarse-throated beggars with ease.

Claudia noted her followers and relaxed. Good old Marcus.

The closer they drew to the Forum, the more incense wafted from open-air shrines. Young blades in their finery swaggered to catch the eyes of promenading maidens with chaplets woven into their hair, a bear danced to the tune from a lyre, cats wailed from the rooftops. On the steps of the Temple of the Divine Julius, conjurors produced rabbits out of felt hats to a shower of coins, and outside the basilica a black man juggled terracotta plates as he danced.

'That was fun,' Erinna said, as they eventually turned to make their way home. It was approaching midnight, and she had freed her long mane of chestnut hair from its bun to hang down her back, shining like a stallion in the light of the torches which burned from sconces set in the walls.

'Why don't you tell Skyles you love him?' Claudia asked.

Erinna stopped short. 'Me? Skyles? That's the most ridiculous thing I've heard this year,' she snapped. 'I've not even been alone with him.'

'Yes,' Claudia said. 'That's what puzzles me.'

Down Pomegranate Lane, the road that led home, a covered dray cart was blocking the street. Shouts of the drivers jammed up behind drowned any chance to talk further and Claudia and Erinna slipped down the parallel lane, Pepper

Alley. Neither noticed that, as their protectors turned into the lane behind them, two cudgels landed blows from a doorway.

The driver of the dray cart geed up his mules. It turned out of Pomegranate Lane and stopped again at the end of Pepper Alley.

Claudia glanced over her shoulder. Strangely, this passageway was completely deserted, and it was oddly reassuring for once that Orbilio's two Security Policemen were behind.

'Erinna,' she began.

Two hulking figures stepped out of the shadows.

'Quick,' she said, spinning Erinna round. 'It's a trap. Run!' Together, they hurtled down the alleyway. Behind them, the two men also broke into a run. 'Help,' she called out to Orbilio's men. 'Help!' But the men had stopped, blocking the alley, and now she drew closer, she saw that they were shorter, and uglier, and not the same pair. Two mounds on the cobbles told the story. She turned again, but the first two were closing in fast.

Before either girl had a chance to scream, sacks were flung over their heads.

The driver of the dray cart flipped up the oilskin covering the wagon. Four men and two squirming bundles were hustled inside, the cover quickly flipped closed. The cart moved off at a cracking pace, and the Saturnalia revellers interpreted the shrieks inside as the squeals of lovers having fun, because this was the season of peace and goodwill, and no one's minds were on evil.

Orbilio opened his eyes, and found himself in a room that was both familiar and unfamiliar at the same time. He closed them again, conscious of a throbbing in his head and a terrible ache in his side. Where was he? He remembered walking down his own street when Angelina confronted him. Recalled only too well the knife in her hand. After that, though, he must have passed out. He forced his eyelids apart, and realized that what he was seeing were his own walls and ceiling, but from a totally different angle. He was lying in the guest room where he'd left Deva, and it was at the back of his mind that it was a good place to recover. She'd want for nothing in this house and also, he decided, his taste in decor was better than he'd given himself credit for.

But there was something he had to do, wasn't there? Something urgent? Struggling to sit up, a burning pain splintered his body, tore it in pieces and scattered them to the four winds. He fell back, panting. Sweat poured from his forehead.

'I could have given you something to dull it,' the herbalist said, applying a soothing lavender compress to his temples, 'but it would have knocked you out cold. Under the circumstances, I couldn't allow that.'

Overriding the lavender was a smell that Orbilio recognized from his days in the army. A mixture of mouldy bread, opobalsam, turpentine and vinegar. The unmistakable smell of dressed wounds. Gingerly he prodded the wadding around his waist. It brought him out in a fresh sweat.

'You were lucky,' the herbalist said, replacing the compress. 'If your pixie had stabbed you on your right side, she'd have punctured your liver.'

Lucky, Orbilio thought, was a relative term.

'What circumstances?' he asked.

'Hm.' The herbalist dried his hands on a towel. Propped a pillow under Marcus's head. 'You know I told you that by burning the house down, your pixie was destroying the fantasy? Well, it occurred to me after you left—'

'Yes, I know. The fantasy was me.'

'Precisely. Which is why I came running after you, and just as well that I did.' The herbalist replaced the stopper on a small onyx bottle. 'Just as I was prising the knife out of her hand, a legionary happened to pass by. She's in jail.'

'And you told me you weren't a hero.'

'I must admit I surprised myself,' the herbalist said. 'But

when it comes to saving the world, I think I'll stick to my potions.'

'And Deva?'

'Still alternating between shakes and shivers, but I moved her to your steward's room, because you needed this bed more.'

'Bring her back,' Marcus rasped, swinging his legs off the couch. 'I'm getting up anyway. There's something urgent I have to do.'

'Yes.' The herbalist smoothed his receding red hair. 'I'm afraid there is.'

'We're back to those circumstances again,' Marcus said, as another explosion of pain ripped him to shreds. 'The reason you couldn't—' (not *didn't*) '—give me a sedative.'

'I'm sorry to put you through this, Marcus, but a note came while you were unconscious.' Exhausted hands picked up a scroll of parchment from the table. 'Since your steward said it was connected with the rapist, I took the liberty of opening it. It's from a young woman called Claudia, and on it is written the name of the beast who tried to destroy my Deva.'

'Just the name?'

'Just the name,' the herbalist nodded.

'She always was one for economizing,' Orbilio said, but his smile turned into a grimace as a fireball tore through his stomach. 'I'll have to borrow your cloak,' he told the physician. The porter's was covered with blood.

'Shall I come with you?' the herbalist asked.

'No.' This was for him and him alone.

'But, Marcus!' he called after him, waving the parchment. 'Don't you want to know who it is?'

'I already do,' Orbilio said thickly.

It was Dymas

Squirming in the arms of her attackers under the cover of the dray cart, Claudia experienced the unmistakable stirrings of panic. These were professionals, but who? Butico? No, he wouldn't risk that. Slave traders, then? Wrong time of year. Slave ships operate when the seas are fully open, they need as many escape routes as they can. And in any case they don't snatch women from Rome when there are coasts all round with unprotected villages to raid. Anyway, this was a sophisticated operation which had been planned in advance. They'd followed Claudia from the house. Deliberately blocked Pomegranate Lane, knowing that she would be forced to cut down the adjacent Pepper Alley, which in turn had been turned into a trap. Men had been stationed in readiness to take care of her bodyguard. Pedestrians had been kept out of the alley by some ruse which, being Saturnalia, wouldn't faze them.

The flutterings of panic grew stronger. Her limbs started to quake. She was snatching air in great quivering gulps.

It had to be ransom. Maybe another ploy by the Wine Merchants' Guild to force her hand? Say to the authorities, look: women need men to look after them and protect them, because how can you trust a woman with business, when you can't trust her to look after herself? But the Guild already believed they'd driven her out by ensnaring her in Butico's felonious hands— As the wheels clacked over the cobbles, Claudia heard a faint animal whimper. It took her a moment to realize that the sound came from her. Out, out, she had to get out. With one furious kick, she brought her heel back on the shin of the bear who was holding her. Yelping, he loosened his grip. She pulled the sack from her head with one hand, pushed at the oilskin with the other, saw people, lots of people, laughing and drinking and having fun in the streets.

'Help!' she called, but they didn't hear her. 'Hel—'

She never got time to finish the word. A cudgel caught her square on the side of her head. Somewhere in the distance, as though down a long tunnel, she heard the herald call the first hour. What a way to start Saturnalia Eve.

Thirty-Four

It was all so obvious with hindsight, Orbilio thought.

With his strength ebbing, he had been forced to take a litter and now he cursed the stupidity that caused its perilously slow progress as the bearers forged their way through the jaunty throng. Dammit, he should have predicted Angelina's violent outburst. *Just as he should have understood that Dymas was the Halcyon Rapist.* Tomorrow was the biggest day of most people's year. It would start with the Great Sacrifice, followed by the public feast and concluding with Games, dancing and wine flowing out of the fountains, and people were happy. For a few treasured days, they could put their problems aside and Orbilio had never felt more alone, more isolated, from the community.

Around him, a sea of jovial faces exchanged pleasantries in a score of incomprehensible tongues, the chill in the air nothing to them, as they wished goodwill and happiness to all men. On his cushions, the bonhomie grated. Perhaps it was the wound in his side straining the herbalist's stitches, but somehow the festive atmosphere highlighted his own shortcomings. Drew attention to his failure as an instrument of the law. His head pounded and his eyes could barely focus. An innocent man had been executed. Girls had been dragged off the streets and brutalized. *And all because of him.*

His mind ranged back over the case. Firstly, how information through street contacts had led to Dymas reporting that he had a suspect. But why should he have questioned the honour of his own people? If you can't trust the Security Police, hell, who can you trust? Realistically, how could he have predicted that, when Dymas shouted out that he'd found the mask beneath the suspect's bed, it had been planted by the investigator himself?

No, no, he couldn't allow himself to get off that lightly. True, that evidence alone might not have convinced him. The suspect, a loner, had protested his innocence and he had owed it to the man to check the facts, but then three of the victims identified him outright as their attacker. Surely all three couldn't be wrong? Lying back on the cushions as his litter crawled its agonizing snail's pace through the streets, sweat streamed down Orbilio's face, and not from the pain which was wracking his side.

Claudia had seen what he had not. What was in front of him all along. That's why she went to visit the victims and had kept her suspicions about Dymas to herself. To brand a man a monster when he was merely odd would leave an irrevocable scar, while for Marcus to arrest his own colleague in a rush to stop further attacks and then be proved to have been wrong would have destroyed both Dymas and him. It was only once the pieces started to fall into place that he realized what tipped the balance of Claudia's scales from supposition to proof. The victims' statements.

Funny, but he could quote them word for word every time and still the penny didn't drop.

'How could you identify the attacker,' he had asked, 'if he was masked?' and each reply was the same.

'By the smell of aniseed, by the way he held himself, by his voice and the shape of his hands.'

That was the point. *Each reply was the same.* As though someone had coached them— And, goddammit, he hadn't picked that up.

'You can drop me here,' he told the head bearer. The Greek's small apartment was one block ahead, he could see a light burning in the window. Could almost picture Dymas hunched over the case notes. Insurance, my arse! He'd kept those files to pore over in his spare moments, relishing every living moment, gloating over his triumphs.

Orbilio checked the dagger in his belt, the knife down the side of his boot.

'This is for you,' he promised the man whose throat had been torn out by the lions.

'Bloody fuck, mate, you gave me a start. Don't you know what time it is?'

Orbilio smiled. 'Did I wake you?'

'Well . . . no. But it's gone midnight, can't it wait?'

'Not really,' Orbilio said mildly, pushing past.

The apartment was small. Cramped, even, and not very clean. Food, probably stew in a past life, had congealed into black tar on top of a pile of unwashed wooden trenchers, shrivelled onions hung on a string on the wall, and a coating of dust took the shine off what little furniture there was. It occurred to him that, if he'd been lowborn and forced to live on Security Police pay, this is the sort of accommodation he could expect to live in.

But if he'd been hoping for the stale smells to be eclipsed by aniseed, he was out of luck. Of course, that was never really on the cards. A man who covered his tracks with such care wouldn't risk leaving the paraphernalia of his trade lying about. The aniseed, the files, the mask, these treasures would be kept in a separate place. A secret place. The Halcyon Rapist's private den, where his trophies could be displayed to their full and glorious triumph. And where the stench of aniseed could be washed off, leaving no trace.

'If you don't mind my saying, you look like shit, mate.'

Orbilio wondered where the hot-food vendor's wife had wounded him. She didn't know. Twisted his testicles, lunged with the knife and ran off before he could get his breath back. 'You look pretty rough, too,' he said happily.

'Crumbs, what d'you expect? It's two in the fucking morning and it's been a tough few days. Drink?'

'That's promotion for you,' Marcus breezed, seating himself in a high-backed wooden chair and waving away the proffered goblet. Ideally, he would have crossed his legs to emphasize the casual nature of his call, but the wound in his side wouldn't permit it. In the end, he was just glad to sit down and felt a small trickle of something sticky run down the inside of his tunic.

'So what happened?' Dymas asked, indicating his colleague's blackened and ragged appearance.

Orbilio steepled his fingers. 'We caught the rapist,' he said.

'Really?' Dymas's eyes lifted at last. 'Well, good on you, Marcus. Sure you won't have that drink?' He swallowed half a glass in one go, and Orbilio noted the effort the Greek had to use to keep the smirk from his face.

'So was I right?' Dymas refilled his goblet. 'Was it some sick copycat bastard?'

Orbilio ran his hand round the back of his neck. 'No, Dymas. Just some sick bastard,' he said, adding, 'with a pathological hatred of women.'

A hatred so bitter, so twisted, that he tormented his victims over and over by making them relive their ordeal in the name of interrogation. Some of the girls naturally recognized his voice – and how Dymas would have relished that moment. Watching the horror on their faces as they realized that the rapist was protected by the Security Police. There could be no justice for them, they would think. Who would believe their stories? His word against theirs? They'd be the accusations of a hysterical woman versus a trusted investigator. It was hopeless. Leaving Dymas to torment them to the brink of despair and treasure in his heart that exquisite moment when they howled, whimpered, quivered or tore at their own flesh with the injustice of it all. How sublime, knowing you had the ability to push someone over the edge into suicide. No wonder he'd been so keen to go back to Deva this morning. He hadn't finished torturing her yet. Silently, Marcus thanked Jupiter for the brainwave which got her out of his clutches.

'Imagine the control he exercised, Dymas. Limiting himself to just fourteen rapes at a run.'

A number specifically chosen to breed panic yet insufficient to run too much risk of detection.

'Over Saturnalia, too,' Dymas said, covering the smirk he could no longer control with the back of his hand. 'Halcyon Days, when people should be happy and without a care in the world.'

'Ah, but he's a spoiler, Dymas. He chose Saturnalia because it's traditionally the happiest time of the year, and he isn't happy, so he wants to ruin it for everyone else.'

A man who submerges his victims in ordure is a man who wants to defile everything. The chair creaked when Marcus leaned back.

'It's the only way someone so small and insignificant can feel big.'

The Greek's hand clenched round the goblet so tight that it shattered.

'Can't agree with you there, mate,' he said, wrapping a linen towel round his hand to staunch the blood. 'Our boy's instigated one of the biggest manhunts in the history of the Security Police, he's outwitted us at every bleeding turn and put the fear of Jupiter into every woman in the city. That's a clever man, Marcus. A very intelligent mind at work.'

'You think?' Orbilio pretended to consider. 'I reckon that if you asked anyone in the Empire, rich or poor, freeborn or slave, what's clever about destroying lives and creating a climate of fear, they'd laugh in your face.'

Dymas's expression darkened. Marcus pressed on.

'Only little men think terror is clever. Big men, important men, the *really* intelligent ones, they have nothing to prove.'

252

'You don't know what you're talking about,' Dymas hissed. 'But anyway, who cares? You got the bastard, you said.'

Orbilio moved across to the window and peered between the gap in the shutters. 'Only because he overreached himself,' he said quietly. 'He got greedy.'

Limiting the rapes, organizing the attacks, entailed enormous self-control, but the pleasure came from the stalking beforehand and the tormenting after, whether or not the victims recognized their attacker. And for those who hadn't recognized his voice, how simple to suggest, in a personal visit, that the Security Police had strong evidence linking a suspect, then stressing that it was only circumstantial. Yes, his clothes reeked of aniseed, yes, they found this mask under his bed – oh, Dymas. How easy it must have been when you held up the grinning face of their attacker. How susceptible they would be then to your coaching. What did you plant in their impressionable minds? How much better it would be if witnesses were able to identify the evil bastard and put him where he belonged, perhaps? In hell. Orbilio could see how quickly the terrified girls would have learned their lines.

'He got careless, you say?' A gloating light danced in Dymas's eyes as he saw history repeating itself. Better and better. Now this patrician, this tall, handsome, wealthy patrician who he so despised because of his caste, would send another man to the arena. And in so doing, would slit his own throat—

Orbilio moved the candle and propped himself against the sill. 'No,' he said. 'I was the careless one. You see, Dymas, for the first time in my life, I took someone else's word, without checking the facts for myself.'

The pause was almost imaginary, but something in Dymas changed. Orbilio felt the hairs stand up on the back of his neck.

'Yeah, but that last guy confessed,' the Greek said,

although the bluster had adopted an edge of wariness now. 'You weren't to know he was the type who'd confess to anything, were you? I told you before, shit happens. Quit beating yourself up about this.'

'Well, that was the thing, Dymas. I didn't actually get a confession last time. No one actually reported the suspect *confessing* to the crimes, only that he signed a confession. There's a difference.'

Dymas's tongue flickered nervously round his lips. 'It's not part of your remit to interrogate suspects once they're under arrest.'

'Nor is it yours.' He stood up, flexed his shoulders. Felt a hundred years old. 'It's over, Dymas. The game's up.'

There was no bluffing. The Greek had worked with Orbilio long enough to know when he was serious. He edged towards the bed. Marcus drew the knife from his boot.

'This will be in your heart before you're halfway.'

'Kill me and you kill yourself,' Dymas sneered. 'They'll say you did it because I was promoted over your head and you couldn't take it, and who's to say otherwise? You have no evidence, nothing to connect me with the rapes. Even with your poncy connections, who'll believe you? Callisunus?' He spat on the floor. 'Yeah, right.'

'Oh, I'm sure that somewhere in this poky apartment there'll be a key. A key to a room where files are spread out permanently, anchored by stones, and where a mask hangs on a wall. A room where a little man, an insignificant little worm of a man, a man who can't get a woman in any normal way, pleasures himself as he relives his victims' torment.'

'Sex? You think this is about *sex*?'

Orbilio didn't, but he said nothing. Dymas had unleashed the beast now. There was only one way this could end.

'Sex is nothing, mate. A dirty, vile, nasty little act by a man who's supposed to love you and care for you but sneaks into your bedroom when you're seven years old and holds your head into the pillow until you can't breathe then tells you he'll throttle you if you tell anyone. No, it's not about sex, mate. This is power.'

Dymas seemed to grow before his eyes.

'Until you experience it, you can't imagine what it's like,' he said, clenching his fists. 'You talk about exercising control when it comes to limiting the attacks, but fuck, that's nothing compared to the control when you've got the little whores whimpering at your feet.'

He laughed. It was the first time Marcus had heard him do so, and it wasn't a sound he much cared for.

'I never harmed one of the little slags, d'you know that? Didn't need to, mind. Showed them the blade, and they were too fucking scared to fight back. Timid, snivelling, cringeing little mice, that's all they are, and they got what was coming to them, the worthless trash.'

'I didn't realize any creature deserved to have their lives ruined, their families put on hold, their emotions suspended for ever.'

'*What* life?' Dymas scoffed. 'You've seen them. Wandering around half-naked, even this time of the year. Harlots, that's what they are. Oho, yes, don't think I haven't seen them, mate. Don't think I haven't watched the little whores and I tell you, that herbalist's no better than a pimp, having Deva showing herself in all weathers. Well, I showed her, mate. I showed all of them. I bloody did, too.'

'Bodices and short skirts are traditional Damascan attire, and Deva didn't invite sex and she certainly didn't invite rape.'

'Yeah, but she won't be waggling her arse at any more men for a while, will she? Filthy little prick-teaser.' Dymas turned a sly eye on his colleague. 'But I'm not finished yet. Not by a long chalk.'

As he dived for the bed, he kicked out at the table. The candle fell and went out. Orbilio's knife whizzed through the air. Thudded harmlessly into the door. Shit. Splinters of pain tore at his side, jarred by the table slamming into his thigh. It had ruined his aim. In the darkness, Dymas laughed. The sound reminded Marcus of a hyena closing on a kill. Silently, he drew his dagger.

Listened.

Heard nothing.

Dymas was employed by the Security Police for his streetwise ways and his cunning, his brute strength and his resilience. Orbilio cursed the man who gave him the job. In the blackness, the only breathing he could hear was his own. Below, in the street, men wished each other goodwill. He remained motionless, straining for sounds. Dymas knew every square inch of this apartment. Orbilio's sole advantage was that he had his back against the wall.

The strike came out of nowhere. At the last moment, he saw the blade plunging through the dark. He ducked. Could not contain the grunt that escaped when the herbalist's stitches snapped as he twisted. One all, he thought dully. Blood dribbled down the outside of his leg and pooled at his feet. He waited. Dymas would have expected him to move. For that reason he hadn't. Seconds dripped by like lead. Then, Jupiter be praised, a lull in the traffic coincided with Dymas's strike. Orbilio swung his dagger. Steel clashed against steel.

'Sloppy, very sloppy.' Dymas was laughing. 'I can fucking smell you.'

Vinegar and turpentine. Of course. The blades locked and Orbilio's free hand balled into a fist, driving into Dymas's side. The Greek jerked like a puppet. So then. That was where the food vendor's wife had landed her blow. Without waiting to think what it would cost him, Orbilio thudded his boot into the wound. Dymas reeled backwards and Orbilio tumbled on top of him. Closing his forearm round the Greek's throat, he forced Dymas's head back, exposing the throat.

'You haven't the strength,' Dymas hissed.

It was true. But Orbilio had the strength to call out. Immediately, four legionaries burst into the room. The one at the back carried a torch.

'Drop the knife, Dymas.'

The Greek had no choice. Reluctantly, he released the dagger in his hand.

Marcus turned his head to the soldiers, was conscious of blood pumping from the wound in his side and sweat pouring down his face to blind his eyes. 'Did you get all that, sergeant?' he rasped.

'Every word, sir,' the soldier said, grinning. 'Although you took your bloody time calling us inside, if you don't mind my saying so.'

When Orbilio released his grip on the rapist, his whole body began to shake like a poplar. 'This was something I had to do myself.'

As one of the soldiers stepped forward with chains, the hobnails on his boots slipped in the pool of Orbilio's blood. It was all the time Dymas needed. He lunged for his dagger. Marcus used every last ounce of his strength to prevent him from falling on it.

'No chance,' he growled. His victims weren't going to be cheated. 'Last time I arranged for the rapist to be executed by lions. For you, Dymas, I'm working on something rather more protracted.'

But for now it was Saturnalia Eve, and despite the hour he owed Claudia a visit. He needed to thank her for talking to the victims today, for helping him out, for taking such an interest in the case, to tell her she was right and—

Who was he kidding?

Hell, he just needed to see her.

Thirty-Five

Claudia opened her eyes to blackness and the sound of a percussion orchestra on their first practice run. It took her a while to work out that the cymbals and drum rolls were inside her head, and that the blackness came from lying face down on a pile of thick fleeces. The fleeces had been washed, and they were soft and comforting, like floating on a cloud, and smelled slightly oily. She tried to sit up, and found that her furs had been stripped from her, her arms tied behind her back, her ankles bound and memories of being trapped down Pepper Alley flooded back. Looking round, shivering from the bitter night air, she realized she was in some sort of shed, possibly a warehouse, lit by a single oil lamp placed on the floor.

'I'm so glad you are able to join us, Mistress Seferius.'

The voice was cultured and deep, imbued with natural authority. With his thumbs looped into his belt, he was tall, well built and, under other circumstances, Claudia would have described him as handsome with his thatch of blond hair and distinctive patrician attire. Beside her, white as a ghost, Erinna had hauled herself into a kneeling position on the fleece cloud.

'My apologies for the rude form of transportation.'

The kidnapper was leaning almost nonchalantly against a stack of soft, bulging sacks and, although Claudia could not make out the colour of his eyes, she recognized triumph dancing in them.

'Unfortunately, I'm not sure a direct invitation would

have been accepted, and—' he indicated Claudia's head '—
I must apologize, too, for my boys' manners. They can be
a little over-enthusiastic at times.'

The air was dry and dusty and she wanted to sneeze.
Instead, she lifted her chin to face him.

'Who are you?' she demanded. 'What do you want with
me?'

But even as she asked the question, she knew it wasn't
for ransom.

And in the end it wasn't the kidnapper who answered.

'His name,' Erinna said quietly, 'is Sextus Valerius Cotta
and it's not you he wants. Is it, Senator?'

Autumn. The air was sticky. Leaves hung limp on the trees
surrounding Cotta's estate in the Alban Hills. Amber.
Scarlet. And rust. Over the horizon to the east, the sun was
just starting to rise. Soft, golden and mellow. A few birds
sang, magpies chattered and an old boar snuffled for acorns.
Rabbits scampered over the clearings as the first slanting
rays of liquid gold penetrated the patchwork canopy, and
the air was ripe with the scent of beechnuts and sweet
chanterelles. Crashing through the undergrowth, the Digger
noticed none of the season's sultry beauty. Fear gave wings
to her heels. Any second now, the news would break. They
would set the dogs on her. The human kind, as well as the
estate hounds, and she remembered what happened last time
she tried to break free.

It had been different then.

For three years, Erinna had worked with the old man as
he concocted his recipe for the Elixir of Immortality. Like
the Senator, she thought it was nonsense, but the old man
was defiant and besides, he would argue, if not life everlasting, then another half century would suffice. Fifty years?
Was he serious? He was bent and crippled as it was, his
chest wheezed like a pair of ancient bellows and his eyes
were rheumy and dim. In five years, never mind fifty, he'd

be blind, shrivelled and bed-bound and what life was that? But Erinna had grown fond of her master and knew the old man cared for her in return. For a slave, a kind master is all you can ask for.

'The Poseidon Powder is the key,' he would cackle merrily. 'Once I've cracked that, I'm immortal.'

Saltpetre, this strange salt of Petra, was apparently the only substance which could adequately dissolve the vermilion cinnabar crystals, which in turn were crucial to the fabled elixir, and it was for just one pouchful of this precious white powder that he had scoured the earth and shelled out a small fortune. What he had bought, though, rendered him almost delirious with delight and he was happier than Erinna had seen in a long time at the prospect of finally fulfilling his dream. That fateful afternoon, Erinna and the old man had been experimenting with the ingredients as usual.

'Are you sure about this, master?'

This wasn't the first time she'd questioned his formula. Recent chest pains had prompted him to start taking short-cuts. Erinna worried, and with good reason. White nitre hadn't been named after the Earth-Shaker for nothing!

'Oh, stop fussing, gel, and pass me the honey.'

He had given up trying to dissolve the red grit a fort-night before. Either the formula was incorrect, he said, or the whole thing was a hoax, and the old man hadn't given credence to the latter. The Orientals possessed the secret of eternal life, this was a fact, and after many years of experimenting, he was absolutely certain that he was finally on the right track.

'This'll make your fortune, gel,' he would tell her. 'When I die, you receive your freedom under the terms of my will. You can sell the formula and be rich.'

Watching the chemicals bubble and fizz, Erinna knew she would never be rich. But freedom . . . ? That was another matter entirely. Around his room, this self-styled laboratory sited as far from the domestic area as his son could organize without insult, bowls and jars, phials and philtres cluttered every available shelf space and table. The Senator claimed he kept the laboratory clear of the house because of the smell, which was pretty noxious, Erinna had to agree. Personally, she tended to think that the Arch-Hawk was ashamed of his father's eccentric dabblings.

'Are you sure you've roasted the iron pyrites correctly?'

'Yes, master,' she'd replied patiently. 'And I collected the vapour and recrystallized it according to your exact instructions.'

No wonder they called it fools' gold! But with each pain in his chest, each wheeze in his lungs, the old man grew progressively tetchy, and his hands were no longer steady enough to hold a spoon to his own mouth without spilling. For three years, Erinna had undertaken the intricacies of his chemical experiments that his failing body could not.

'Hmph.' A bony finger tapped impatiently. 'Then *I* don't know what's wrong.'

This was a regular exchange, and Erinna saw no more reason to pay particular attention that afternoon to his grumblings than to any of its predecessors.

'Maybe that Arab didn't give us the true salt of Petra,' he suddenly said. 'That's it! I've been swindled, this isn't Poseidon Powder at all! That dirty wog bastard has diddled me!'

'Calm down, master.' He was getting overexcited again. Any moment and another claw would rip at his heart. 'The Arab didn't cheat you, you watched yourself when he scooped up the powder.'

But the old man was beyond listening. 'I'll have to test it,' he said. 'Light that brazier, gel.'

'Let's test it tomorrow,' Erinna suggested.

She hadn't liked the look of the old man's colour, but knew he wouldn't have the estate physician near his laboratory, not after the names he had called the elixir, and the master was a proud old duffer, for all that.

'*Now!* I'm going to test it *now*,' he said shrilly. 'If the powder burns with a purple flame, then it's genuine. If not, I'm going back to Petra and have that Arab's intestines strung out on a clothes line.'

Slaves cannot argue with their masters. They can only render the place as safe as possible. Leaving him poring over his brew of realgar, honey and sulphur above a brazier which she hadn't yet lit, Erinna scooped up the limewood box, the only orderly apparatus in the room, and took it away for safe keeping in his bedroom. Accidents had happened before. Acid burns, fires, small explosions inside the cauldron. They could laugh about it now, but at the time it wasn't funny, having your eyebrows singed ginger and watching your dinner explode! Senator Cotta had no idea of the amount of furniture that had been quietly smuggled out in smouldering pieces.

Returning from his quarters, Erinna was walking along the shade of the portico when she was blown backwards off her feet. The old man, too impatient to wait for her return to test out his powder, had lit the brazier himself. Poseidon, the Earth-Shaker, had spoken.

Even as the dust rained down on her head, Erinna was astute enough to realize that, had she not removed the limewood box, she and the whole house would have blown up. Hundreds of lives would have been lost. Very little saltpetre, she had learned, was required to create an explosion. It was the combination of the ingredients which rendered them volatile. That, and the fact they were mixed in a small, metal container. When the container exploded, so did everything round it, and paradoxically, the smaller the container, the greater the explosion.

Erinna did the only thing she could think of. She ran.

They caught her, of course. Just outside Frascati, and she knew the Senator would execute her for murder, because the old man had most certainly not died from natural causes. She had screamed her bloody head off, kicked and screeched and called for help, because with the old man's death she was officially a freewoman now, she was entitled to trial by jury. But the townspeople decided this was none of their business. They viewed her desperate fight only in terms of light entertainment. *The bastards had actually laughed.*

To her surprise – no, to her astonishment – the Senator didn't charge her with murder when they dragged her back. Instead he shut her in a storeroom and asked her, very politely, what formula the old man had used. And in that moment, Erinna understood everything. She saw that, in the explosion, the Arch-Hawk had seen a fast track to his expansion plans—

Terrified now, truly terrified, she prevaricated. Told him she didn't know the precise formula, that the master wouldn't disclose his secrets to a mere slave, but the Senator wasn't fooled. They both knew she had been his instrument.

Three days passed. Cotta tried every trick in the book and it didn't matter to him that she was free now. He needed the formula and Erinna was the only person who possessed it. How much saltpetre to sulphur, what ratio of honey to realgar, and so on. As she continued to bluff it out, he offered riches and made threats in return. But Erinna wasn't stupid. His patience would not last for ever and he would turn to other methods to extract the information he needed. Hand twisting or the bastinado. In any case, Erinna was dead. He would not, could not, afford to let her live now. Whatever he promised.

Her only chance lay in escape.

Strangely, it wasn't that hard. Like most sensible interrogators, Cotta employed violence as a last resort. More results were obtained by keeping the questioning friendly, and for that reason Erinna was allowed a certain privacy for her ablutions. Foolish. Very foolish. Claiming an urgent need for the latrines, she knocked her jailer unconscious with a block of wood and picked up a couple of small, but precious objects from the atrium as she fled. Cotta owed her that much, she thought. With that gold statuette and the ivory carving, she could get to Alexandria and disappear.

As dawn turned to daylight, birdsong filled the woods. Erinna had no plan. She didn't know which direction she was headed, only that she must get away. Hitch a lift on a cart, anything, to put distance between this terrible place and herself. Juno be praised, there was only one other person on the road this early. A young woman with a cloak of dark hair and shabby clothes, whose face was a picture of burning resentment. The girl stopped when she saw Erinna.

'What's wrong, love?' she asked, and Erinna hadn't realized she'd been crying until the woman pointed it out.

Even now, she didn't know what possessed her to go babbling off to a stranger. Stress, she supposed. The desperate need to confide after the horrendous few days. Oh, she didn't let on about Cotta's secret; of course, that would go with her to the grave. But Erinna couldn't halt the sudden outpouring of emotion, and it all came gushing out. How urgently she needed to reach the coast. Book a passage on a ship. Any ship. To Athens, Massilia, anywhere.

At what point had the stranger's concern twisted into something darker? It was only afterwards that Erinna remembered the scowl, the expression of burning resentment that had been on her face when she first saw her walking towards her on the road. Compassion, she discovered later, had been instinctive – but fleeting.

'How will you pay for your passage?' the stranger had asked, and there had been a shrewd look in her eye. Again, something Erinna paid no heed to at the time. Vulnerable and afraid, the desire to trust and be trusted was overwhelming. She showed the woman the gold statuette and the carving under her cloak.

'Then I think I can help you,' the dark-haired woman said, brightening. 'Come with me.'

Taking Erinna's arm in sisterly solidarity, she had led her up past the post house, and Erinna barely noticed the spade leaning against the wall at the time. She had heard only the snicker of horses, reminding her that any minute, Cotta's men would come charging through the dawn mist towards her. She felt sick to her stomach, yet safe. Safe in the hands of this woman, this sister who understood and who *cared*.

When she looked back over her shoulder to check on possible pursuers, she did notice that the spade had gone, although there was still no sign of the ostler.

'I'm an actress,' the stranger explained. 'With a few tricks of the trade and the aid of cosmetics, I can change your appearance to the point where your own mother wouldn't recognize you.' And as she led Erinna down into the woods, where this miraculous transformation would take place, she explained how the group of strolling players she had been with had split up. The very bitterness and venom in her voice should have alerted Erinna, but she was too bound up in her own sorrows. Still grieving for her dead master, for herself, for the predicament for which – hallelujah! – she had found a solution, but heavy with the knowledge that Cotta would stop at nothing to find her. Down the hill, near a stream, her companion paused. Set down her bundle and covered it carefully with her cloak. Erinna caught the clang of something metallic, but yet again paid no attention. To give yourself up to someone else's ministrations was a luxury she'd never experienced before.

'Look at those beautiful butterflies!' the actress gasped, using both hands to point to the profusion of painted ladies heading south through the canopy. 'Don't they take your breath away, the way they dance through the trees?'

Erinna looked up and saw hope dancing among the profusion of painted ladies. 'They're beautif—'

Her breath was cut off. Two hands clasped round her

neck and began squeezing, and suddenly the dance of the butterflies had turned into a macabre dance of death. Even as they fought, Erinna knew she was losing the battle. The actress had the advantage of surprise and her hands, strong from hauling scenery, pressed deeper into Erinna's throat. She fell to her knees, heard a hideous gurgling sound and knew it was her last breath.

Why fight? Give in, you're dead anyway, a little voice said. Let go, Erinna.

But the need to survive was stronger than the voice in her head. Erinna desperately wanted to live and, as she twisted and writhed, a red mist closing over her eyes, she saw the spade. The cloak, which had been kicked aside in the struggle, exposed its shiny, deadly metallic blade. In that second, that single split second, Erinna turned into a killer.

A transformation, she realized belatedly, that was far worse than death at the hands of a stranger.

And the body in the grave screamed, 'You bitch! You killed me, you bitch, caved my bloody head in. Don't you see that with that statuette and the carving, I could have done so *well* for myself! I could have bought fine clothes and jewels and secured myself the protection of a man who would demand only my body in payment – and what did you do? You wasted those treasures! Instead of selling them and making a comfortable life for yourself, you climbed into my old threadbare clothes, put my pack on your back and hooked up with a troupe of losers! Caspar threw me out, did you know that? Said the company was fed up with my carping, that it undermined their morale, and even the splinter group wouldn't take me. *Bitch*. With that gold, I could have been happy. Really happy. I hope you rot in hell for what you've done!'

The curse was more successful than she could have predicted.

Not a day passed when the Digger didn't regret swinging that shovel. The more she bonded with the Spectaculars, and the more they accepted her without question, the more accute the pain.

And then there was Skyles—

She should have listened to that little voice inside her head, the one which told her to give in, stop fighting, let go. But she'd fought back and survived to dance solo among the butterflies in the woods, and now there was only one solution to ending the torment that locked her in eternal autumn.

Once Saturnalia was over and she had discharged her obligations to perform, there would be one final spilling of blood.

Erinna's own.

Thirty-Six

Despite her head pounding like thunder and the bitter cold chilling her bones, Claudia picked up most of the situation. What Erinna glossed over, Cotta filled in, and frankly she wondered why he bothered. He didn't seem a particularly vain man, who enjoyed speaking just to hear the sound of his own cultured voice. Then she realized.

He was explaining for the same reason that he hadn't just let her go.

You could forgive his heavies for snatching both women back in that alley. In the dark, in a hurry, in a crowd, time was not on their side. They could decide later which of the women was which. So why hadn't the Arch-Hawk let Claudia go? If he'd had Erinna followed, then he obviously knew who Claudia was, and it would have been a simple matter to have his 'boys' dump her somewhere while she was still unconscious. She would never have known then who had taken Erinna, much less where or, more importantly, why. Instead, he was dotting the Is and crossing the Ts, briefing his captive in true military style. He had even explained to Claudia how he came to locate the last missing piece of his puzzle.

'Jupiter alone knows how hard my men tried to find her,' he said. 'It was as though Erinna had disappeared from the face of the earth.'

He had expected to trace her through the stolen objects, he added, but inexplicably none of the missing objects turned up. She had simply vanished into thin air, taking with her his plans for the expansion of Rome.

'How,' he asked, smiling, 'could I hope to blow up the Senate House now? With a plentiful supply of the Poseidon Powder, I could have experimented to my heart's content, but *one pouch*?'

Claudia didn't understand. Blow up the Senate? What was he talking about? Blitzing one building would hardly change the course of the Empire. With a rush of freezing ice to her veins, she knew there was only one way history could be altered with one blast. Sweet Janus! Three hundred men would be packed inside, debating, laughing, jeering. With no idea they had minutes to live— No, wait. Cotta would want more. He would be wanting three hundred and one. History could not be changed without changing the Emperor.

She thought of his own history. General to Senator to Emperor in three simple steps.

'You're crazy,' she said, but even as she spoke the words, she knew it wasn't true. Sextus Valerius Cotta was sane. Excruciatingly sane, in fact. He merely saw the Senate as a dam to be breached. An obstacle to be erased in the name of progress.

'Then a letter arrived from Frascati,' Cotta said, as though accusations of psychosis were hurled at him three times a day. 'A woodsman reported that he'd found the body of my runaway slave and he thought I should know.'

Tactics was one key to winning a battle. Thoroughness another, he added.

'I had no reason to doubt the woodsman's account, but felt it sensible to send my steward to verify the discovery. Confirm once and for all that the corpse was Erinna's.'

Once again, the Arch-Hawk's celebrated attention to detail had paid off.

'You can see how the woodsman was mistaken. The body in the grave had long hair, but it was black. Jet black.' Cotta prised himself away from the soft, bulging sacks and strolled nonchalantly over towards the two women. Wooden boards reverberated dully under his tread, but Claudia could not hear for the drumming inside her head. 'Erinna's hair, as you can see,' he said, stroking it, 'is pure chestnut.'

Erinna did not flinch when he touched her. She just continued to stare at him, her white face quite without expression. Cotta, on the other hand, looked faintly amused. It took a couple of seconds for Claudia to realize that his overriding emotion was satisfaction. Immense satisfaction. Like his father before him, he was on the point of realizing his dream. And Claudia, goddammit, was the catalyst.

'I recognized you from the Temple of Janus,' he told Erinna, lifting her chin with his finger. 'Oh, not at the time. Unfortunately.'

He'd been minding his own business, dutifully attending the Festival of the Lambs, he explained, when boredom was suddenly alleviated by a group of strolling players launching into an impromptu performance. Fortune had smiled on the Arch-Hawk that day. Had he not attended (and let's be frank, he only went because the ceremony was less boring than his dear wife), but had he not attended, he would not have been able to put the pieces together.

'It was, in fact, this magnificent cloak of chestnut hair that triggered my memory. The way you always eschewed fashion in favour of coiling it into a bun.'

Even though the girl outside the Temple of Janus had been veiled, when her tunic came away in Ion's hands, Cotta had glimpsed the bun. At the time, it hadn't registered as significant, but his memory was trained to recall details. Reading the result of his steward's investigation, another snippet of gossip came back. About the troupe of strolling players who had been hiring in Frascati last October. At which point, everything fell into place.

'Caspar's Spectaculars,' he said silkily. 'Sponsored by one Claudia Seferius.'

'Let her go,' Erinna pleaded. 'Please, Senator. Let her go.'

Claudia swallowed. 'He can't,' she said thickly. Why the hell did Erinna think he was telling Claudia this?

'She doesn't know anything about the experiments,' Erinna continued. 'I'm the only one who knows the secret.'

Claudia's teeth began to chatter, and not from the cold. Erinna still didn't get it, did she? Sextus Valerius Cotta, that handsome Arch-Hawk of the Senate, had tried every trick in the book to make her disclose the formula that would blow the Senate House into three thousand pieces. In his storeroom back in Frascati, he'd tried bribing her, he'd made threats, and although he hadn't tortured her, he had little hope that she would actually impart the knowledge he so desperately sought.

But there was a way. There was always a way. The solution was in front of him now.

From the depths of his toga he drew out a candle, lit the wick from the solitary oil lamp. Oh, god. Panic filled Claudia's veins. Not burns. Oh, please. Anything but that. Please. *Not burns.*

Slowly, with the flame flickering like a yellow demonic tongue, Cotta advanced towards her. She tried to wriggle out of his range, just as Erinna, seeing what was about to happen, squirmed backwards as fast as she could. Cotta didn't bother with his ex-slave girl. A strong hand reached out and grabbed Claudia's hair, jerked her spine so hard against his thigh that she cried out. With his prisoner bound hand and foot, Cotta was still taking no chances. The boot pressing down on her calves was implacable.

Like a hare petrified into immobility by a night torch, Erinna stared open-mouthed at the tableau of horror. 'D–don't. I beg you, Senator. Don't do this.'

He had, at last, found her weak point. Out of stubbornness, honour, who knows what, Erinna might hold out against whatever he threw at her. But few people can stand by while an innocent third party is tortured.

Cotta ripped away the cloth from Claudia's shoulder.

'Master, please. I beg you.' Tears coursed down Erinna's cheek. 'She's done nothing, let her go.'

'If you give me the formula, you have my word, Erinna, that Claudia will go free.'

Meeting Erinna's terrified eye, Claudia shook her head as far as Cotta's grip would allow. His word meant nothing. He was going to kill them both anyway. No point in letting him take three hundred more lives. Or rather, three hundred and one.

'No?' Cotta sighed. 'That is a pity, Erinna. A real pity.'

At first, Claudia felt nothing but the heat from the flame. Then an excruciating pain shot up her neck and she heard someone screaming. There was an acrid smell in her nostrils. A combination of burned linen and charred skin, and she thought she was going to be sick.

'For gods' sake, woman, do you think this gives me pleasure?' Cotta rasped. 'Erinna, I am going to get my formula in the end, so I beg you, the quicker you tell me, the easier it will be for her.'

In front of her, Erinna opened her mouth to speak.

'The only thing you will tell him,' Claudia said, amazed that there was no sign of fear in her voice, 'is to go to hell. Understood?'

Tearful and terrified, Erinna didn't know what to do. Claudia skewered with her eyes. Finally, Erinna nodded. Turned her face up to Cotta. 'No matter what you do, I will not give you the secret,' she said sadly.

'No?' The Arch-Hawk wasn't convinced. One burn was merely a start. There were the hands, yet, the soles of the feet, the breasts, the face, ah yes, the face. When Erinna saw Claudia's pretty features melt like beeswax, she would talk.

He applied the candle to another part of her shoulder, and was surprised at how hard he had to grip the girl to keep her upright. Poor bitch, she didn't deserve this. Too much pain for just one woman's stubbornness. But his heart was hardened. One girl suffers, but millions of people gain. All the same. Cotta swallowed. It did not have to be like this—

'For heaven's sake, Erinna, have you no pity?'

The only reply was an animal whimper from deep in Erinna's throat.

With her skin on fire, Claudia prayed. She didn't know who to pray to in times like this, so she prayed to them all. To Diana the huntress, that she would strike Cotta dead with her arrows. To armoured, striding, strident Minerva, that she would smite him with her dagger to avenge her sisters. And, in desperation, to Lua, who wards off calamity.

'Don't make me do this, Erinna,' Cotta growled, but there was no shake to the candle flame as he held it high to show her Claudia's burns.

That was his mistake. In lifting the tallow, he revealed what Erinna had not been able to see before. That he was holding them prisoner on the upper floor of a warehouse. In the circle of light cast by the yellow flame, she saw the brown stone walls, an array of pulleys, winches, cogs and handles, hooks and ropes. More importantly she could see the edge of the platform on which the fleeces were stacked. Dropping away into nothingness—

Claudia watched the change on her face. Erinna's beauty became suffused with a peace and radiance she had not seen before and in that terrible, heart-stopping instant, she realized what Erinna was planning.

By jumping, Erinna could not hope to save Claudia's life, but she could save her from prolonged and hideous torment, and the Assembly and the Emperor would be safe. Death was the one thing Erinna did not fear. Every night and every day, she relived the moment when she rolled the bloodied corpse into its unmarked shallow grave. Now, with one final lurch, she could find the release that she craved.

Her expression was calm, her lips almost smiling, as she turned glistening eyes upon Claudia. She mouthed one word. 'Sorry.' Then launched herself over the side.

'*NO-O-O-O-O-O!*'

The scream which followed was primal and shocking. Visceral in its intensity, deafening in its volume, the sound chilled Claudia to her marrow. It filled the warehouse, reverberated its wooden floorboards, jerked the winches into motion. She had never known a sound so animal, so gut-wrenching in its agony, that it could move machinery, but beside her, the rope was definitely swinging.

'*No-o-o-o-o-o!*'

But screams can't turn cogs, however primitive they might be. The only way machinery moves is when someone operates it, and Claudia's second surprise was that the scream wasn't coming from Cotta's throat.

When Erinna threw herself off the edge, he had raced to the side of the platform and he, too, had been disorientated by the echoing yells. The Hades effect, Claudia realized. Just as she had expected the sound to have come from him, furious at having his plans thwarted, so Cotta had interpreted the scream to have been Erinna's soul being wrenched from her body. In that moment of shock, he hadn't understood that the reverberations were footsteps. That the pulleys were being operated by two strong hands.

That the scream was only the start of one man's outpourings of grief.

Kneeling on the edge of the platform peering into the dark, he didn't hear the swing of the winch. Only when he heard a hiss and a whoosh did the Arch-Hawk look round. Too late. The giant hook caught him square on the jaw. His neck snapped like a twig.

Claudia blinked. It had happened in seconds. Literally. *Seconds.* She couldn't believe it.

One minute, Erinna was alive. The next—

And Cotta. A heartbeat ago he was burning her flesh with a flame. Now his handsome, blond head lay at an angle hideously out of line with the rest of his body.

How quickly human life could be extinguished. How precious that which had been spared . . .

Above, the hook ceased to swing.

Creak, creak, creak. Slowly the cranking of the machinery died away. Then finally, nothing.

Nothing, save a primeval howl.

Skyles. No one else would mourn Erinna like that.

Shaking uncontrollably, Claudia fell back against the fleeces, her face wet with tears. She was safe now. No more pain. It was finished. Over. Her life was spared. She could go home. Why, then, lying on this soft, fluffy cloud, did she feel no relief? Oh my god. She sat up.

'Skyles! Skyles, quick.'

'I'm coming,' he sniffed. 'Give me a minute.'

'Not me, you big oaf. Erinna!'

For heaven's sake, this was a wool warehouse. Up here was where the fleeces were stacked. Which meant downstairs was where they stored the wool. No wonder Cotta hadn't roared with frustration. No wonder he had simply knelt at the edge of the platform, peering into the darkness below. He was the Arch-Hawk, the Arch-Tactician of military campaigns, for heaven's sake. He would have planned for *every* contingency.

As if to confirm it, a low moan filtered up from below.

Skyles' scream was no less loud than before. But this time it was a yelp of pure joy.

Thirty-Seven

'It occurs to me,' a melodious baritone murmured, 'that you should forget all about theatrical productions and turn this place into a hospital.'

Claudia opened her eyes. She expected to be torn apart by the pain. Instead she felt only a lightness, as though she was floating outside of her body.

'What happened?' she asked. This was her own room. Her own bed. Even her own cat stood on the table, tail bushy, hackles raised, growling at everyone and everything, but refusing point blank to leave.

'Ah—' Skyles began.

'You passed out,' a face with receding red hair cut in cheerfully.

This was the herbalist, Claudia presumed, noting that his left hand bore four bright-red parallel scratch marks. Good old Drusilla. Orbilio she could (just about) tolerate in the house. But a *stranger* in her mistress's room?

'Skyles carried you home,' the baritone said, and Claudia thought she caught a note of pique in Orbilio's voice. He looked ghastly. His skin was a hideous grey colour, and he was leaning against a chair for support. A thick wad padded out the left side of his tunic, and he smelled of balsam and mouldy bread.

'What about Erinna?' she asked. Strange, but she'd grown kind of used to the sandalwood. And that hint of rosemary, where his clothes had been rinsed.

'She's fine,' Skyles said. 'Really. Her pride was hurt far

276

more than her body. The fall was cushioned by a huge pile of blankets.'

Cotta would have put them there, of course. Just in case. The only contingency he couldn't have predicted was Skyles. Skyles who was so deeply in love with Erinna that he had found a way out of the house and followed her, just to be near her. Skyles who was so deeply in love with Erinna that he was scared to let his emotions show. Hence the lack of expression he had schooled himself to wear whenever he looked at her. Hence his asking her out in secret. In a company where everything was shared openly, Erinna was so precious, so dear to him, that he wanted her all to himself. Secrets, secrets, so many secrets, she thought.

> *One day a stranger*
> *Rode into our valley,*
> *Ravaged with scars of hard battles long past.*
> *His eyes, they were weary,*
> *He was tired of running,*
> *But the law was behind him and catching up fast.*

Instinctively, perhaps runaway to runaway, Erinna had read Skyles' past in his face and had even written the song about him. He recognized himself and tackled her about it, but even then he could not see the truth staring him back in the face.

> *I know not what befell him,*
> *I hope he found freedom,*
> *But I'll always bear him a love that is true.*

Erinna, too, had fallen. So deeply, so violently, that she dare not give in to it. She was a killer, she deserved the pain she was suffering and deserved the end she planned for herself, and she could not afford to let Skyles into her heart.

How many times had Claudia felt like clashing their thick heads together?

Skyles was on the run, which is why he'd changed his name, shaved his head. Who can connect a runaway slave, who had more than likely killed the master who had inflicted those vicious beatings, with a laughing, clowning, bald-headed Buffoon? That was why Claudia needed to find out who he was from her agent. To protect him. She had seen the way his face scanned the crowds with such intensity. Had anyone recognized him, he was wondering. Were they making their way through the crowds towards him out of adulation – or to take him back to face summary execution? Act, act, act. Pretend, pretend, pretend. How exhausting such a role must be on a man, how draining. With Erinna, though, he could dispense with all that weighty pretence. With Erinna, Skyles could just be himself.

For her part, Erinna believed Skyles went with the women after the shows to maintain his macho persona and impress his peers. Far from it, Claudia thought. He accepted their favours because he was lonely. For a few minutes he could escape to yet another fantasy world. A world of rich tapestries and rare woods, vintage wines and fine foods, where damask sheets perpetually covered the beds and chandeliers hung from tall, vaulted ceilings. Another role to immerse himself in, and in those few moments, Skyles was wanted. Genuinely wanted. The weight of his burden was lifted. Loneliness, he discovered, like many men before him, could be assuaged with hot sex.

Yet all he wanted was just one woman. His soulmate.

Don't we all, Claudia thought.

'You rest,' the herbalist said, patting her head like a child. 'I'm going to see how Deva's coming along, and I'll return later to check up on my patient.'

Claudia waited until he was gone before swinging her legs out of bed.

'Whoa! Where do you think you're going?' Skyles asked.

'It's Saturnalia Eve,' she reminded him. Incredibly, her only sensation was that of walking on air. 'In a few hours' time, twenty guests will troop in to watch a troupe of twenty.'

She could easily disguise the gauze bandage round her neck and she'd picked up enough acting techniques to know that, by the time her personal performance was done, no one would have noticed a thing.

'That's ridiculous,' he protested.

'No, that's Claudia,' Orbilio laughed. 'You might just as well try turning the tide, Skyles. Incidentally, how did you get that wound in your side?'

'It's not a wound, it's a cracked rib,' Skyles said, adding with a low chuckle, 'Probably two, after lugging her lady-ship home.'

'You didn't answer my question,' Marcus said.

'Oh, for heaven's sake, will you two stop gossiping like fishwives? Skyles, go and give Caspar a hand, we're running late enough as it is.'

Secrets, secrets, so many secrets, and the last thing Claudia wanted bandied abroad was how he got that wretched rib cracked. Oh, Flavia, Flavia, what a nasty spoiled child you are underneath! Skyles would have gone to that tavern at the Capena Gate, but you don't let a girl like Flavia down gently. Not one so entrenched in having her way. *What?* A lowborn, common actor spurning her virginity? *Her?* The child of a wealthy wine merchant, the stepdaughter of Claudia Seferius, the foster child of Marcellus, the architect! Claudia could almost hear the clatter as the stool splintered against his ribcage. Followed immediately by violent sobs of contrition! Silly cow. Let her stew in her misery for a couple of days. *Then* see who they could field as a husband . . .

'Will they be able to perform tonight?' Orbilio asked, his knuckles white from gripping the chair.

Claudia wondered how deep the knife had gone in.

Wondered, too, who had done it, and why, and whether he had caught Dymas in time, and most of all, why the thought of his injury should make her feel sick. He was only a policeman, for heaven's sake. This was his job.

'With all the walking wounded, you mean?' She smiled. 'That lot would have to be dead before they cancelled a show!'

'Caspar has a stunning black eye and quite a bad limp. I don't suppose you know how he got that?'

'Me? No idea.'

Secrets, secrets, so many secrets – and small wonder Julia wanted bolts fitted to her door. But it was Caspar she felt sorry for. He truly believed he was doing the old boot a favour by sneaking into her room in the dead of the night to perform the task he thought Marcellus was neglecting. He, for whom no woman could be too plump, too joyful, too wobbly, must have felt truly a hero as he slipped under the blankets of Julia's bed, and oh what a pity mother and daughter weren't the type to swap stories! What a treat for the fly on the wall, hearing them both confess to beating up men in their bedrooms!

'Just as you've no idea how Doris pulled a muscle?' Marcus asked dryly.

'None at all.'

Claudia smiled. Doris, Doris, who never told a lie . . .

Oh, and then there was Ion. Big, bearded, macho Ion, who had been gripped by the most terrible depressions of late, and why? Because Jupiter had fallen in love! It happened all the time in tight-knit groups, of course. Allegiances form, friendships develop, love blooms and when four people share a room, you learn so much about one another. What a shock for Ion, finding how closely life imitates legend. Jupiter fell in love with Ganymede, and Ion, he who epitomized manly love, had fallen for a sinuous youth whose eyes bore traces of kohl and whose bracelets jangled ever so softly.

Claudia almost laughed aloud. What a shock when he discovers Doris's secret. Those fine chiselled cheekbones, those effeminate hands, those eyelashes like a giraffe . . .

'What's your real name?' Claudia had asked.

And what was the reply? Tongue in cheek and designed to mislead, the reply had still come straight from the heart. Daphne. Doris was not a man, but a girl. She disguised it with over-the-top feminine gestures and who would guess from strong muscles built up from hauling on scenery? But unless she wanted to contain herself to musical farce, it was the only way a woman could appear on the stage. And Doris (Daphne!) was a natural actor. She played the Miser to comic perfection. No doubt, she would play tragedy to wring out the tears—

Yet even as she was picturing the moment Ion found out about the bandages binding her breasts, there seemed to be something wrong with Claudia's legs. They just weren't getting the message to walk and were setting off in directions all of their own. She put her hand up to the lump where that thug had knocked her out on the dray cart, and as she did so she brushed another, much larger bump on her temple.

'What happ—?'

Her knees buckled. As Orbilio staggered towards her, his face white with concern, she found herself clutching at bedclothes.

'That's why Skyles had to carry you home,' Marcus said, and she hoped it was the blood thundering in her ears, but dammit, it sounded for all the world like he was laughing.

'As he whooped for joy at Erinna's survival, he – um – accidentally set the hook in motion again.'

It was always going to be like this with Orbilio, she realized, as she reeled sideways on to the floor. Ups and downs, storms and torrents, it would never be a smooth ride with this man. He wouldn't get the credit for saving the Empire, either, because there was no credit to take. When Cotta died, the evidence died with him and the Senate would sincerely mourn their Arch-Hawk, whose life was tragically snuffed out by an accident in his warehouse, where a carelessly tied hoist had swung loose. Marcus would always be fighting for his seat in the Senate, just as she would always be fighting to maintain her position as a woman in trade.

Aristocrat in a pleb's world.

Woman in a man's world.

They were more alike than she'd realized.

She tried to laugh with him at the absurdity of the second bump, at the ridiculous mass of walking wounded downstairs, at the sheer farce played out within a farce, but the pull of the blackness was stronger. She had to tell him, though. She had to tell him, before she passed out again. Make him understand—

'You're right,' she whispered, as oblivion rushed up to meet her. 'You *are* the best friend I've ever had.'

Orbilio shouted to someone to call the herbalist back quickly. Claudia Seferius was clearly delirious.